Marie Belloc Lowndes

The Story of Ivy

e-artnow 2020

Marie Belloc Lowndes
The Story of Ivy

Murder Mystery Novel

e-artnow, 2020
Contact: info@e-artnow.org

ISBN 978-80-273-3807-8

Contents

Prologue	11
Chapter one	15
Chapter two	22
Chapter three	29
Chapter four	36
Chapter five	40
Chapter six	48
Chapter seven	55
Chapter eight	59
Chapter nine	66
Chapter ten	71
Chapter Eleven	75
Chapter Twelve	83
Chapter Thirteen	87
Chapter Fourteen	93
Chapter Fifteen	100
Chapter Sixteen	105
Chapter Seventeen	110
Chapter Eighteen	114
Chapter Nineteen	120
Chapter Twenty	127
Chapter Twenty-one	133
Chapter Twenty-two	137
Epilogue	145

Prologue

"Tell me something about the Lextons, Mary. Where did you pick them up?" asked Lady Flora Desmond of her hostess, Mrs. Hampton. "As I looked at Mrs. Lexton during dinner, I thought I had never seen a prettier face. When I was a child, your little friend would have been what people then called a professional beauty."

"She certainly is very pretty, and a regular honey-pot! Look at her now, with Miles Rushworth?"

The speaker nodded towards the wide-open French window of the high-ceilinged, oval eighteenth-century sitting-room. She and two other women were sitting there together after dinner, on the Saturday evening of what Mrs. Hampton thought promised to be a very successful week-end party.

The window gave access to a broad stone terrace. Beyond the terrace lay a wide lawn, bathed in bright moonlight, and across the lawn sauntered very slowly two figures, that of a tall man, and that of a slender woman dressed in a light-coloured frock. They were moving away from the beautiful old country-house where they were both staying as guests, making for an avenue of beeches.

Mary Hampton went on, speaking not unkindly, but with a certain tartness: "He took her out in his motor after tea, so she might have left him alone after dinner."

"You oughtn't to complain, my dear! You told me this morning that you had asked the Lextons this week-end so that they could make friends with your millionaire," observed Joan Rodney.

She was a sharp-tongued, clever spinster who enjoyed putting her friends right, and telling them home truths. Much was forgiven to Miss Rodney because she was, if sharp-tongued, fundamentally kind-hearted.

"My millionaire, as you call him, is one of the finest amateur billiard-players in England. I made Jack get hold of the best of the young 'pros.' He could only spare us this evening, and now that all the men, and two of the women, are either playing or watching the play in the billiard-room, Miles is philandering with Ivy Lexton in the garden!"

"Not philandering, Mary," observed Lady Flora, smiling. "Mr. Rushworth never philanders."

"Well! You know what I mean. It's my fault, of course. I ought to have known that no party would be big enough to hold Ivy Lexton and another attraction. Last time she was here she snatched such a nice boy from his best girl, and stopped, I'm afraid, a proposal."

Lady Flora looked sorry. A plain woman herself, she admired, without a touch of envy, physical beauty more than she admired anything else in the world.

"I don't suppose Mrs. Lexton can help attracting men. It's human nature after all——"

Quoted Joan Rodney, with a sharp edge to her voice:

"It's human nature but, if so, oh!
Isn't human nature low?"

"Little Ivy isn't exactly low; at least I hope not," observed little Ivy's hostess reflectively. "But I do feel that there's a curiously soulless quality about her. Though she's not what people call clever, there's something baffling about Ivy Lexton. I liked her much better when I first knew her."

"She mayn't be what silly people call clever, but she's plenty of what used to be called 'nous,'" said Miss Rodney drily. "She engineered her stroll with Mr. Rushworth very cleverly to-night. Your husband was determined to get him into the billiard-room——"

"She had a good excuse for that, Joan. As I told you yesterday, Jervis Lexton has been looking out for something to do for a long while."

Mrs. Hampton turned to her other friend. "It suddenly occurred to me, Flora, that Miles Rushworth, who must have many jobs in his gift, might find Jervis Lexton something to do.

Ivy knows that I asked them both for this week-end on purpose that they might meet him. It isn't easy to get hold of him for this kind of party."

"Have you known the Lextons long, Mary?" asked Lady Flora.

She felt genuinely interested in Mrs. Jervis Lexton. The quiet, old-fashioned, some would have said very limited, middle-aged widow, and lovely, restless, self-absorbed, and very modern Ivy Lexton, had "made friends."

"I have known Jervis ever since he was born. His father was a friend of my father's. But I had not seen him for years till I ran across him, in town, about three months ago. The last time I had seen him was early in the war, when his father had just died, and he had been given a fortnight's leave. He's what Jack calls quite a good sort; but it's bad for a young man to become his own master at twenty. He seems to have married this lovely little thing when he was twenty-two. That's six years ago."

"They seem to get on very well," observed Lady Flora.

"I think they do, though I'm afraid they've muddled away most of his money in having what Ivy considers a good time. He must have come into a fair fortune, for his father had sold their place just before the war."

"What fools young people seem to be today—I mean compared to the old days!" exclaimed Joan Rodney harshly.

She went on: "John Oram-you know, Mary, the big solicitor-once told me that of ten men who sell their land at any given time, only two have anything of the purchase-price left at the end of ten years."

"Jervis Lexton won't be one of those two men," said his hostess regretfully. "Ivy told me today that they're fearfully hard up."

"People often say that when it is laughably untrue! It's the fashion to pretend one's poor. Mrs. Lexton dresses beautifully. She must spend a great deal of money on her clothes," interjected Joan Rodney.

"I'm afraid there was no pretence about what Ivy told me this morning. She looked really worried, poor little thing! I do hope she will get something good for Jervis out of Miles Rushworth."

"She makes most of her frocks herself; it's so easy nowadays," said Lady Flora. And then she added: "She was telling me today about her girlhood. Her father failed in business, through no fault of his own, and for a little while she was on the stage——"

"Only a walking-on part in a musical comedy," observed Joan Rodney, "if what her husband, who strikes me as an honest young fellow, told me is true. However, I'm surprised, even so, that she didn't do better for herself in what I have heard described as the straight road to the peeresses' gallery, to say nothing of 'another place.'"

"Joan! Joan!" cried Mrs. Hampton deprecatingly.

Miss Rodney got up and came across to where her hostess sat under a heavily-shaded lamp.

She put her left elbow on the marble mantelpiece, and looking down into the other's now upturned face, "I don't like your little friend," she said deliberately. "I've been studying her closely ever since she arrived on Thursday afternoon, though she didn't seem aware of my existence till after lunch today. When I was in America last year, they'd invented a name for that sort of young woman. She's out, all the time, for what she can get. 'A gold-digger'—that's the slang American term for that kind of young person, Mary. I know what I'm talking about."

"How can you possibly know?"

"By instinct, my dear! If I were you I should give pretty Mrs. Lexton a very wide berth."

And then, rather to the relief of the other two, she exclaimed, "Having done what's always foolish-that is, said exactly what I think—I'm off to watch the champion billiard-player."

After she had left the room, Mrs. Hampton said slowly, "It's sad to hear a good woman, for Joan is really a good woman, say such cruel, unkind things."

"It's odd, too, for no one can show more real understanding sympathy when one's in trouble," answered Lady Flora in a low voice. She was remembering a time of frightful sorrow in her own life, when Joan Rodney had been one of the few friends whose presence had not jarred on her.

"Ah, well! She's devoted to you. Also, you're an angel, Flora, so there's no great merit in being kind to you. What Joan Rodney can't forgive in another woman is youth, happiness——"

"And, I suppose, beauty," interjected Lady Flora. "Yet to me there is something so disarming, so pathetic, about Mrs. Lexton."

"Then Joan has such a poor opinion of human nature," went on Mrs. Hampton in a vexed tone. "You heard with what delight she quoted that horrid little bit of doggerel. Still, quite between ourselves, Flora, I must admit that, in a sense, she is more right than she knows about Ivy Lexton."

Lady Flora looked dismayed. "In what way, Mary?"

"Ivy is very fond of money, or rather of spending it. In fact she is idiotically extravagant. She is dancing mad, and belongs to the two most expensive night clubs in town. It's her fault that they've frittered away a lot of Jervis Lexton's capital. Also, there's a side to her, for all her pretty manners, that isn't pretty at all."

"How d'you mean?" and the other looked puzzled.

Mrs. Hampton hesitated. Then she smiled a little ruefully. "My maid told me that when Ivy arrived she was quite rude to Annie-you know, my nice old housemaid? —because there was no bottle of scent on her dressing-table! There was one, it seems, last time she was here. It had been left by some visitor—I don't undertake to provide such luxuries."

"That doesn't sound very nice, certainly," Lady Flora looked naïvely surprised.

"Then, if I'm to be really honest, my dear, there's no doubt that one reason why Joan Rodney has taken such a ferocious dislike to Ivy Lexton is owing to the fact that I stupidly told Ivy this morning of Joan's marvellous bit of luck—I mean of that big legacy from the American cousin. I'm afraid that's why Ivy, who behaved all yesterday as if Joan hardly existed, began at once to make up to her! But pretty ways are very much lost on our Joan."

She began to laugh. She really couldn't help it, remembering the way her friend had received the younger woman's overtures of friendship.

Lady Flora looked disturbed, for she was one of those rare human beings to whom it is a pain to think ill of anybody.

"After all, Joan's money is of no good to anyone but herself, Mary? I don't see why you should suppose poor little Mrs. Lexton made up to her because of that legacy."

The other looked at her fixedly.

"Ivy Lexton has a good deal in common with the heroine of Jack's favourite drawing-room story."

"What story?" asked Lady Flora. Her host's rather sly sense of humour had never appealed to her, though they were quite good friends.

"The story of the lady who said to her husband, 'Oh, do let's go and see them; they're so rich!' to be met with the answer, 'My dear, I would if it was catching!'"

Lady Flora looked a little puzzled. "He was quite right. Money is not catching, though I suppose most people wish it were."

"A great many people are convinced that it is, Flora, and our little Ivy is among them. I'm sure she feels that if she rubs herself up against it close enough, a little will certainly come off. And I'm not sure, in her case, that she's not right!"

But Lady Flora could be obstinate in her mild way.

"I like Mrs. Lexton," she said gently. "I'm going to call on her when we're all in town again. She's promised to take me to a nice quiet night club. I've always longed to see one. I want my sister-in-law, I mean Jenny, to know her. Jenny loves young people. She gives amusing little dances——"

"I think you'll make a mistake if you introduce Ivy to the Duchess."

"I don't see why, my dear? After all, Mary, your little friend has been very sweet to me, and that though she knows I'm really poor."

The other woman gave a quick look at her friend. Sometimes she thought Flora Desmond too good, too simple, even for human nature's daily food.

Chapter one

The July sun shone slantwise into the ugly, almost sordid-looking bedroom where Ivy Lexton, still only half dressed, had just begun making up her lovely face in front of a tarnished, dust-powdered toilet-glass.

It was nine o'clock in the morning; an hour ago she had had her cup of tea and-mindful of her figure-the hard biscuit which was the only thing she allowed herself by way of breakfast. Her husband, hopelessly idle, easy-natured, well-bred Jervis Lexton, was still fast asleep in the little back bedroom his wife called his dressing-room, but which was their box-room and general "glory-hole."

Everything that had been of any real value there had gradually disappeared in the last few weeks, for Ivy and Jervis Lexton, to use their own rueful expression, were indeed stony-broke.

Yet they had started their married life, six years before, with a capital of sixty-eight thousand pounds. Now they were almost penniless. Indeed, what Ivy called to herself with greater truth than was usual "her little all," that is, a pound note, and twelve shillings and sixpence in silver, lay on the stained, discoloured mahogany dressing-table before which she was now standing.

How amazed would her still large circle of friends and acquaintances have been had they learnt how desperate and how hopeless was her own and her husband's financial position. Yesterday she had even tried to sell two charming frocks brought back for her by a good-natured friend from Paris. But she had only been offered a few shillings for the two, so she had brought them home again.

And now, as her eyes fell on the pound note and tiny heap of silver, they filled with angry tears. How she loathed these sordid, hateful lodgings! What a terrible, even a terrifying thing, it was to have fallen so low as to have to live here, in two shabby, ill-kept bedrooms, where there wasn't even a hanging cupboard for her pretty clothes, and where the drawers of the painted deal chest of drawers would neither shut nor open.

The Lextons had come there for two reasons. One, a stupid reason, because their landlady was the widow of a man who had been employed as a lad in the stables of Jervis Lexton's father. A better reason was that, owing to there being no bathroom in the house, the rooms were amazingly, fantastically cheap. The Lextons had already been camping here, as Ivy's husband put it, for some months, but they rarely gave any of their friends their address. Jervis still belonged to a famous club to which some of his rich men acquaintances would have given much to belong; and Ivy had a guinea subscription to a small bridge club from which her letters were forwarded each day.

There came a knock at the bedroom door. It was a funny, fumbling knock, and she knew it for that of the landlady's little boy.

Flinging a pale pink lace-trimmed wrapper round her, "Come in," she called out sharply. The child came in, holding in his grubby hand two letters.

She took them from him, and quickly glanced at the envelopes. The one, inscribed in a firm masculine handwriting to her present, Pimlico, address, she put down on the dressing-table unopened. She knew, or thought she knew, so well what it contained.

There had been a time, not so very long ago, when Ivy Lexton's beautiful eyes would have shone at the sight of that handwriting. A time when she would have torn that envelope open at once, so that her senses could absorb with delight the ardent protestations of love written on the large plain sheet of paper that envelope contained.

But she no longer felt "like that" towards her daily correspondent, Roger Gretorex. Also she was going to see him this morning in the hope, nay, the certainty, that he would help to tide over this horrid moment of difficulty, by giving her whatever money he could put his hands on.

Gretorex was of a very different stamp from the men who had up to now fallen in love with her. He worshipped her with all his heart and soul, while yet conscious that he was now doing what, before he had been tempted, he would have unhesitatingly condemned in another man. As to that, and other matters of less moment, he was what Ivy Lexton felt to be ludicrously

15

old-fashioned, and she had soon become weary of him, and satiated with the jealous devotion he lavished on her.

Also, Roger Gretorex was poor; not poor as Ivy's husband had become, largely through his own fault and hers, but through that of his father, a great Sussex squire, who had gambled and muddled away his only son's inheritance. That was why Gretorex was a doctor, and not what the woman he loved would have liked him to be, an idle young man of means.

The other envelope was addressed in a woman's flowing hand, and it had been sent on from Ivy's bridge club.

The writer of the many sheets this thick, cream-laid envelope contained was named Rose Arundell. She was a well-to-do, generous, rather foolish young widow, who had taken a great fancy to lovely Mrs. Jervis Lexton. Mrs. Arundell had been, nay, was, a most useful friend, and a look of dismay shadowed Ivy Lexton's face as she read on and on, till she reached the end of the long letter.

Wednesday afternoon.

Ivy, darling, I have the most astounding news to tell you!

I'll begin at the beginning. Besides, I can't help thinking-for I know you're rather worried just now, poor dear-that it may be of help to you. D'you remember my telling you last time we met at that tiresome fête where we couldn't see each other for a moment alone, that I'd had a wonderful adventure? That I'd been to a fortune-teller? Her name is Mrs. Thrawn. She lives at No. 1 Ranelagh Reach on the Embankment. Her fee is a pound-and I feel inclined to send her a thousand pounds when I think of what she has done for me!

I don't mind telling you now that I was on the point of taking that silly boy, Ronny. No one knows but myself how horribly lonely I've been. Well, I thought I'd go and see this Mrs. Thrawn and hear what she'd got to say; for, after all, I didn't love Ronny, and I always had a dreadful suspicion it was my money he liked, rather than me.

Well, my dear, I went off trembling. But I can't tell you how wonderful she was! She described Ronny and warned me against him. Then she said that an extraordinary change was coming over my life, and that if I would only be patient and wait, everything I had most longed for would come to pass. She was most awfully kind-really kind. She said that if I was sensible and did what she said —I mean refuse Ronny —I should take a long journey very soon to a place that she, Mrs. Thrawn, knew well and loved; and that I should be very, very happy there. That place was India, as I knew, for the woman who first told me about Mrs. Thrawn said she was the widow of a missionary!

And then, oh, Ivy, what do you think happened? I wonder if you remember all I told you about the soldier who was my first love? The man whom my mother would not let me marry and who did so splendidly in the war? He's home on leave from India, where he has a splendid appointment. We ran across one another in the street, and I asked him to come and see me. You can guess the rest!

His leave is up by the end of next week. We shall be married very quietly on Thursday, and sail for India on Friday.

I'm in a whirl, as you can imagine. I'd love to have you at my wedding, darling, for you really are my dearest friend. But he doesn't want anyone there who didn't know us both in the old days, before the war. He hasn't a bean, but, thank God, I've plenty for us both!

Your devoted
Rose.

Ivy Lexton put the long letter she had just read down on the dressing-table. Then she took up the other, still unopened, envelope, and stuffed it into her bag. After all she could read the letter it contained in the omnibus, on her way to see Roger Gretorex. He had taken over for a friend a slum practice in Westminster, and he lived in what Ivy called a horrid little street named Ferry Place.

She turned again towards the looking-glass, and began once more making up her face at the point where she had been interrupted. She was so used to the process that she worked quickly, mechanically, though taking a great deal of intelligent care, far more care than did most of her young married women friends.

With regard to everything that concerned herself, Ivy Lexton was quick, uncannily shrewd, and instinctively clever. She knew how to exploit to the very best advantage her exceptional physical beauty, her natural charm of manner, and, above all, her extraordinary allure for men.

And yet, so unsuspicious is human nature in that stratum of the financially, easy, agreeably self-absorbed, and pleasure-loving world in which Ivy played a not unimportant part, that all the men, and many of the women, who came across her in that world, would have told you that Ivy Lexton was "a dear little thing," "a regular sport," "a good plucked one," and "a splendid wife to that rotter Lexton."

When she had finished what was always to her an interesting and pleasant task, she stood still, and did nothing, for a moment. She longed to get away from this hateful room and this horrible house, yet Roger Gretorex would not be free of his poorer patients for quite a long while. This was the more tiresome as she always went into his tiny mid-Victorian house by the back way, through the surgery, which gave into a blind alley.

Suddenly her eyes fell on "her little all." Why shouldn't she take that pound note, and call on Rose Arundell's wonderful fortune-teller on her way to Ferry Place? After all, she, too, might have an unexpected bit of luck waiting for her round the corner.

She slipped on a cool pale-pink cotton frock given her by that same generous friend who was now, to her regret, going out of her life. Then she jammed a little brown straw hat on her fair, naturally wavy, shingled head, and, tiptoeing down the carpetless stairs, she hurried through the dirty hall into the sunshiny street.

Ranelagh Reach consisted of a row of six early nineteenth-century houses on that part of the Embankment which forms a link between Westminster and Chelsea. Two of the houses had evidently been taken over lately by well-to-do people, for they had been repainted, and their window-boxes were now filled with ivy-leaved geraniums. The four other houses were shabby-looking and dilapidated, and it was in one of these that there dwelt the woman who had taken as her professional name that of Janet Thrawn. The blinds of No. 1 were down, the brown paint on the front door had peeled, and the steps had evidently not been "done" for days. Everything looked so poverty-stricken that Ivy felt surprised when a very neat and capable-looking maid opened the door in answer to her pull at the old-fashioned bell. She had expected to see a slatternly little girl.

"I've come to see Mrs. Thrawn; Mrs. Arundell sent me."

"I'm not sure that Mrs. Thrawn can see you, miss, unless you've made an appointment. But please come in, while I go and see."

The inside of the little house was in its way as much of a surprise as the maid; it was very different from what the outside would have led the visitor to expect. There was a fine Persian rug on the floor of the narrow hall, and plenty of light came in from a window half-way up the staircase. Affixed to the red walls were plaster casts of hands, forming a curious, uncanny kind of decoration.

After the maid had gone upstairs Ivy Lexton felt a sudden impulse "to cut and run." A pound note meant a great deal to her just now. But as she was turning towards the front door, the woman came down the steep stairs of the old house.

"Mrs. Thrawn will see you," she said. Then she turned and preceded the visitor up the staircase.

As they reached the landing the maid murmured:

"Mrs. Thrawn won't be a moment."

Ivy Lexton looked round her nervously. There were evidently two rooms on this floor-the front room, of which the blinds were down, and a back room, of which the door was masked by a heavy embroidered green silk curtain. On the patch of wall which formed the third side of the landing was a dark oil painting, bearing on its tarnished gold frame the inscription in black letters, "The Witch." The subject was that of a white-haired woman being burnt alive, while an evil-looking crowd gloated over the hideous sight.

There came the tinkle of a bell.

"Mrs. Thrawn will see you now," said the woman shortly, drawing back the curtain to show a door already ajar.

"Come in!" called a full, resonant voice.

Feeling excited and curious, for this was the first time she had ever been to a fortune-teller, Ivy brushed past the maid.

Then she felt a pang of disappointment. The room before her was so very ordinary-just an old-fashioned back drawing-room, containing one or two good pieces of furniture, while on the chimney-piece stood a row of silver-gilt Indian ornaments.

Even the soothsayer, the obvious owner of this room, impressed her client as being almost commonplace. At any rate there was nothing mysterious or romantic about her appearance. She was a tall, powerful-looking woman, nearer sixty than fifty. Her grey hair was cut short, and she was clad in an old-fashioned tea-gown, of bright blue cashmere, which fell from her neck to her feet in heavy folds.

The most remarkable feature of Mrs. Thrawn's face was her eyes. They were light hazel, luminous, compelling eyes, and as Ivy Lexton advanced rather timidly towards her they became dilated, as if with a sudden shock of gripping, overwhelming surprise.

Yet nothing could have appeared at once more simple and more attractive than this lovely girl who wanted to take a peep into the future. Ivy Lexton looked almost a child in her flesh-coloured cotton frock and the simple pull-on brown hat which framed her exquisite little face.

Making a determined effort over herself, Mrs. Thrawn withdrew her astonished and, indeed, affrighted, glance from her visitor, and said coldly, "I cannot give you long this morning, for I have an appointment"—she looked at her wrist-watch—"in twenty minutes. I suppose you know my fee is a pound, paid in advance?"

Ivy felt a touch of resentment. Only twenty minutes for a whole pound? Yet she was beginning to feel the compelling power of the woman, and so, slowly, she took the one-pound note that remained to her out of her bag.

Mrs. Thrawn slipped the note into one of the patch pockets of her gown, and motioned her visitor to a low stool, while she sat down, herself, in a big arm-chair opposite. For a moment Ivy felt as she had felt when as a little girl she was going to be scolded.

"We will begin with your hands. No! Not like that. Your left hand first, please, and the back to start with."

As she took Ivy's hand in her cool firm grasp Mrs. Thrawn said quietly, "I need not tell you that you have amazing powers of-well, keeping your own counsel, when it suits you to do so."

Then she turned the hand she held over, and taking a small lens out of the pocket where now lay Ivy's one-pound note, she closely scrutinised the lines criss-crossing the rosy palm.

"You've the most extraordinary fate-line that I've ever seen-and that's saying a very great deal," she observed.

"What I want to know," began Ivy eagerly, "is ——"

"Whether there is going to be any change for the better in your life?"

The fortune-teller waited a moment, and, lifting her head, she gave her client a long measuring look. "Yes, there is going to be a great change in your life. But as to whether it will be for the better or for the worse ——?"

Mrs. Thrawn hesitated for what seemed to the other a long time. But at last she exclaimed, "From your point of view I should say 'for the better,' for I see money, a great deal of money, coming your way."

Ivy turned crimson, so great were her surprise and joy.

"Will it be soon?" she asked eagerly.

"Very soon-in a few hours from now."

"Are you sure?"

"Quite sure."

Mrs. Thrawn lifted her great head, and again she looked at her visitor fixedly.

"May I speak plainly? Will you try not to be offended at what I'm going to say?"

"Nothing you say could offend me," cried Ivy in her prettiest manner. "You don't know how happy you've made me!"

"I do know. But, though I don't suppose you will ever believe it, money is not everything, Mrs. ——"

"—Lexton."

The name slipped out. After all, why shouldn't she tell Mrs. Thrawn her name? Yet she was sorry she had done so a few moments later, for the fortune-teller, leaning forward, exclaimed harshly:

"Now for the powder after the jam! I sense that you are engaged in an illicit love affair fraught to you, and to others also, with frightful danger."

Once more Ivy's face crimsoned under her clever make-up, but this time with fear and dismay. Her eyes fell before the other woman's hard scrutiny.

"Wrong is, of course, a matter of conscience, and I know you think you have nothing to be ashamed of. But you are leading a fine soul astray, and evil influences are gathering round you."

"I know that I've done wrong," faltered Ivy, frightened and perplexed by Mrs. Thrawn's manner, rather than by her warning.

The other said sharply, "You know nothing of the sort! You've not got what I call a conscience, Mrs. Lexton. But a conscience nowadays is a very old-fashioned attribute. Many a young woman would hardly know what to do with one if she had it!"

Ivy did not know what to answer, and felt sorry indeed that she had let this censorious, disagreeable person know her name.

"For your own sake," went on Mrs. Thrawn earnestly, "break with this man who loves you. For one thing, 'it's well to be off with the old love before you are on with the new.'"

"Then there is going to be another man in my life?" Ivy asked eagerly.

"I see a stranger coming into your life within a few hours from now. Whether his valuable friendship for you endures will entirely depend on yourself."

Mrs. Thrawn got up from her chair.

"As we haven't much time, I will now look into the crystal."

She drew down the blind of the one window in the room, and, going across to the writing-table, she took off it a heavy, round glass ball which looked like, and might indeed have been sold for, a paper-weight. Then, moving forward a small, low table, she put it between herself and her visitor.

"Don't speak," she said quickly. "Try to empty your mind of all thought."

Bending her head, she gazed into the crystal, and what seemed to Ivy Lexton a long time went by.

In reality, it might have been as long as two minutes before Mrs. Thrawn began speaking again, this time in a quick, muffled voice.

"I see you both now, you and the dark young man on whom you will bring unutterable misery and shame, and who will bring you distress and disappointment, if you do not break with him now, today. The safe way is still open to you, Mrs. Lexton, but soon it will be closed, and you will find yourself in a prison of your own making, and trapped-trapped like a rat in a sinking ship."

Again there was a long, tense silence, and again Ivy began to feel vaguely frightened.

The prediction of shame and misery to another meant very little, if indeed anything, to her. But distress and disappointment to herself? Ah! that was another thing altogether. Ivy very much disliked meeting with even trifling disappointments.

Mrs. Thrawn looked up. All the brilliance had gone out of her curious, luminous eyes.

"I fear you will not follow the better way," she said slowly. "Indeed, I sense that you are making up your mind not to follow it, unless the doing so falls in with your other plans. I see this dark young man's destiny closely intertwined with your life. He will bear the scars you are about to inflict on him to his grave, and that whether he lives but a few months, or a long lifetime. You do not what you call love him any more. But he loves you as you have never yet been loved, and never will be."

Her voice softened and became low and pitiful, for the girl who was now gazing at her with a surprised, frightened expression on her exquisite face looked too young to be what the soothsayer believed her to be, that is, already doomed, unless she altered her whole way of life, to suffer terrible things.

"As woman to woman, let me give you a word of advice, Mrs. Lexton. For your own sake try to follow it."

"I will!" cried Ivy sincerely.

"Do not be afraid of poverty——" And then, as she saw the other's instinctive recoil, "Poverty does not touch the likes of you with its cold finger," and Mrs. Thrawn gave an eerie laugh. "If you are wise, if you do what is still open to you to do, you will have ups and downs, but the ups will predominate, and there will always be some man, even when you become what I should call an old woman, who will be proud, yes, proud, to be your banker."

"Do you see something nice coming for me soon in that glass ball?" asked Ivy nervously.

She longed, secretly, to be told something more of the new man who was coming into her life.

Mrs. Thrawn bent over the cloudy crystal. Then she muttered:

"The pictures are forming. They are coming thick and fast. And-but no, I will not tell you what I see, for what I am seeing may not concern you at all. It may concern the future of the woman who is now on my doorstep——"

And, as she said the word "doorstep," the old-fashioned house-bell pealed through the house.

Mrs. Thrawn rose and put her crystal back on the writing-table. Then she pulled up the blind.

"We've only a few moments left. But I'm going, for my own satisfaction," she interjected in a singular tone, "to tell your fortune by the cards."

As she spoke she took a pack of cards out of the drawer of her writing-table, and sank down again into her chair.

"Now, cut."

After Ivy had obeyed, the soothsayer rapidly dealt out the cards. Then she put down her finger on the queen of hearts.

"This card stands for you," she dragged her finger along. "And here is the king of diamonds, the man who is coming into your life, and who will give you money, much money. Even so——" she shook her head, "you will never be able to count on him as you can count on the man who is still bound to you, and whom I bid you cast out of your life at once-at once."

She swept the cards together and rose from her chair.

"I saw trouble in your hand; I saw trouble in the crystal; I saw great trouble in the cards. Yet, Mrs. Lexton, you are not a woman who troubles trouble before trouble troubles you. Even so, unless you follow my advice about your present lover, I see misfortune galloping towards you like a riderless horse."

"But you do still believe that I'm going to get a lot of money?" Ivy asked pleadingly. "Did the cards tell you that also?"

"Yes, the cards told me that also."

From outside the door came the sound of footsteps.

"One last word-one last warning. When you came into this room you were not alone, Mrs. Lexton."

Ivy stared at her. What could Mrs. Thrawn mean? Of course she had been alone!

"You were accompanied, surrounded, by a huge mob of men and women, invisible to you, but visible to me. Are you an actress?"

"I was an actress, for a little while, before I married," said Ivy, smiling. "And I'd love to go back on the stage, but only as a leading lady, of course."

"Given certain eventualities, you will become of great moment, of absorbing interest, to hundreds of thousands of people. Men and women will fight over you-the newspapers will record your every movement."

Ivy smiled self-consciously. This last unexpected prediction gave her a thrill of pleasurable excitement. What could it mean but a triumphant return to the stage, of which she had been hitherto only a humble and transient ornament?

"There is a woman already in your life —I see her now standing behind you. She is a grey-haired, worn-looking old woman. If you fail to do what I advise you to do, she will play an overwhelming part in your destiny. Indeed it is she who may determine your fate."

Then she turned, and taking a tiny silver-gilt bell off the mantelpiece she rang it sharply.

The door opened, and the maid pulled aside the heavy curtain. There was no stranger waiting on the landing. Ivy looked so surprised that the woman smiled. "Mrs. Thrawn doesn't like her clients to cross one another. The lady who has just come in is waiting in the front room."

As Mrs. Thrawn's late visitor walked quickly down the Embankment towards the place for which she was bound, she felt more really light-hearted than she had felt for, oh! such a long time. Money coming her way-and a new man in her life? That was all Ivy Lexton really remembered of that curious interview. The warnings Mrs. Thrawn had given her she put down to the soothsayer's conventional outlook on life.

As for the woman's advice concerning Roger Gretorex, she ought to have known, being a fortune-teller, that she, Ivy, had already made up her mind to break with her secret lover. She could not, however, break with him today, for two reasons. First, she was going to ask him for a little money, and secondly, he was giving a theatre-party this evening. She, Ivy, her friend Rose Arundell, and Jervis Lexton were to be Gretorex's guests, and he was taking them on, after the play, to supper at the Savoy. That had been settled days ago.

Rose Arundell? She told herself vexedly that Rose would certainly "chuck." In fact it was plain that Rose had forgotten all about to-night's engagement, or she would have mentioned it in her letter. They would be three instead of four. But perhaps, after all, that didn't really matter, for Jervis was quite fond of Roger.

There was, however, a fly, albeit a small fly, in the ointment. There was no such person, there never had been, or, it seemed to her, could be, in her life, as a worn-looking, grey-haired woman. This fact made her feel a little doubtful, a little anxious, as to the truth of the fortune-teller's other predictions.

Chapter two

"Why, there's Mr. Rushworth! Do go over and ask him to join us for coffee."

Ivy Lexton was smiling at her husband —a delicious, roguish smile. As he smiled back, he told himself with conscious satisfaction that his little wife was far the prettiest woman here to-night.

Her sleekly brushed-back auburn hair, white skin, violet eyes, and slender rounded figure were wont to remind those few of her admirers familiar with the art of Romney of a certain portrait of Nelson's Emma, spinning.

Ivy's husband was pleasantly aware that she was not only the prettiest, but also one of the smartest looking, of the women supping at the Savoy to-night. This was the more commendable, from simple Jervis Lexton's point of view, as they were so hard up-stony-broke, in fact.

He generally did at once anything Ivy asked him to do, but now he waited for a few moments. "D'you mean that chap we met at the Hamptons? *I* don't see him."

"Don't be stupid, darling! He's over in that corner, with two dowdy-looking women, looking bored to death. I'm sure he'll be delighted to join us for coffee."

There had come an edge of irritation in her seductive voice. Ivy had a peculiar and very individual intonation, and many a man had found it the most enchanting voice in the world.

At last Lexton rose, just a thought unwillingly. He had been enjoying himself to-night, forgetting the money anxieties which had at last become desperately pressing, while listening to his wife's gay chatter concerning the well-known people who were also supping at the Savoy this July night.

The young man liked a party of just three friends much better than the big noisy suppers to which he sometimes escorted his wife. In a way it was funny that their host, a grim-looking young doctor named Roger Gretorex, was their friend, for even Lexton realised that, though he and Gretorex were both country-bred, and belonged to the now vanishing old county gentry class, they had nothing else in common.

The host had hardly said a word during the whole evening, either at the theatre, or since they had come on here. So taciturn had he been that Lexton supposed the poor chap was glum because the pretty widow, Mrs. Arundell, whom they were to have brought with them to make a fourth, had fallen out. He knew that Ivy suspected that Gretorex liked Mrs. Arundell quite a little bit. If so, the young man was out of luck, for he was the last sort of chap an attractive widow was likely to fancy.

As he threaded his way between the crowded round tables, there came over Jervis Lexton a queer and very definite feeling of unwillingness to obey his wife. He remembered that he and Ivy had met this man, Miles Rushworth, about three weeks ago at a week-end country house party, and that Ivy had taken quite a fancy to him. But he, Jervis, remembered that he himself had not taken to Rushworth. For one thing, he had thought the man too damn clever and pleased with himself.

Rushworth was, however, an enormously rich man, and Ivy had spent most of the Saturday evening of that long week-end out in the moonlit garden, pacing up and down with him. Late that same night she had told her husband, excitedly, that her new friend had said he thought he could find what Lexton had long been looking for-an easy, well-paid job.

But Ivy's husband, simple though he might be, had learnt a thing or two since they had joined the ranks of what some call "the new poor." One was that, though his wife could twist most men round her little finger, it didn't follow she could make them do much to help him. This time he had been so far wrong that on the Monday morning this chap Rushworth, after motoring them both back to town, when saying good-bye had muttered something to Ivy as to "setting your husband on his feet again." But this had happened a good three weeks ago, and their new acquaintance had given no further sign of life.

After Lexton had risen from the little round table, the two he had left sitting there kept silence for what seemed, to the woman, a long time. Then suddenly Gretorex exclaimed, in a low tense voice, "How I hate hearing you call that man 'darling'!"

Ivy Lexton made no answer to that statement. She was picking up the tiny crumbs left by her fairy bread from the side of her plate, and arranging them in a diamond pattern on the tablecloth. But, though she seemed intent on her babyish task, she was angrily, impatiently aware that her companion was gazing at her with unhappy, frowning eyes. His words had cut across her pleasant thoughts-her joyful relief at having seen Miles Rushworth, at knowing that in a few moments he would be here, with her.

"I'm sorry I made this plan about to-night," she said at last, scarcely moving her lips. "It was stupid of me."

"It was more than stupid of me to agree to it," muttered Gretorex savagely. "I've never been more wretched in my life than I've been to-night!"

She told herself, with a touch of contempt, that what he had just said was not only stupid, but utterly untrue. Why should the presence of her good-humoured, easy-going husband make Roger wretched? But she kept her feeling of irritation in check.

She glanced round at him-it was a pleading, tender glance-and his heart leapt. How wondrous beautiful she was, and-how divinely kind!

And then a curious thing happened to Roger Gretorex. In that softly illumined, flower-scented, luxurious London restaurant, it was as if he saw in a vision the wistful and plain, if intelligent, face of a girl he had known the whole of her short life. Her name was Enid Dent, and she was now twenty-one. Had he not met Ivy Lexton seven months ago, he and Enid Dent would now have been engaged to be married . . . .

So strong was the half-hallucination that he shut his eyes. When he opened them again the vision was gone, and he was hearing the voice which meant more to him than any other voice would ever mean to him in this world murmur gently, "It hasn't been exactly cheerful for me."

Impulsively he exclaimed, "You're an angel, and I'm a selfish brute, Ivy——"

She smiled, but it was a mirthless smile.

"Not a brute, Roger, only just a little selfish. I was a fool to ask you to ask us to-night——"

For the first time this evening Ivy Lexton had uttered a few true, sincere words. She knew now that it had been a stupid act on her part to bring her husband and this strong-natured, not over good-tempered, young man who loved her together this evening. But after all they had to meet now and again! Poor Jervis quite liked Roger Gretorex. Why couldn't Roger like Jervis, too?

Ivy was really fond of her husband. He was so kindly, so unsuspicious, on the whole so easy to manage, and still so absolutely devoted to her. And yet of late she often thought, deep in her heart, what a glorious life she might be leading now, if Jervis, less or more devoted, had granted her, two years ago, an arranged divorce. There had been a rich young man who had adored her. But Jervis had angrily refused to fall in with her scheme. It had led, in fact, to their only real quarrel. But "all that" was now forgiven and forgotten.

She stole a look at the occupants of the other tables and, as she did so, she felt a sharp stab of envy. They all seemed so prosperous, so care-free! Each woman had that peculiar, indefinable appearance which only a happy sense of material security bestows, each man, in his measure, looked like a lord of life. . . . But what was this Roger Gretorex was saying as he bent towards her? "I sometimes wonder if you really know, dearest, how much I love you?"

The ardent words were whispered low, but she heard them very clearly, and she smiled. Though she was growing very weary of Roger Gretorex, it is always sweet to a woman to feel she is loved as this man loved her.

Still, she felt relieved when she saw her husband, and the three she had sent him for, threading their way through the narrow lane left between the beflowered tables.

Miles Rushworth was leading the little company. He was the kind of man who always does lead the way. Though he was now only two or three tables off, Ivy realised that he had not yet seen her, and so she was able to cast on him a long measuring glance.

Mary Hampton, the woman at whose house they had met, had said that he was a millionaire. The word millionaire fascinated Ivy Lexton. And then all at once she told herself that it was Rushworth, of course it must be, who was the stranger coming into her life.

Miles Rushworth was tall and well built but, had he not kept himself in good condition, he would have been a stout man. He had a healthy, almost a ruddy, complexion; brown eyes; what is called a good nose; a large, firm mouth; and perfect teeth. His short-clipped brown hair was already slightly streaked with grey, though he was only thirty-six.

He was not in, and did not care to be in, what to herself Ivy called "society." Neither was he nearly so much a man of the world as was, for instance, her own rather foolish husband. Yet Miles Rushworth had that undeniable air of authority, that power of making himself attended to at once, which always spells brains and character, as well as what old-fashioned folk call a good conceit of oneself.

She glanced also, with quick scrutiny, at Rushworth's guests. They were probably a mother and daughter, and, though dowdily dressed, obviously well-bred women. The older lady was wearing a black lace gown of antiquated make; the lace was caught at her breast with an early-Victorian brooch made of fine diamonds. Hung round her long, thin neck was an emerald necklace. The girl had a pleasant, animated face, and a good figure. Her long hair was still dressed as it had been when she was eighteen—a fact that marked her age as being about seven-or eight-and-twenty. She was wearing an unbecoming pale mauve dress, and there came over Ivy a fear that she might be a widow. Lovely Ivy Lexton shared the elder Mr. Weller's opinion concerning widows.

The younger lady's only ornament was a string of real pearls. The pearls, though not large, were beautifully matched.

As Miles Rushworth came close up to the table, Ivy Lexton rose from her chair, and her face broke into an enchanting expression of pleasure and welcoming surprise. As she held out her hand she exclaimed: "Jervis felt sure it was you! Thank you so much for coming over here. It is most kind of your friends to come too."

Rushworth took her little hand in his strong grasp. He gazed down into her upturned face with a look which, to her at least, proved she had not been mistaken, and that, in spite of his broken promise, already she meant something to him.

He turned round: "May I introduce my friend Mrs. Lexton, Lady Dale?" And then, more lightly, he exclaimed: "Bella, I want you to know Mrs. Lexton!"

As she held out her hand, "Bella" smiled and looked, with unenvious admiration, at the lovely young woman before her. This pleased Ivy, for she had an almost morbid desire that all those about her should like her, feel attracted to her, and think well of her, whatever their relation to herself might happen to be.

A moment later Bella Dale found herself sitting next to a gloomy-looking young man who somehow interested her because he looked clever, as well as gloomy. Jervis Lexton was talking pleasantly, happily, to Lady Dale. As for Miles Rushworth, he had lowered himself into a chair which he had unceremoniously seized from another table, and which he had put a little apart from the rest of the party, and close to Mrs. Lexton.

"I have forgotten all you told me, and what I promised you," he said in a low tone. "But I only came back to town this morning, and I've been fearfully busy all the time I've been away."

He waited a moment, then he asked her what she felt to be a momentous question. "Would your husband take a job away from London?"

A feeling of acute dismay swept over her. It would be dreadful if this big powerful man-powerful in every sense-were to arrange suddenly that she and Jervis should go to live in some dreary, dull town in the north of England! So, after a perceptible pause, she answered frankly,

"I don't think I should like to leave London, and as for my husband, I'm afraid he'd be like a fish out of water, anywhere else."

Miles Rushworth looked across to where Jervis Lexton was now sipping slowly a liqueur brandy. "The chap looks a regular slacker," he said to himself contemptuously.

He considered it a tragic thing that the deliciously pretty, sweet-natured, little woman now sitting so close to him that they nearly touched, should be married to "that."

He heard her whisper hesitatingly, "But Jervis must get something to do very soon now, Mr. Rushworth, or I don't know what we shall do. We're so horribly hard up," and her mouth, that most revealing feature, quivered.

His strong face-the face he believed to be so shrewd, and which was shrewd where "business" was concerned-became filled with warm sympathy.

"That can't be allowed to go on!" he exclaimed a little awkwardly.

During their last moonlit walk and talk in the dark, scented garden of the house where they had first met, Ivy Lexton had told him the pathetic story of her life. How, when she and Jervis Lexton had first married, they had been quite well off, but that a dishonest lawyer had somehow muddled away all "poor Jervis's money."

She had further confessed that now they were really "up against it," hard-driven as they had never been before.

"An idle man," she had said, speaking in that tremulous, husky voice which nearly always touched a listener's heart-strings, "can't help spending money. I would give anything to get my husband a job!"

Miles Rushworth remembered, now, that pathetic cry from the heart, and he felt much ashamed that he had not attended to the matter ere this. But he had not forgotten this dear little woman, and, had they not met to-night, she would have heard from him within a day or two.

All at once, by what was a real accident, his fingers touched her bare arm. They lay on her soft flesh for the fraction of a minute, and it was as if she could feel the thrill which ran through him.

She did not move, she scarcely breathed. Neither could have said how long it was before those hard, cool fingers slid down and grasped her soft hand. He crushed her hand in his strong grasp, then let it go.

"I suppose you would like Mr. Lexton to start work this autumn?" he said at last. "There isn't much doing during August and September."

His voice sounded strangely caressing and possessive, even to himself. But he felt sure that Ivy, a "nice" woman, had no suspicion of how much he had been moved by that casual, unexpected touch.

Miles Rushworth told himself that he must mind his step, for this seductive little creature, God help him, was another man's wife, and he "wasn't that sort." Neither, he would have staked his life on it, was she.

And yet? Was it he? —sensible, prudent, nay, where women were concerned, over-cautious — Miles Rushworth, or some tricksy, bold entity outside himself which uttered the words: "By the way, what are you doing next month? If you're doing nothing in particular, I do wish you'd both join my yachting party. Lady Dale and her daughter are coming, together with two or three others."

A look of real, almost child-like, joy and pleasure flashed into Ivy Lexton's face and, once more, the man sitting so closely by her side felt shaken to the depths. Tenderness was now added to the feeling of passionate attraction of which he was already half uncomfortably, half exultantly, aware. How young she looked, how innocent-now, at this moment, like a happy little girl.

"D'you really mean that?" she cried. "I've always longed to go yachting! But I've never even been in a yacht. Jervis is awfully fond of the sea, too; he was at Cowes when the war broke out!"

"Then that settles it," exclaimed Rushworth delightedly. "We join the *Dark Lady* at Southampton on August the 5th! By the way, perhaps I ought to tell you that we're not going on any specially wonderful trip. We're only going to cruise about the coast of France.

I'm afraid Lady Dale and her daughter will have to leave us fairly soon-they've promised to stay with some people near Dieppe."

"It will be heavenly-heavenly!"

Ivy whispered those five words almost in his ear, for she was exceedingly anxious that Roger Gretorex should hear nothing of this delightful plan. She had promised the young man she would spend a week, during August, alone with him and his mother in the Sussex manor house which was still his own, though all the land up to the park gates had been sold.

As she gave a quick surreptitious glance at the host who was her dangerously jealous lover-even jealous, grotesque thought, of her husband, entirely unsuspicious Jervis —a feeling of sharp irritation again swept over Ivy Lexton.

She told herself angrily that, though Roger Gretorex might belong by birth to grand people (to her surprise he made no effort to keep up with them), he had never been taught to behave as a young man should always behave in pleasant company. Even now, he still had what Ivy called "his thundercloud face," and he was scarcely paying any attention to the girl sitting by him.

Ivy, not for the first time, realised that she had been a fool indeed to allow herself to become attracted to a man who was so little of her own sort. And yet Gretorex had been such a wonderful wooer! And his ardour had moved and excited her all the more because, at times, he had been as if overwhelmed with what had seemed to her an absurd kind of remorse at the knowledge that the woman he loved was another man's wife.

Dismissing the distasteful thought of Gretorex from her mind, she turned to Rushworth.

"Don't say anything to my husband about this delightful plan," she murmured. "I shall have to bring him round to the idea. You see, he's so awfully eager to start work at once."

The lights were now being turned off one by one, so Ivy smiled across at Lady Dale, and rose from the chair which touched that on which Rushworth was still sitting as if lost in a dream.

As, a few moments later, they all stood together outside in the cool night air-all, that is, but Roger Gretorex who, after having uttered a curt good-night, had gone back to the now fast-emptying restaurant to pay his bill-Miles Rushworth exclaimed: "We can all squeeze into my car, or, if not, I'll go outside."

Ivy was delighted. She very much disliked the spending of any unnecessary ready money just now; and the thought of going home in a crowded omnibus on this fine July night had been unbearable.

In the end it was Jervis Lexton who sat outside by the chauffeur, while inside the car the other four discussed their coming yachting tour.

At last the Rolls-Royce drew up before the shabby-looking, stucco-fronted house in Pimlico, and Rushworth helped Ivy Lexton out of his car with a strong, careful hand.

"Don't ring," she said hurriedly; "Jervis has a latchkey. This house belongs to an old servant of the Lexton family; that's why we are living here."

As Ivy's husband opened the door, Ivy's new friend caught a glimpse of the dirty, gaslit hall, and his heart swelled with mingled disgust and pity. He must get this sweet, dainty little woman out of this horrible place at once-at once. Taking her hand in his, he held it just a thought longer than is perhaps usual even when a man is bidding good-night to an exceptionally pretty woman.

Long, long after Jervis Lexton was fast asleep in his crowded little back room, Ivy lay awake on the hard, lumpy, small double bed which took up most of the space in the front room.

She was tired, and with fatigue had come a feeling of depression. Miles Rushworth had said nothing as to their next meeting. He had forgotten her before-he might forget her again. As for Mrs. Thrawn-all that woman had told her might be fudge. The hard, shrewd side of Ivy's nature came uppermost, and whispered that she had probably been very silly to spend a pound on a fortune-teller, and sillier still to believe in her predictions.

As she lay there, moving restlessly about, for it was a hot night, there came over her a feeling of revolt, almost of despair, at the conditions of her present day-to-day life. She was vividly aware of her own beauty-what beautiful young woman is not? In a certain set, the world of the smart night clubs, she was known as "the lovely Mrs. Lexton." Further, she was popular, well liked by all sorts of people, women as well as men, and dowered by nature with a keen appreciation of all that makes civilised life decorous, orderly, and attractive.

Unlike some of her friends, she hated and despised Bohemian ways. She had tasted something of what Bohemia can offer her subjects during the few weeks she had spent in the chorus of a musical comedy. Yet now she was condemned-she sincerely believed through no fault of her own-to lead an existence full of sordid shifts, and of expedients so ignoble that even she sometimes shrank from them, while always on her slender shoulders lay the dead weight of her husband, a completely idle, extravagant, and yes, well she knew it, very stupid young man.

With angry distress she now asked herself a question of immediate moment. How was she to procure even the very simplest clothes suitable for life on a yacht? For a long time, now, she had had to pay ready money where she had once been welcome to unlimited credit.

Then in the darkness her face lightened. She had remembered Roger Gretorex! Poor though he was, he could always find money for her at a pinch. He had done so this very morning, and would of course do so again.

Then her face shadowed. Though Roger had his uses, he was becoming a tiresome, even a dangerous, complication in her life. Yet had it not been for him, had he not taken them to the Savoy to-night, she might never again have seen the man on whom now all her hopes centred.

Ivy Lexton had an intimate knowledge of the ugly, sinister sides of human nature. Her own father, a big man of business, had failed when she was seventeen. He had killed himself to avoid legal proceedings which would have led to a term of imprisonment. Their large circle of acquaintances (of real friends they had none) were some kind, some cruel, to the feckless, foolish, still pretty widow, and her lovely young daughter. The widow had soon married again, to die within a year. Ivy, after drifting about rudderless for a while, had obtained the "walking-on" part which had introduced her to an idle, pleasure-seeking, rich class of young men. By the time she was twenty she could have married half a dozen times. Her choice finally fell on Jervis Lexton, partly because he was of a superior social world to the other men who made love to her, but far more because at that time he had been undisputed owner of what had seemed to her a large fortune. Yet that fortune had melted like snow, lasting the two of them barely six years . . . .

Tossing about in her hot bed, Ivy reminded herself with a dawning feeling of hope, almost of security, that dull Lady Flora, who was no gossip, had said, during the week-end they had first met, that Miles Rushworth's income was over a hundred thousand a year . . . .

As she was drinking her cup of tea the next morning, there was brought up to her an envelope, marked "Personal," which had come by hand.

Eagerly tearing it open, at once she saw that, in addition to a letter, it contained a small plain envelope:

The Albany,

Friday morning.

My Dear Mrs. Lexton,
I have already thought of a job for your husband, but the earliest moment he can begin work would be the third week in September, say a week after our return from our yachting trip. This being so, I hope you will forgive me for sending you the enclosed cheque for a hundred pounds, which he can pay me back at his convenience after he has begun to draw his salary.

I shall be so pleased if you and he will lunch with me tomorrow at the Carlton Grill. We can then make our final arrangements as to meeting at Southampton on August 5th.

Yours very sincerely,

Miles Rushworth.

As Ivy drew out of the smaller envelope an uncrossed cheque made out to "self," and endorsed "Miles Rushworth," tears of joy rose to her eyes.

She ran into the next room, and excitedly told her husband the good news. But she said that the cheque their generous new friend had sent them "on account" was for fifty pounds.

Jervis Lexton leapt out of bed. "How splendid!" he exclaimed. And then, seizing her in his arms, he pirouetted in the tiny space left in the middle of the garret. "You are the cleverest as well as the prettiest little woman in the whole world!" he cried.

Chapter three

"Do look at Mrs. Lexton! Isn't she absolutely lovely, Miles?"

"Yes, Bella-and as good as she is pretty, I really do believe," was the half-joking answer.

Look at her? Rushworth had done very little else since Ivy had come out of her state-room this morning.

The two speakers were standing on the deck of the *Dark Lady*, and three yards away Ivy Lexton, lying back in a deck-chair, was talking animatedly to one of her fellow-guests, a good-looking young man named Quirk, who after having done well in the war, had been very nearly down and out by 1921, when he had been found and succoured by Rushworth. He now had his own 'plane, his air-taxi as he called it, and, thanks again to Rushworth, he never lacked good customers.

It was true that Mrs. Lexton looked lovely today. All the lovelier because she was thoroughly enjoying her new rôle, that of a perfectly turned out yachts-woman.

But Miles Rushworth had already told himself more than once, in the last hour, that he would be cool, detached, impartial, when considering this special guest.

"I suppose you couldn't say a word to her, just pointing out that she's quite pretty enough to do without lipstick and rouge? I wish you'd tell her they don't look, somehow, the right thing on a yacht."

Bella Dale smiled and shook her head. "If you want me to make friends with her, that would be a very poor beginning——"

He said suddenly, "I am afraid Lady Dale doesn't care for Mrs. Lexton?"

The colour deepened in his companion's cheeks, and she looked embarrassed.

"Mother hasn't had much of a chance of talking to her yet."

Bella Dale was uncomfortably aware that her mother had taken an instant dislike to Ivy Lexton on the evening they had first met at the Savoy; and she knew that Lady Dale's feeling had increased, rather than lessened, since the Lextons had joined Miles Rushworth's yacht, for she had exclaimed to her daughter in the privacy of their state-room: "It's foolish to be too good-natured, Bella. That young woman is a regular little minx!"

But Bella Dale, at this time of her life, saw everything through Miles Rushworth's eyes. She liked what he liked, admired what he admired, and at any rate tried to believe good what he believed good. He had asked her earnestly to make friends with Mrs. Lexton, and he had told her something of the struggle the poor, pretty, little thing had gone through. Also he had let her see how great was his contempt for Ivy's worthless, extravagant, idle husband . . . .

Rushworth had always had from childhood a passion for the sea. His had been an old-fashioned home, and everything had been done by his parents to promote what they thought was for his happiness from the day he was born; but not once had he been asked what he wished to do in life. His path had been marked out for him almost, it may be said, before his birth. His father would have been surprised as well as dismayed to learn that, both as a child and as a youth, his great wish had been to enter the Navy. During the war he had given to naval charities what would have crippled a lesser fortune than his own.

His fine yacht was his one personal extravagance, and on the *Dark Lady* he spent by far the happiest hours of his life. But he had deliberately so arranged the accommodation that it was impossible for him to have a really big party aboard. Eight to ten, including himself, was his limit, and the same people were generally asked by him each year. Lady Dale and her daughter, together with an old-fashioned couple belonging to a rather older generation than himself, who looked forward the whole year through to this August yachting fortnight, always came. To these he had added this summer the flying man, the latter's bride, and the Lextons.

Acting as hostess was a middle-aged spinster cousin of his mother's, who, like himself, had a passion for the sea. Charlotte Chattle was a pleasant woman of the world, speaking both French and Italian well, and clever in organising expeditions for those of his guests who cared for land jaunts. But the only people who counted in Rushworth's mind on this summer cruise were Lady Dale and her daughter, and Ivy Lexton and Ivy Lexton's husband.

Ivy's half-presentiment at the Savoy had been perhaps a case of thought transference, for Miles Rushworth, just about that time, had been thinking seriously of marrying Bella Dale. Indeed, had that meeting with the Lextons not taken place, he would almost certainly have been engaged by now to Bella, and he still so far deceived himself as to wish that the girl he thought he loved, and whom he intended to become Mrs. Miles Rushworth, should make friends with Ivy Lexton.

Bella Dale had done her best in the last three days to fall in with his wishes, but she found it difficult to get further than a mild acquaintanceship with Miles Rushworth's beautiful guest. She knew nothing of the night club, dancing, racing life, which was all that both the Lextons knew and thought worth living for. And Ivy, on her side, was entirely ignorant of, and would have despised, had she known of them, the manifold social and general interests which filled the life of even so quiet a girl as Bella Dale. Also Bella, who was no fool, realised with some discomfort that Mrs. Lexton had very quickly become aware that Lady Dale did not like or approve of her.

And Ivy herself? Ivy was counting the hours-to her intense relief they had now become hours instead of days-to the time when Lady Dale and her daughter would leave the yacht at Dieppe.

During the three weeks that had elapsed since their memorable meeting at the Savoy, Ivy Lexton and Miles Rushworth had been constantly together. It had all been very much above board-indeed, quite as often as not, Jervis Lexton had been of the company when the two lunched or dined, went to the play, or, pleasanter still, motored down to Ranelagh to spend an enchanting evening.

But Rushworth had a definite philosophy of life. To pursue a woman who, whatever the undercurrents to her life might be, appeared happily married, would have seemed to him a despicable, as well as a cruel and unmanly thing to do. Also, he prided himself on being able, when he chose to do so, to resist temptation, and he felt convinced he could handle what might become a delicate situation not only with sense, but even with comfort to himself. This was made the easier to him because he put Ivy Lexton on a pedestal. God alone knew how he idealised her, how completely he believed her soul matched her delicately perfect, ethereal-looking body.

While Ivy was chatting gaily to her companion, she was yet almost painfully aware of the two who stood talking together in so earnest and intimate a way. She was feeling what she had never felt in her life of twenty-six years: that is, bitterly, angrily jealous of a girl whom she thought stupid, dull, and unattractive.

Miles Rushworth's attitude to herself disconcerted her. She could not, to use her own jargon, get the hang of him. It was so strange, in a sense so disturbing, that he never made love to her. Then, now and again, she would remember Mrs. Thrawn, and Mrs. Thrawn's predictions.

She had followed the fortune-teller's advice with regard to Roger Gretorex. She had insisted that it would be better for them both neither to see nor to write to each other till she came back to London in September; and he had had perforce to agree to her conditions.

The yacht made Dieppe the next morning, and at breakfast there rose a discussion as to how the party could spend their time on shore to the best advantage. Rushworth at once observed that he would not be able to take part in any expedition ashore. He had received important business telegrams, and he had a number of letters to dictate to a stenographer whose services he had already secured.

Miss Chattle, who knew he would value a quiet working day, suggested a motor expedition to a celebrated shrine a hundred kilometres inland from Dieppe. She declared that if they started at once they could be back in comfortable time for dinner.

And then it was that Ivy, as in a lightning flash, made up her mind as to how she would spend today.

"I get so tired motoring, so I'd rather stay behind." She turned to her host, "While you're doing your work, I can take a walk in the town. Though I've been to Paris two or three times, I've never been anywhere else in France."

"That's a good idea! We might meet at the Hotel Royal about one o'clock, and have lunch together."

Half an hour later Miss Chattle shepherded the rest of the party into two roomy cars, while Rushworth escorted Lady Dale and her daughter on to the quay, where a carriage was waiting for them.

Lady Dale went forward to speak to the driver, and Rushworth turned to the girl he still intended should be his wife.

"If we don't meet again before the end of September, I do want just to say one thing to you, Bella."

He spoke in so peculiar, and in so very earnest, a tone, that Bella's heart began to beat.

"What is it you want to say?" she asked, her voice sinking almost to a whisper.

"I've said it before, and now I want to say it again — —"

Bella looked at him fixedly. Thank God, she hadn't betrayed herself. But what was this he was saying?

"I do want you to make real friends with Mrs. Lexton — I mean, of course, after you and Lady Dale are back at Hampton Court, when Jervis Lexton will have begun work in my London office. His wife, poor little soul, hasn't any real friends, from what I can make out."

"Yet she seems to know a good many people, Miles. When we were looking through those picture papers yesterday, she seemed to know almost everyone who had been snapshotted at Goodwood!"

"I was thinking of real friends-not of those stupid gadabouts who are here, there, and everywhere," he said with a touch of irritation.

And then they heard Lady Dale's voice.

"I think we ought to be off, Bella. It's nearly half-past ten, and you know they lunch early at the château."

Rushworth wrung Bella's hand. "I'm sorry you've had to leave the yacht so soon."

But his voice had become perceptibly colder. He was disappointed, even a little hurt. He had always thought his friend Bella not only kind, but full of sympathy and understanding. Yet she had spoken of his new friend with a curious lack even of liking, let alone sympathy.

When Miles Rushworth came back from seeing the Dales off, he found Ivy Lexton sitting on the now deserted deck. There was a pile of newspapers on the little table which had been brought up close to her deck-chair, and she was pretending to read the Paris *New York Herald*. Convinced that Miles Rushworth intended to be with her the whole of the long sunny morning, she was not only surprised, but also very disappointed, when he said cheerfully:

"Well, lovely lady, I've a hard mornin's work before me, for there's a whole pile of letters and telegrams waiting to be answered. Cook's man has found me an excellent shorthand writer, so I hope to be through in a couple of hours."

Her face suddenly became overcast, and he felt tempted, for a moment, to throw aside his work. But he resisted the temptation.

"Would you rather laze about here or take a walk and meet me at the Royal?"

"I'll go into the town. There are one or two little things I want to buy. What time shall I be at the hotel?"

He hadn't meant to meet her till one o'clock. But for once the old Adam triumphed.

"Let me see? It's half-past ten now, let's meet at twelve-thirty. We'll have an early French lunch, and then we'll go for a motor drive, or do anything else that you feel like doing. From what I can make out, the others can't be back till seven, if then."

Ivy waited till she had seen him disappear into the state-room which was the one retreat on the yacht where Rushworth never asked any of his guests to join him, and about which they all felt a certain curiosity. Then she put down the paper she still held in her hand, and, closing her eyes, she began to think.

What manner of man was this new friend of hers? He must "like" her surely? "Like" was the ambiguous term Ivy Lexton used to herself when she meant something very different from "liking." Yet he had never said to her the sort of thing that the men she met almost always did say, and on the shortest acquaintance. Stranger still, he had never asked anything of her in exchange for what had become considerable and frequent benefactions. True, Rushworth's gifts had almost always been useful gifts. He had never, so to speak, "said it with flowers." That had puzzled her a little, made her sometimes wonder as to what his real feelings could be. Never once-she had made a note of it in her own mind-had he mentioned Bella Dale during the three weeks when they had been so much together in London.

So it had been a disagreeable shock to find Lady Dale and her daughter already established on the yacht, and on the happiest terms of old friendship with everyone on board. Again and again during the week's cruise, Ivy had asked herself anxiously whether Miles Rushworth could really "like" such a dowdy, matter-of-fact girl as was Miss Dale? Yet now and again when she saw them together, talking in an intimate, happy way, and when she heard them alluding to events which had happened long before she knew Rushworth, there would come over her a tremor of icy fear, for well she knew that, from her point of view, a man friend married was a man friend marred.

It was to her a new experience to be in close touch with such a real worker as was Miles Rushworth. There was nothing in common between him and the idle, often vicious, and for the most part mindless young men who drifted in and out of the spendthrift world in which she and Jervis had both been so popular as long as their money had lasted.

She got up at last, and went into her luxurious state-room to fetch a parasol. It was a charming costly trifle, matching the blue coat and skirt she was wearing, but large enough to shelter her face from the sun. Her quaint little sailor hat, a throw-back to a mode of long ago, while very becoming, was quite useless from that point of view.

She walked slowly along the deck, hoping against hope that Rushworth would see her and, leaving his work, join her; but as she passed his state-room she heard his voice dictating.

The French of all ages and both sexes are lovers of beauty, so in a small way Ivy Lexton's progress through the picturesque old town of Dieppe was a triumphal progress. Most of the people she passed turned and looked after her with unaffected admiration and one man-she felt instinctively that he was some important person-followed her for quite a long way. But it was very hot, and in time she grew weary of the crowded streets. Taking as her guides a couple who were carrying their bathing costumes and towels, she went after them up a shady by-way and so through the old gateway leading to the wide lawns along the sea-front, which are the great charm of Dieppe.

What an amusing, lively, delightful place! Against the deep blue sky rose the white Casino, and the parking place was crowded with serried rows of motors. Along the front groups of Frenchwomen, for the most part wearing white coats and skirts, strolled about with their attendant cavaliers.

Her spirits bounded up; she felt herself to be once more what she had not felt herself to be at all on Rushworth's yacht, in her own natural atmosphere again. And, to add to her satisfaction, she soon spied out the Hotel Royal, brilliant with flowers and blue and white sun-blinds.

The Angelus chimes rang out from one of the old churches, and the gay crowd began to move slowly towards the villas and hotels which form the sea-front side of the incongruously-named Boulevard de Verdun.

Ivy walked into the cool hall of the hotel, and sat down in an easy chair with a sigh of pleasure.

How she wished she was staying here instead of on the yacht! She delighted in the atmosphere of gay bustle and care-free wealth and prosperity of all the happy-looking people who were strolling past her on their way to the restaurant. She enjoyed the glances of covert, and in some cases of insolent, admiration thrown her way; in fact she was kept so well amused that she gave quite a start when she heard Rushworth's voice exclaim, "So here you are, little lady! I've been looking for you everywhere. I thought you'd be out of doors."

She got up, and then he said something which filled her with dismay.

"Among my letters this morning there was one from a very old friend of mine, a man with whom I worked during the war. He and his wife have a room in some back street, for they're not at all well off. So I thought it would be a good plan to take them for a drive this afternoon. I felt sure you wouldn't mind?"

"Of course not!"

She felt bitterly disappointed, but she would have been more than disappointed had she known that Rushworth had deliberately asked these old friends to join them, in order to put temptation out of his way.

He added, a little quickly, "I felt rather a brute not asking them to lunch, but I was so looking forward to my lunch alone with you."

"I'd been looking forward to it, too," she said in a low voice.

And then there did come across him a sharp, unavailing pang of regret that he had been so stupidly quixotic, and instantly he made up his mind that their drive should not last more than two hours. After all, he and Ivy were both decent people, and dear friends to boot; why shouldn't they go back to the yacht to spend a quiet happy hour or two, alone together, before the others returned?

They had a delicious lunch, the sort of lunch that Ivy enjoyed, in an airy room full of chattering, merry, prosperous-looking couples.

Then, after they had had coffee, they went out and slowly sauntered to the little garden at the foot of a great cliff on which stands an ancient stronghold. It was cool and quiet there, and the only person with whom they shared the garden was an old lady exercising her Persian cat on a lead.

They sat down in silence. Rushworth was smoking a cigar, Ivy a cigarette. Suddenly he threw away his cigar, for there had come over him a wild, mad impulse to put his arms round her. But, instead, he moved a little farther away.

She, too, suddenly flung away her cigarette, and turned to him, "I sometimes wonder, Mr. Rushworth, if you know how awfully grateful I am to you for all you've done for me-and for Jervis."

He saw that tears were in her eyes, and he took her hand and clasped it closely. He was saying to himself, "Poor little darling, it would be the act of a cad, of a cur, to take advantage of her gratitude and-and loneliness."

"You've nothing to be grateful for," he said quietly, and then he released the soft hand he held. "It's a great privilege to meet someone who really deserves a little help. A man who is known to have money is there to be shot at," he smiled a little grimly. "Any number of what are called deserving objects are presented to his view. The real problem is to find the people who want helping, and who won't ask for help."

He sincerely believed that the woman to whom he was addressing those words fell within that rare category.

Suddenly he got up. "I see the Actons," he exclaimed. "I told them three o'clock in front of the Casino-they're a little before their time."

It was a wonderful drive to Tréport, and Ivy, rather to her own surprise, enjoyed it. Partly, perhaps, because Rushworth's old friend, James Acton, "fell for" her at once, to the amusement of his good-humoured, clever, middle-aged wife. They stopped at the Trianon Hotel on their way back and had some early tea; but even so it was only five o'clock when they returned to Dieppe and dropped the Actons.

Dismissing the car, they began walking towards the harbour. At last-at last they were alone.

In the Grande Rue Ivy stopped, instinctively, before a minute shop, a branch of a famous house of the same name at Cannes and Deauville.

The window contained but one object, to Rushworth's masculine eyes a rather absurd-looking trifle, for it consisted of a lady's vanity bag which looked like a tiny bolster of mother-of-pearl. The clasp consisted of a large emerald set with pearls.

"What a lovely little bag!' exclaimed Ivy ecstatically.

"D'you like it?" Rushworth was filled with a kind of tender amusement. What a baby she was, after all!

"Like it? I adore it!"

"Then I'll give it you-for next Christmas!"

"You mustn't! It must be fearfully expensive," she cried.

But he had already gone into the shop. With something like awe, she watched him from the pavement shovelling out bundles of thousand franc notes on to the narrow counter behind which stood a white-haired woman.

How rich, how enormously rich Miles Rushworth must be!

As he joined her, Ivy saw that the precious bag was now enclosed in a soft leather case which had evidently been made for its protection. He put his delightful gift into her eager hands, and said, smiling:

"The elegant old dame in there-she looked like a marquise herself-declares that the clasp of this bag was once a brooch belonging to the Princesse de Lamballe, Marie Antoinette's friend."

"How wonderful!"

He looked at her quizzically, "I said I hoped it wouldn't bring you bad luck! She quite understood the allusion," which was more than Ivy did.

"It was made, it seems, to the order of a lady who supplied the jewel for the clasp. She's suddenly gone into mourning, and as they had made it they consented to try and sell it for her. It was being sent on to their Deauville branch this very afternoon. It's been here a week, and the old lady admitted that she hadn't had a single inquiry for it!"

Ivy had now opened, the case and taken out the wonderful little bag, her eyes dancing with pleasure and gratitude. She told herself with satisfaction, that, given the right kind of frock, she could use it by day as well as by night.

There was a very practical, shrewd side to Mrs. Jervis Lexton. But it was a side of her nature which she was slow to reveal to her men friends.

As they went on board the yacht a telegram was handed to Rushworth. Carelessly he tore it open, read it through, and then handed it to his guest:

Tremendous affair taking place here tomorrow midday. French President unveiling monument to fallen. We propose staying the night in excellent hotel. Shall be back by tea-time.

Charlotte Chattle.

Ivy looked up. There was joy in Rushworth's face-and more than joy, for the eager, half-shamed look Ivy had so often seen on a man's face was there also. But all he said was:

"This means that we shall have a quiet little dinner alone together, you and I."

"That will be very nice," she answered quietly.

"I've a good deal more work to get through so shall we say half-past eight? We might have dinner in what I call my sea-study. I always dine there, when I'm alone on the yacht."

Just as she was leaving him, she turned and said gently:

"Don't you think you ought to have a little rest after all the work you did this morning? Why not wait till tomorrow?"

There was such a sweet solicitude in the tone in which she uttered those words that Rushworth felt touched.

"Work's the only thing that makes time go by quickly," he answered, and then, in a low, ardent tone, he added, "When I'm not with you, I'd far rather be working than idling— —"

A sensation of intense, secret triumph swept over Ivy Lexton. She felt that the gateless barrier Miles Rushworth had thrown up between them was giving way at last. To-night would surely come her opportunity of lifting their ambiguous relationship from the dull plane of friendship to the exciting plane of what she called love.

She turned away, and then, a moment later, she stayed her steps, and looked back to where he was still standing . . . .

Small wonder that during the three hours that followed that informal parting, Rushworth, while mechanically dictating business letters, was gazing inwardly at a lovely vision-an exquisite flower-like face and beseeching, beckoning eyes.

Chapter four

When Ivy came out of her state-room at half-past eight, the great heat of the day had gone, and old Dieppe harbour was bathed in a mysterious, enchanting twilight. She had put on to-night a white chiffon frock which made her look childishly young, and, as she floated wraithlike down the deck towards him, Rushworth caught his breath.

He had been waiting for her-he would have been ashamed to acknowledge to himself for how long, though he knew that she was never late. Jervis had no sense of time, but punctuality was one of Ivy's virtues.

"I'm afraid you'll think my sea-study rather austere!"

"Austere?"

His lovely friend hardly knew the meaning of this, to her unusual, word. Eagerly she walked through into what was the floating workshop of a very busy man, though something had been done this evening to disguise its real character. Two great bowls of variously coloured roses stood on the writing-table; and in the centre of the state-room was a small table set for two. On an Italian plate in the centre of the table was heaped up some fine fruit.

"How delicious!" She clapped her hands. "Who would ever think we were on board a ship?"

"You are the first guest of mine who has ever come through this door."

He longed to tell her, he wanted her to know, that she held a place apart from any other human being in his life.

"How about Miss Chattle?"

"Charlotte least of all! Once she was free of this room, I should never be able to get her out."

"Not Miss Dale even?"

The colour rushed into Rushworth's sunburnt face, and Ivy noted it with a jealous pang, as he answered more gravely, "No, not even Bella. I made up my mind-and I'm a man who once he has made up his mind, well, sticks to it-that this state-room should be my bolt-hole, as well as my study. It's understood by everyone on board that when I'm in here, I won't be disturbed."

He pointed to a telephone instrument. "If the yacht catches fire, my skipper has permission to ring me up."

The short dinner was served well and quickly by Rushworth's own steward; but neither of the two felt in the mood for talking in the presence of even the most unobtrusive third. Each was longing, consciously longing, to be alone with the other.

During that half hour when he had been waiting for her, aching for her, Miles Rushworth had faced up to the fact that he was madly in love with Ivy Lexton, and that he would give everything he valued most in the world to have her for his own.

But his passion for another man's wife-so again and again he assured himself-was of an exalted, noble, and spiritual quality. Never would he allow that passion to become earthly. He admitted, at long last, that, as regarded his own peace of mind, he had been unwise to see as much of Ivy as he had done in London. But he had dreamt, fool that he had been, of a friendship which should be prolonged even after his marriage to another woman. During those three weeks he had also thought often of the girl whom he meant to make his wife. Ivy should be his friend and Bella's friend-their dear, dear friend.

But since they had all come together on his yacht Rushworth had had a rude awakening. He knew now that Bella Dale was his dear, dear friend, but Ivy Lexton was the woman he loved.

At last dinner, which had seemed to them both intolerably long, was over.

"Would you like coffee served on deck?" asked Rushworth.

But before Ivy could answer, the steward intervened. "It's just begun to rain, sir," and as he said the word "rain," there came a flash of lightning, followed by a peal of thunder.

Ivy's host turned to her. "We shall have to stay here, unless you'd rather go into the saloon?"

"I'd rather stay here," she said in a low voice.

"Shall I pull down the blind, sir?"

"You may as well."

In a minute the man brought in coffee, and then they heard him running along the deck through the pelting rain.

Ivy's hand lay on the table. She looked at it-her fingers were twitching. She felt, with joy and triumph, the tenseness of the atmosphere between them, and, for the first time, something in her responded to Rushworth's still voiceless passion.

"I don't want any coffee," she murmured.

"Neither do I."

They both rose. He looked across at her. "You'll find that sofa over there comfortable, I think."

He uttered the commonplace words in a strained, preoccupied tone. The summer storm outside seemed at one with him, shutting them off from the world.

Ivy walked across to the little couch, which was just large enough for two, and, after a perceptible moment of hesitation, he followed her.

For a moment he stood silently gazing down into her upturned face. Then he began moving forward a chair.

"Won't you sit down here, by me?" she asked, looking at him with her dove-like eyes.

"Shall I? Is there room?"

"Plenty of room," she said tremulously.

As he sat down, there came another vivid flash of lightning, followed by a peal of thunder louder than the one before.

He turned quickly to her: "You're not frightened, are you?"

"I am—a little."

And then all at once she was in his arms, and he was murmuring low, passionate words of endearment and of reassurance between each long, trembling, clinging kiss.

How he loved her! And how wonderful to know that she, poor darling, loved him too. He felt as may feel a man who, after wandering for days in the desert, suddenly comes on an oasis and a cool stream.

But even now, when every barrier between them seemed miraculously broken down, Rushworth kept a certain measure of control over himself.

"I'm going to pull up the blind and put out the light," he whispered at last.

A moment later they were in darkness, though now and again a vivid flash of lightning illuminated the harbour through sheets of blinding, torrential rain.

He strode back to the little couch, and sank down again by her; but he resisted the aching longing to take her once more into his arms. Instead he took her soft hand in his, while he muttered in a broken voice, "I've been a brute! You must forgive me."

She answered in a stifled voice, "There is nothing to forgive."

"I've been to blame all through!"

Then, in a tone he strove to lighten, "I ought to have labelled you 'dangerous' from the first moment I saw you."

She melted into tears, and remorsefully he whispered, "Have I hurt you by saying that?"

She shook her head; but she pulled her hand away.

"Listen, Ivy?"

It was the first time Miles Rushworth had called her by her name, and for that, Jervis, poor fool, had thought him old-fashioned and over-formal.

"Yes," she whispered submissively.

"We've got to talk this out-you and I."

"Yes," she said again, wondering what he meant by those strange words, and longing, consciously, even exultantly, longing, for him to take her again in his strong arms.

"I'll begin by telling you something I've never told to any living being."

He uttered those words in so serious a tone that Ivy felt a thrill of fear, of doubt, go through her. Had he a woman in his life whom he would not, or could not, give up?

"I was twenty when my father died, and before his death we had a long private talk. Quite at the end of our talk, he made me give him a solemn promise."

Rushworth stopped a moment. He was remembering what had been the most moving passage up to now in his thirty-five years of life. It was as if he heard the very tones of his father's firm, if feeble, voice.

"At the time my promise seemed easy to keep. Indeed, I was surprised he thought it necessary to exact it."

"What was your promise?" Ivy whispered, and she came a little, only a little, nearer to him.

"My promise was never to allow myself to fall in love with a married woman. Though it hasn't always been as easy as I thought it would be, till now I have kept that promise. But now I've broken it, for I love you. Love you? Why I adore you, my darling——"

Again he waited, and Ivy felt oppressed, bewildered. Many men had said that they adored her. But no man had made that delightful, exciting admission, without showing strong apparent emotion.

Rushworth had uttered the words calmly, collectedly, and staring straight before him.

"And I can't help myself-that's the rub," he went on, in the same matter-of-fact voice. "Indeed, I'm afraid I'm going to go on loving you all my life," he smiled a rueful smile in the soft darkness which encompassed them.

"But of course I knew, even then, when I was a cub of twenty, what my father really meant. There is a part of my promise to him I can keep; and what's more-by God, I intend to keep it!"

She was moved, thrown off her usual calculating balance, by the strength of his sincerity, and also made afraid.

"What d'you mean?" she faltered.

"It's true that I love you—I didn't know there could be such love in the world as that which I feel for you, Ivy. If it would do you any good for me to jump into that harbour out there and be drowned, I'd do it! But I'm going to keep my love for you sacred, and I'm going not only to save myself, but I'm going to save you, my darling, darling love."

He took her hand again, and this time he kissed it.

Ivy burst into bitter tears, and Rushworth put his arm around her.

"I know how you're feeling," he whispered brokenly. "My poor little darling! But for God's sake don't cry. I can't bear it. You've nothing to be ashamed of-it's been all my fault."

"Can't we go on being friends? It's been so wonderful having you for a friend!" she sobbed.

"Of course we'll go on being friends-dear, dear friends. But lovers-no! I'm going right away-it's the only thing to do."

He was telling himself that of course she did not understand-how could she, gentle and pure if yet passionate creature that she was? —the strength of his temptation. She would never know, indeed, he must never allow her to know, what she meant to him, and all he was about to give up for her sake. A sweet, loving wife, children, in a word, a happy, normal life-all that Bella Dale had stood for in the secret places of his heart.

He was brought back to the present by her agitated, agonised, "Going away? Surely you're not going away, now?"

He waited a moment without answering her. A frightful struggle was going on in his heart, his conscience. Then, at last, he answered the, to him, piteous question.

"Do you remember my once telling you of my sister? Of how I longed for you to know her-but that she was too ill for me to take you to her."

"Yes," she murmured, trying to remember.

She had not been really interested, only secretly glad that Rushworth's widowed sister was not well enough to see her. Ivy Lexton did not care to be brought in contact with her men friends' mothers or sisters. They never liked her, and she never liked them.

"My sister saw a new specialist this week, and he says she ought to winter in South Africa. She's horribly lonely-her husband was killed in the war, and-and now I've made up my mind to go with her. You do agree that it's the best thing-indeed, the only thing for me to do?"

There was something in his tone as he uttered the question that made her feel that, for the moment, at any rate, no plea would move him.

"I hate your going so far away," she moaned.

"It's the only thing to do," he repeated in a hard tone.

"I'm afraid you despise me," she said very low.

"Despise you? Good God! I honour you ——"

And then all at once she was again in his arms.

Moved out of her false selfish self by the strength and reality of his emotion, "I love you," she murmured, clinging to him between their kisses. "I shall always love you," and believed she spoke the truth.

Surely, surely, he wouldn't go away now?

The door opened, and in the darkness they sprang apart.

"The hotel has sent the car for you, sir. It is now on the quay."

"The car?"

A feeling of surprise and despondency swept over Ivy.

Rushworth got up. For a moment or two, it seemed like eternity to him, he found he could not speak.

Then he said, "I'm afraid I must go now, Mrs. Lexton. I'm sleeping at the Hotel Royal to-night. A business friend of mine is staying there, and we are going to have a talk before turning in. He is going to Paris tomorrow morning."

Addressing his servant: "I'll be coming in a minute. The storm's over, isn't it?" he added.

"I think it is, sir."

"Then put on the light again, and take the despatch-box that's over there on my writing-table to the car."

Rushworth waited till the sounds of footsteps on the deck outside had grown faint. Then he came back to Ivy, but he had once more regained possession of himself.

"I want to tell you, now, what I didn't mean to tell you till the last day of our trip. Some cousins of mine have a charming flat in the Duke of Kent Mansion, close to Kensington Gardens. They want to let it for six months, and I've just taken it in the hope that you and your husband will live there till you have found something you like better."

"You're too good to me."

She looked crushed, defeated, humiliated.

"Ivy! My precious darling ——" the yearning cry escaped him.

Slowly she lifted her head, and her eyes, swimming in tears, her trembling mouth, longing for his kisses, beckoned.

He leapt forward, and she fell upon his breast. "Must you go away? I don't know how I shall live without you," she sobbed.

As at last he tore himself from her arms, "Oh God," he exclaimed. "If only you were free!"

Chapter five

"Look at lucky Olive Larnoch. A month ago she didn't know where to turn for sixpence!"

Ivy Lexton, and one of her young married women friends, Janet Horley, were lunching together at the Embassy Club.

Every place in the great room was occupied. At the next table an American diplomat was being lunched by one of the younger Ministers of the Crown; and close by a popular actor-manager was entertaining a pretty young duchess. Two sisters, who had just leapt into musical comedy fame, were laughing at the top of their voices, while being gaily chaffed by their host, an elderly peer who had entertained two generations of charming women by the daring quality of his wit.

Olive Larnoch? Ivy gazed eagerly across at a couple sitting at right angles from where she sat herself.

"Look at her string of pearls studded with huge diamonds! They're all real!" went on Mrs. Horley excitedly. "As for the emerald Jock Larnoch gave her the day they became engaged, it's worth five thousand pounds — —"

"I'm sure I've seen her before," exclaimed Ivy.

"Of course you must have often seen her, in the old days, when she was Olive Ryde, a war widow without a bob — —"

" —and a stocking-shop in North Bolton Street?"

"You've got it in one! And her stockings always laddered, too. Well, one evening, she met a Scotch man of business here at the Embassy, named Jock Larnoch. He'd never been in a night-club before, so I suppose it went to his head! I happen to know the people who brought him here, and the funny thing is that they hadn't an idea he was made of money. They just thought him comfortably off. Yet his first love-gift to Olive was a Baby Rolls-she didn't know what to do with it, poor dear!"

Ivy gazed with absorbed interest at the fortunate bride of the Scotch millionaire. How marvellous it must be to have everything one wants, including an adoring husband! She sighed a quick, bitter little secret sigh. The sight of this fortunate young woman had brought back to her poignant memories and a sudden realisation of what her life might be now, had she been, a few weeks ago, what Miles Rushworth called "free."

"Is that nice-looking man her spouse?"

"Heavens, no! That's Bob Crickle, who wrote the book of *T'wee-t'we*. Jock Larnoch spends every other week 'at the works'; there never was such a lucky girl as Olive!"

Again, with a sensation almost of despair, Ivy thought of Rushworth, and of all that he might have meant in her life by now if he hadn't been so-so old-fashioned and queer in his ideas.

The Lextons had been settled down in London for nearly two months, and Jervis was going to Rushworth's City office each morning. As for Ivy, she was once more a popular member of the happy-go-lucky, while for the most part financially solid, set with whom she had danced, played bridge, lunched, and supped through life, in the days when she and her husband were still living on what remained of Jervis's fortune.

But woman does not live by amusement alone. Ivy loved being loved, so she had "made it up" with Roger Gretorex.

Rushworth was far away, and though he wrote to her by every mail, his letters, as she sometimes pettishly told herself, might have been read aloud at Charing Cross. So it was that, though she had really done with Gretorex, she still went, now and again, to Ferry Place, but far less often than in the days when she had been utterly down on her luck, and at odds with Fate.

And yet, though the Lextons' troubles seemed over, black care was again beginning to dog Ivy's light footsteps, for she was once more what she called, to herself, very hard up.

True, the couple were now living in what appeared to Ivy's husband extreme comfort, and even luxury. Not only was their flat one of the best in the fine block called the Duke of Kent Mansion, charmingly furnished; but an excellent cook, and a good day-maid had been left there by Miles Rushworth's cousins. So what might have been called the Lextons' home-life ran as if on wheels.

From the moment, however, that Ivy had come back to London, secure in the knowledge that her husband was now earning a thousand pounds a year, paid monthly, she had again fallen into the way of buying, or, better still, of ordering on account, any pretty costly trifle, any becoming frock or hat, that took her fancy. She also, in a way that seemed modest to herself, had at once begun to entertain.

It was such fun to give lively little luncheon parties to her women friends-lunch being followed as often as not by bridge! One, sometimes even two, bridge tables would be set out in the attractive drawing-room and, in due course, a bountiful tea would be served by the smiling day-maid, for those of Ivy's guests who were not afraid of getting fat.

The good-natured old cook had not been used to so much work, and she had very soon declared, not unreasonably, that she must have extra help in the kitchen.

Lexton, who was rather pathetically anxious "to make good," always went down to the City each morning by the Underground. But he came back by omnibus, and he invariably dropped in at his club on his way home, and, as he was an open-hearted fellow, he often asked one of his new business acquaintances to drop in too. That, also, meant entertaining, but on a far more modest scale than that in which Ivy indulged.

Though Mrs. Jervis Lexton had learnt long ago the fine art of living on credit, there are a great many things which even in London a prosperous young couple with a good address cannot obtain, as it were, for nothing. Each week many pounds slipped through pretty, popular Ivy's fingers, and she honestly could not have told you how or why. So it was inevitable that she should again begin to feel short of money-short, even, of petty cash.

Often she told herself that it was maddening to feel that if Rushworth were in England she could almost certainly have had all the money she needed, and that without too great a sacrifice of her pride, or, what was far more important, his good opinion of her. Just before leaving for South Africa he had given her a hundred pounds as "a birthday gift." How good he was, how generous! Her heart thrilled with real gratitude when she thought of Miles Rushworth.

Late in the same day that his wife had lunched at the Embassy Club, Lexton, who was going out to what he called a stag party that evening, came back from the City to find an unpleasantly threatening letter, this time from a tailor to whom he had owed for years a huge bill, and who had evidently just heard of his new-found prosperity.

For once Ivy's husband looked ruffled and cross, and she, also for once, felt very angry indeed. Jervis had begun, so she told herself with rage, to put on airs, just because he had a job —a job that she was too clever and tactful ever to remind him was entirely owing to her friendship with his employer.

At last he left the flat and, with a feeling of relief, she went off, too, by omnibus, to the tiny house where Roger Gretorex lived and practised his profession. It was in what might have been called a slum, though each of the mid-Victorian, two-storied, cottage-like dwellings were now inhabited by decent working people and their families.

Ivy had not been to No. 6 Ferry Place for nearly a fortnight, and her lover had written her a long, reproachful letter, imploring her to come and see him there, if for only a few moments. It made him feel so wretched, so he wrote, never to see her now, except in the company of people and in surroundings which filled him with contemptuous dislike, or, in a sense worse still, only in the presence of her husband.

When everything was going well with Ivy Lexton, she felt bored, often even irritated, with Roger Gretorex and his great love for her. But the moment she was under the weather and worried, as she was again beginning to be, then she found it a comfort to be with a man who not only worshipped her, but who never wanted her to make any effort to amuse or flatter him, as did all the other men with whom she was now once more thrown in contact.

So it was that this late afternoon, immediately after Jervis had left the flat, she telephoned and told the enraptured Gretorex that as she happened to have this evening free, she would come and have dinner with him at Ferry Place.

And yet, as she sat in the almost empty omnibus on her way to Westminster, her heart and her imagination were full of Miles Rushworth, and not once did she even throw a fleeting thought to the man she was going to see. Gretorex had become to Ivy Lexton what she had once heard a friend of hers funnily describe as a kind of "Stepney" to her husband. Sometimes she felt that she really preferred Jervis to Roger. Jervis was so kindly, easy-going, unexacting.

Still to-night she felt cross with Jervis, because of the scrap they had had over the tailor's bill, so the thought of secret revenge was sweet.

But the image securely throned in her inmost heart was that of Miles Rushworth.

The knowledge that Rushworth, a man possessed of great, to her imagination limitless, wealth, was loving her, longing for her, and yet, owing to his over-sensitive, absurdly scrupulous, conscience, hopelessly out of her reach, awoke in Ivy Lexton a feeling of fierce, passionate exasperation.

At last she stepped lightly out of the omnibus, the conductor, and an old gentleman who had been her only fellow-passenger, eagerly assisting her. She smiled at them both. Even the most trifling tribute to her beauty always gave her a touch of genuine pleasure. She was looking very pretty to-night in a charming frock, and in her hand she held the curious little bolster bag which Rushworth had bought for her at Dieppe.

Eight o'clock boomed from Big Ben, and Roger Gretorex, his arm round Ivy's shoulder, led her into the tiny dining-room, where had been prepared in haste an attractive little meal. She had been what the man who loved her with so devoted and absorbing a passion, called "kind," and he felt happy and at peace.

After they had finished dinner they sat on at table for a while, and, as she looked across at him, Ivy told herself that her lover was indeed a splendid-looking man—a man many a woman would envy her.

"Sometimes," he said in a low voice, "I dream such a wonderful dream, my dearest. I dreamt it last night——"

She looked at him roguishly. "Tell me your dream!"

"I dreamt that you were free, and that we were married, you and I——"

She made no answer to that remark, only shook her head, a little pettishly. For one thing, she always felt a trifle cross, as well as bored, when Gretorex talked in what she called to herself a sloppy, sentimental way. Could he seriously suppose that, if she had the good fortune to be what he called "free," she would marry a poverty-stricken doctor who was forced to live and work in a slum? He evidently did suppose that; and the fact that he did so made her feel uncomfortable.

"I don't set out to be particularly good, Roger, but I do think it awfully wrong to talk like that!"

He said slowly, "I agree, it is."

"It makes me feel I oughtn't to come and see you like this, in your own house. Jervis would be very much put out if he knew I ever came here."

Gretorex, wincing inwardly, made no answer to that observation. Sometimes this woman, who was all his life, would say something that made him experience a violent feeling of recoil.

She had got up as she spoke, and with a sensation of relief she put on her hat. It was still early, and she had suddenly remembered an amusing bachelor girl named Judy Swinston, who lived not far from here, in Queen Anne's Mansions. Judy had said that she was always at home after dinner on Thursdays, so why shouldn't she, Ivy, go along there now? She could telephone from a call office to find out if it was really true that the Bohemian crowd who formed Judy Swinston's circle didn't bother to dress.

In some ways Ivy Lexton was very conventional. She would have disliked making part of any gathering which could be called a party, in her present day-frock and walking shoes, charming as were both the frock and the shoes. It was a perfect St. Martin's summer evening, more like June than the first of November.

"You're not going yet?" asked Gretorex, in a tone almost of anguish.

"Jervis said he'd try and be back by half-past ten, so I knew I'd have to be home early."

"I see. All right. You won't mind my walking with you a little way?"

And then she turned and faced him, angry at his obtuseness. How utterly selfish men were!

"I should mind-mind very much indeed! Whenever we've left the place together, I've always felt uncomfortable. Taxis go all sorts of ways nowadays-just to make their fares bigger, I suppose. The other day a taxi brought Jervis and me down close here, past the end of this street, though it was quite out of our way. I should hate it, if he met us walking together at this time of night. He would think it so queer."

Again he said sorely, "I see. All right."

Suddenly there came the sound of raucous cries echoing down Ferry Place.

" . . . Verdict in the Branksome Case. . . . All the winners!"

"I thought they weren't allowed to cry papers now?" said Ivy, as the shouts drew nearer and nearer.

"They cry them down here. As for the Branksome Case, to my mind the verdict is a foregone conclusion. The man will hang, and they'll let the woman off-though she ought to hang too!"

"A lot of people were talking about the Branksome mystery where I was lunching today," exclaimed Ivy. "I knew nothing about it, so I felt rather a fool. The truth is, I'm not a bit interested in murders, Roger. I think it's morbid to want to know about such things."

"Do you, darling? Then I'm afraid I'm morbid. This Branksome Case is of peculiar interest to every medical man, owing to the simple fact that there is a great deal of secret poisoning going on nowadays."

"What a horrid idea!" And Ivy Lexton did indeed think it very horrid.

"Horrid, no doubt. But I'm afraid unquestionably true. In fact I heard the question put only the other day, as to what a doctor ought to do if he suspects anything of the sort is going on?"

She looked at him with a certain curiosity. "What would you do, Roger?"

"I've never been able to make up my mind. Of course, this Branksome story was complicated by the fact that two were in it—a husband and a wife. They'd got everything they could out of the woman's lover, so they made up their minds to do away with him. They were awfully clever, and it's a marvel they were ever found out."

"How did they do it?" she asked, eager at last.

"With arsenic-fly papers."

"Fly papers?"

He laughed. "Wonderful what people will do sometimes, isn't it? Steeping fly papers in water has long been a common way of ridding oneself of a tiresome husband. There's arsenic in almost everything we use-at least, that's what's said."

"Arsenic?" Ivy pronounced the word very carefully. It was a new word in her limited vocabulary.

He smiled across at her. Every moment of her presence was precious to him, so he talked on, eager too. "There's plenty of the stuff in my surgery, at any rate. It's a splendid tonic, as well as a poison."

"What a funny thing!" and she smiled at him, apparently rather amused at the notion.

Looking back, for even Ivy Lexton looked back now and again to certain crucial moments of her life, she realised it must have been at that very moment that a certain as yet vague and formless plan slipped into her mind.

"As a matter of fact," Gretorex smiled back at her, "I've got to make up and send off this very evening a mixture which will contain arsenic — —"

"I must be off now," Ivy said, a thought regretfully.

They walked down the short passage, and through the two doors which separated the house from the surgery. Once there he turned up the light. Anything-anything to keep her a few moments longer in his company!

He went quickly across from the door to the left corner of the bare, low-ceilinged room, now his surgery, which had once been an outhouse. There he unlocked the cupboard where he kept his dangerous drugs, and lifted down a jar on which was printed on a red label the word "ARSENIC." Placing it on a deal table above which was a hanging bookcase, he exclaimed, "If you would like to see, darling, what ——"

And then there came a thunderous knock at the front door of the tiny house.

"Wait one moment! Don't go yet, dearest," he said hastily. "I won't be a minute!"

He rushed away, though even in his haste he did not forget to shut both the doors which separated the surgery from the rest of the house.

Ivy Lexton gave a quick look round the sordid-looking stone-flagged walled space, through which her eager little feet had so often carried her last winter, at a time when she had been in love, really in love, with Roger Gretorex.

She noted that there was no blind to the little square window. But, even in the unlikely event of anyone looking in through that window, no one standing outside could see, while she stood by the table, what she was doing, or was about to do.

Standing very still, she listened. From the consulting-room at the other end of the passage there came the sound of voices, raised in argument.

Hesitatingly she took up the jar Gretorex had placed on the table. Then she looked at it with avid curiosity. How strange and exciting to know that Death was in that jar-prisoned, but ready to escape and become the servant of any quick-witted, determined human being.

When, at last, she put the jar down again, she noticed what she had not seen till now, that a glass spoon lay on the table.

Once more she looked round the bare surgery. Once more she listened intently, only to hear again Gretorex's voice, far away, raised in argument.

All at once and in feverish haste she began unscrewing the top of the jar. Once this was achieved, she pressed the jewelled top of her bolster bag, and as it sprang open, she took her powder puff out of its *pochette*. Then, taking the glass spoon off the table, with its help she began shaking into the little white leather-lined pocket a quantity of the powder which she knew to be a deadly poison.

After snapping-to the bag, she replaced its cap on the jar labelled "Arsenic" and screwed it tight. Then she stepped back from the table a little way, and stood quite still, thinking of what she had just done.

Why had she done that-to herself she called it "funny" thing? Deep in her heart she knew quite well the answer to her own wordless question. But she did not admit her purpose, even to herself.

All at once she heard sounds just behind her-the sounds made by slippered, shuffling feet.

Filled with a sudden shock of sick terror, she turned slowly round to see Roger Gretorex's old charwoman, Mrs. Huntley, standing uncertainly in the middle of the room.

The woman had evidently let herself in from the back alley with a latchkey. But how long had she been here? And how much had she seen?

"Why, Mrs. Huntley," said Ivy in a shaken voice. "You did startle me!"

"Did I, ma'am? I beg your pardon, I'm sure. I just come in to see if the doctor wanted anything," the old woman spoke in a pleasant, refined voice.

"He'll be here in a minute ——"

"I won't disturb him now, ma'am. I'll come in later."

Opening the door through which she had entered, she slipped through it into the gathering darkness. Then she shut the door noiselessly behind her.

Ivy moved again close to the deal table. She felt violently disturbed, even terrified. Yet the old woman had looked absolutely placid, though a little taken aback at finding a lady where she had expected to see nobody, excepting maybe her employer, and him only if he were engaged in making up medicines.

Hardly knowing what she was doing, Ivy Lexton glanced up at the row of books in the shabby little bookcase above the table by which she was standing, and she saw that among them was one entitled, "Poisons."

She was just about to take it down when she heard quick footsteps in the short passage, and Gretorex opened the surgery door.

"I won't be more than a few moments now! You will stay, my dearest, won't you, till I've done with this chap?"

"Of course I will. Don't hurry," she answered, in a soft, kindly tone.

She took down the book and hurriedly she turned to the index.

Yes! Here was the word she sought. There were a number of references-half a dozen at least-and she turned up, "Effects of Arsenic; page 154."

A famous case of secret poisoning was quoted, with every detail set out, and she read it with intense, absorbed interest. It told her what she had so much wanted to know, and feared to ask Roger Gretorex, how a secret poisoner went to work, and also how long the process took before-before-even to herself she did not end the question . . . .

As she put the volume back on the bookshelf her mind travelled into the future-the now possible, now probable, future.

Standing there, in Gretorex's barely furnished surgery, she saw herself the cherished wife of Miles Rushworth, and not only rich beyond the dreams of even her desire, but also secure from every conceivable earthly ill.

Had Ivy Lexton belonged to another generation, she would doubtless have called what had just happened to herself "providential." As it was, she just thought it a piece of astounding, almost incredible, good luck.

She next took down from the shelf a thin little book dealing with infantile paralysis. But she had only just time to open it, and to glance, with a feeling of shrinking distaste, at one of the illustrations, when Gretorex burst into the surgery. "The poor chap's gone at last! What are you reading, darling?"

"A book about children, dear."

There came a pathetic look into her eyes, and Gretorex gently took the thin volume from her hand. Then he kissed that lovely, soft little hand.

She had told him, very early in their acquaintance, that her husband hated the idea of children, as if they had a child it would surely interfere with the kind of idle, gay life that he, Jervis, loved. For the hundredth time Gretorex cursed Lexton for a heartless brute.

She allowed him to take her in his arms. For a few moments they clung together, and she kissed him with real passion, responding as she had not responded for what seemed to Gretorex an eternity of frustrate longing.

Ivy had been frightened, very much frightened, just now. It was surprisingly comfortable and reassuring to feel his strong arms round her, to know that he loved her-loved her.

"Did you buy an evening paper?" she asked at last, disengaging herself from his close embrace.

"No, but the chap who came to see me had one in his hand, and I believe he left it behind. Would you like me to give it you to read in the omnibus?"

"It would hurt my eyes to do that. I was only wondering what had happened about that Branksome Case?"

"I can tell you that without looking at the paper, darling. In fact I did tell you-but you've forgotten, my pet."

"What was it that you told me?"

"That they'll hang the man, and let the woman off!"

He spoke quite confidently. "There's not a doubt but that she really planned the whole thing out. But he, poor wretch, bought the fly papers. Most of the secret poisoning that goes on is done by women."

45

"How dreadful!"

"A great many dreadful things go on in this strange world, my darling love."

"You mean things that are not found out?"

He nodded, almost gaily. He was glad, so glad, to find a subject that interested her, and that might make her stay a few moments longer.

So, "I'm afraid that only one secret poisoner is found out for six that go scot free," he went on. "Even now it's difficult to tell the difference between the effect produced by, say, arsenic, and a very ordinary ailment. A post-mortem only takes place if there's already reason to suspect foul play."

"Post-mortem?"

The word meant nothing to Ivy Lexton.

"In the vast majority of cases the danger is negligible," he continued. "The secret poisoner, especially if a woman, is never even suspected, and if she is ——"

"If she is?" echoed Ivy uncertainly.

"The doctor, nine times out of ten, gives her the benefit of the doubt!"

He ended his careless sentence with a laugh. It was of her, of her dear nearness, of her kind, soft, loving manner, that he was thinking, and not at all of what he was saying.

"Would you let her off, Roger?"

He grew suddenly grave. "Well, no, I don't think I would. You see it wouldn't be right. For one thing, she might try the same game over again."

She looked at him coldly. Few men were as set on doing right as was apparently this man.

Then she smiled, a curiously subtle, sweet little smile. She knew, if no one else did, the weak place in his defences. It was pleasant to know that no other woman would ever have that knowledge. Ivy believed, rightly or wrongly, that a man does not love twice as this man, Gretorex, loved her.

"Well, I must go now," she said at last. And then, for she saw the sudden darkening of his face, "You may as well come with me as far as the corner of Great Smith Street, Roger. It's quite dark now."

Once more she allowed him to kiss her. Once more there came from her the response which had now for so long been lacking, and of which the lack made him feel so desolate.

As they walked along the now shrouded, deserted little back streets of old Westminster, Ivy Lexton was very gentle in her manner to the man who loved her with so whole-hearted and selfless a devotion.

She had quite decided that soon they must part, never to meet again. And yet, though Gretorex would never know it, it was to him, albeit indirectly, that she would owe her splendid freedom, and all that freedom was to bring to her. It was that knowledge, maybe, that made her manner so gentle and so kind.

When at last Jervis Lexton came in, he found his wife playing patience in the pretty sitting-room where she spent so little of her time.

He felt a little surprised, for unless she happened to be out, as was the case six nights out of seven, Ivy always went to bed early.

"Thank God, I'm safe home again!" he exclaimed. "It was the most awful show. The grub wasn't bad, but the champagne was like syrup. I've 'some thirst,' I can tell you!"

"Wait a minute, and"—she smiled a gay little smile—"I'll mix you a highball, old boy. Would you like a Bizzy Izzy, just as a treat?"

"The answer, ma'am, is 'yes'!"

She went off into the dining-room, and took from the fine old mahogany brass-bound wine-cooler a bottle of rye whisky and a bottle of sherry. Then, carefully, she poured a small wineglass of each into a tall glass.

With the glass in her hand she hurried down the passage, and so into the bright, clean, empty kitchen. There she soon found some ice, and, after having chipped off a number of small pieces, she waited a moment and listened intently, for she did not want to be surprised in what she was about to do.

But the old cook was lying sound asleep in the bedroom which lay beyond the kitchen. Ivy could even hear her long, drawn-out snores.

Opening a cupboard door very, very quietly, she found a syphon, and filled up the glass almost to the top with soda-water. Then, quickly, she mixed in with a clean wooden spoon a good pinch of the powder she had secreted in the *pochette* of her bag.

"A perfect Bizzy Izzy!" Ivy called out gaily as she swiftly went down the corridor, holding in her steady hand the tall glass, now full almost to the brim.

Through the hall and back into the sitting-room she hurried, and then she watched, with an odd sensation of excitement, her husband toss off the delicious iced drink.

"This soda fizz has got a bitter tang to it," he exclaimed, "but it's none the worse for that!"

Ivy stayed awake for a long time that night. She had suddenly begun to feel afraid, she hardly knew of what. But at last she dropped off to sleep.

At nine o'clock the next morning she awoke. What was it that had happened last night? Then she remembered.

Leaping out of bed she rushed across the dressing-table, on which there lay the mother-of-pearl bolster bag she had had out with her last night. Opening it she took out her handkerchief, her powder puff, and her purse. Then she put the bag, now quite empty save for the white powder the tiny white leather-lined inner recess contained, into an old despatch-box which had belonged to her father.

It was the only "lock up" Ivy Lexton possessed; at no time of her life had she been so foolish as to keep dangerous love-letters more than a very short time. She put the despatch-box in what was the empty half of a huge Victorian inlaid wardrobe. Then she got into bed again, and rang the bell.

A moment later the day-maid opened the bedroom door.

"Mr. Lexton was ill in the night, ma'am. He thinks he ate something last evening that didn't agree with him. He asked me to tell you that he's not going to the office this morning."

Chapter six

It was the eighth of November, a day which, though she never realised it, altered the whole of Ivy Lexton's life. And this was the more extraordinary because she was usually quick enough to realise the importance of everything that concerned herself.

But on this day she was feeling secretly excited, anxious, and what to herself she called "nervy," for her husband's illness, though it had only lasted just over a week, seemed to her intolerably long-drawn-out.

Jervis Lexton, poor devil, was putting up a grim, instinctive fight for life. Coming of a long line of sporting, out-of-door, country squires and their placid wives, he was magnificently healthy, hard-bitten, and possessed of reserves of physical strength on which he was now drawing daily larger and larger drafts.

On the morning when she had first been told that Jervis had been taken ill in the night, Ivy had gone down to Rushworth's city office. There, as she put it afterwards when telling the invalid of her interview with Mr. James, the man he called his boss, "red carpets had been put down for her," and no difficulty at all had been made as to Lexton's staying away.

As a matter of fact, the young man had very soon been sized up as being, from a business point of view, hopeless. But his pleasant, easy manners, and his inexhaustible fund of small talk and of good stories, amused the boss. Also-and that, naturally, was the one thing that mattered-Jervis Lexton was a pet of Miles Rushworth.

After Mrs. Jervis Lexton's visit to the office, however, what had seemed a mystery had been at any rate partially explained. What man, so Rushworth's London agent asked himself smiling, could resist that deliciously pretty and sweet-mannered little woman? No wonder a job had been invented for her husband, who was, after all, a decent chap.

A day was to come when Mr. James would try to remember how Ivy Lexton had impressed him, and when all he would succeed in remembering, very vividly, was how agreeable that impression had been, and how touchingly the lovely lady had revealed her devotion to her husband, fortunate Jervis Lexton.

On the second day Jervis had said he felt so queer that he would like to see their old friend, Dr. Lancaster. And by now, after five days, that genial general practitioner, though utterly unsuspicious of the truth, was nevertheless becoming slightly uneasy at the persistence of the illness.

He had insisted, much against Ivy's will, on sending in a nurse, a placid, kindly woman named Bradfield, who had often nursed for the doctor before.

Small wonder that the patient's wife was also becoming just a little fretful, and more than a little anxious. How long, she often asked herself restlessly, was her ordeal going to last?

Yet another fact added to Ivy Lexton's discomfort during those long days of waiting.

That fact, or rather problem, concerned Roger Gretorex. She found it increasingly difficult to prevent him from coming to the flat. When alone with her he made no secret of his dislike of meeting her husband on "Hail fellow, well met!" terms, and yet he longed to be with her every moment of his scanty leisure.

At times she felt she almost hated him, for by now her whole mind was filled with the thought of Rushworth, and of all that she felt convinced Rushworth was going to mean in her life. But she could not yet afford to break with Gretorex. Afford, indeed, was still the right word, for again he was supplying her with what had always been to Ivy the staff of life-petty cash.

But she came to one great resolution, and that was to go no more to the humble little house in the Westminster slum with which she had now a secret, terrifying association. And so, as her slightest wish was law to Gretorex, the two began meeting now in a picture gallery, or, when it was a fine day, in Kensington Gardens, which was conveniently near the charming flat the Lextons owed to the generous kindness of Miles Rushworth.

So far Ivy had managed to conceal her husband's illness from Gretorex. With regard to that mysterious illness, it was of her lover, and of her lover alone, that up to now she had felt afraid.

As a matter of fact Roger Gretorex had already completely forgotten that idle talk of theirs concerning the Branksome poisoning mystery. But every word that had been uttered during the evening when she had had supper at Ferry Place, and every moment that she had spent in the surgery, remained uncannily present to Ivy's mind.

And now, on this eighth of November, she had been out for an hour, looking into the shop windows which line Kensington High Street. She had even gone into one famous emporium and bought a new, and very expensive, black model hat. Though quite unobtrusive in shape, it was at once as simple and as unusual as only a French model hat can be. She had felt that she might have cause to be really very much put out if that perfect little hat were bought, over her head so to speak, during the next few days.

At last, feeling more cheerful, she walked briskly back to the Duke of Kent Mansion. The pleasant-spoken porter-all men, even lift porters, were always pleasant-spoken to Ivy Lexton-took her up in the lift. She let herself in with her latchkey, for she always liked slipping in and out of the flat alone.

As she went through the hall towards her charming bedroom, the door of her husband's room opened, and Nurse Bradfield came out, looking flustered and worried.

"Mr. Lexton doesn't seem so well, and as we haven't seen Dr. Lancaster for two days, I telephoned to say I'd like him to come now. But oh, Mrs. Lexton, such a dreadful thing has happened!"

Under her delicately applied rouge, the colour drifted from Ivy's face.

"Something dreadful?" she repeated mechanically.

"Yes, indeed, for Dr. Lancaster has gone and broken his leg playing golf! He was staying with his brother-in-law at Seaford, for one night only, but now he's laid up there, and they don't know for how long."

Ivy's first feeling was one of relief. She had been so dreadfully frightened just now lest "something" should have been found out.

But even so, as the nurse went on speaking, there did come over her a slight feeling of misgiving.

"However, Dr. Berwick, the doctor who works in with Dr. Lancaster, so to speak, is coming round instead!" Nurse Bradfield continued.

"I hope he's nice," said Ivy earnestly.

The accident to Dr. Lancaster was real bad luck. He was a dear old thing, and so truly fond of her. When they had been almost penniless, he had attended her twice for nothing.

There came a curious look over the nurse's face. She hesitated, and then made up her mind to be frank.

"To tell you the truth, Mrs. Lexton, I don't much like Dr. Berwick! But then I'm prejudiced, for I once had a nasty little scrap with him when I was nursing another case for Dr. Lancaster. I consider that Dr. Berwick was very rude to me."

"How horrid of him!" exclaimed Ivy sympathetically, although she had not really been attending to what Nurse Bradfield was saying.

But she did listen, with startled attention, when the nurse suddenly added:

"However, he's said to be very clever, and he's much more up-to-date than Dr. Lancaster. I shouldn't be a bit surprised if Dr. Berwick finds out what really is the matter with Mr. Lexton!"

Ivy stared fearfully at the speaker, and again there swept over her a strong feeling of misgiving, if not of fear.

Thus was effected the entrance of Dr. Berwick into the lives of Ivy Lexton and her husband.

In spite of his shrewdness and long professional experience, it took the new doctor some days to become even vaguely puzzled-so true is it that murder is the one chink in the armour of a civilised community-over certain unusual features in his patient's case.

On the occasion of his first visit to Jervis Lexton, Dr. Berwick had been in a great hurry, and though he had seen his new patient's wife for a few moments, he had impatiently dismissed her from his mind as a foolish, frivolous little woman. Indeed, considering the manner of man he was, he could hardly have told, after that brief interview in the dimly lighted hall, whether young Mrs. Lexton was pretty, or just ordinary, though he had noticed, with disapproval, that she was very much made up.

Ivy on her side, if feeling slightly surprised by the doctor's lack of interest in her attractive self, was at the same time reassured by the fact that Dr. Berwick evidently thought her husband only suffering from a temporary, if obstinate ailment, brought on, most probably, by something he had eaten during the evening which had preceded the night he had first been taken ill.

And yet her feeling of misgiving prevailed so far that she deliberately tried to keep out of the new doctor's way. This was quite easy, for she was out to most meals, and owing to Lexton's illness she had stopped giving her pleasant little bridge-parties at the flat.

But as the days dragged on, as Jervis Lexton, instead of responding to treatment, grew steadily worse, Dr. Berwick began to feel really puzzled. He made up his mind one day to see Mrs. Lexton. On that day Ivy was going to be motored to Brighton by a new admirer, and she had said she would come in after lunch to fetch her fur coat. So the doctor, believing she would be back soon, waited for her. But the moments became minutes, and the minutes mounted up to close on half an hour.

Feeling very much annoyed, he was just about to leave the flat, when Ivy walked into the drawing-room, looking, as he instantly acknowledged to himself, charmingly pretty and gay.

"I waited to see you, Mrs. Lexton, because I am not satisfied with your husband's condition. From what the nurse tells me, Dr. Lancaster was puzzled too, though he said nothing of that in the notes he sent me concerning the case."

Then, almost in spite of himself, he was touched by the look of distress which at once shadowed her lovely face, and it was in a kinder tone that he went on:

"If he does not pick up in the next day or two, I should very much like to have another opinion. Will you try to persuade him to see a specialist?"

"Of course I will," she said quickly. "Though he can't bear any fuss made over him, poor old boy! He very much objected to our having a nurse; but she's such a comfort to me."

Dr. Berwick disliked Nurse Bradfield. He thought her slow and old-fashioned. So now he told himself that, though she might be a comfort to Mrs. Lexton, he would far prefer a different kind of nurse to tend one as ill as he now realised Jervis Lexton to be.

He looked fixedly at his patient's wife, debating within himself whether he ought to impart to her a suspicion which was beginning, only beginning, to touch his mind. Now and again, during the last two days, he had felt a slight, half-doubting suspicion as to whether certain untoward symptoms could possibly mean that Lexton was absorbing some form of irritant poison. But even to hint or half-imply such possibility is a very serious thing to do from a doctor's point of view, and so he fell back on what seemed the wiser course of recommending a second opinion.

"Do you think Dr. Lancaster will be away long?" asked Ivy. "He's such an old friend of mine," and she smiled, a pretty, disarming little smile. "I know you're ever so much more clever than he is——"

Dr. Berwick interrupted harshly, "That's quite untrue! Dr. Lancaster has had ten times the experience I've had, and I take my hat off to him every time. But I fear he's not likely to be back for a long time. You see, he's no longer a young man, and it is a great chance for him to be invalided away from home, and where he can't be got at by the kind attentions of friends and-patients."

The next day an untoward thing happened which, though it seemed at the time of very little account, was yet to prove of considerable moment.

Roger Gretorex ran across a Mrs. Horley, whom he had often met in Ivy's company in the now far-away days when he would go anywhere, and everywhere, just to see her, and to hold her hand for a moment. Mrs. Horley naturally alluded to Jervis Lexton's illness, and was evidently much surprised to find that it was all news to him. To everyone but Gretorex, Ivy constantly mentioned her husband's unfortunate condition, and expressed some measure of anxiety.

Though only half believing Mrs. Horley's tale, or rather believing that Lexton was suffering from some slight indisposition, Gretorex went off to the flat, only to find that Ivy was out, as usual.

The cook had opened the front door. She knew Gretorex quite well by sight, for in the early days of the Lextons being there, he had been an occasional visitor.

He listened to her wordy account of "the master's" illness; and then the nurse, hearing voices in the hall, opened her patient's door.

"Nurse! This is Dr. Gretorex, a great friend of the master and missus," said cook, retreating down the corridor towards her kitchen.

Nurse Bradfield, who found life very dull just now, was pleased to see the fine-looking young man —a doctor, too.

"Will you ask Mr. Lexton if he would care to see me?" asked Gretorex.

He felt he could do nothing less, as he was there, and Ivy was out.

Poor Jervis eagerly, even joyfully, welcomed the suggestion, and the nurse left the two young men together. They talked of all kinds of things-things that interested Lexton rather than Gretorex.

At last the visitor rose. "I'll be going now ——"

"Must you? I get so bored lying here. I wish, old chap, you could think of something that would make me feel the thing again? I don't think much of Ivy's Dr. Lancaster. Besides, he's just broken his leg!"

Then he went into details of what had become his wretched case, and, after having heard him out, Gretorex produced a paper pad and a fountain pen. Rapidly he began writing out a prescription, and he was so absorbed in what he was doing that he did not hear the bedroom door open.

Dr. Berwick, who was tired, having been up all night over an anxious case, stared with anger, as well as amazement, at his as yet unknown colleague.

"Hallo!" cried Jervis, trying to lift himself up from the pillow, for he had become very weak. "Here's a lark! An impromptu consultation, eh?"

Then, as even he realised that Dr. Berwick looked like a thundercloud, as he afterwards expressed it to the nurse, he went on, apologetically: "I was joking of course! Gretorex, this is Dr. Berwick, who has taken over Dr. Lancaster's patients."

Then, looking at Berwick, he went on: "Dr. Gretorex is a great friend of mine and Ivy's. He came in just now, and I told him about my poor dry throat and asked him if he could think of something that might give me a little relief. You don't mind, do you?"

Dr. Berwick waited a moment. Then he said, in far from a pleasant tone:

"Well, to tell you the truth, I do mind. You are my patient, Mr. Lexton, not Dr. Gretorex's patient."

Gretorex rose from the chair on which he had been sitting close to the sick man's bed. The colour rushed up all over his dark face. He said stiffly, cursing Lexton for a fool the while:

"Mr. Lexton had just told me that Dr. Lancaster has broken his leg. I had no idea that someone else had already taken over the case ——"

There followed an awkward silence between the two men. Dr. Berwick was waiting for the formal apology which the other did not consider it necessary to tender to him.

At last Gretorex took the piece of paper on which he had written out a prescription for a soothing mixture and tore it in two.

"Well, Lexton," he exclaimed, "I'll be off now, leaving you, I'm sure, in excellent hands! Tell Mrs. Lexton I came in. I've been so awfully busy this last fortnight that I haven't had a minute to myself. I've taken over for a friend a practice in Westminster for a bit. It's in a slum, and means a lot of work ——"

"And precious little pay, eh?" said Lexton.

Roger Gretorex smiled grimly, "But it's all experience."

Then he went out of the room, with just a cool nod to the other doctor.

It was a very different Dr. Berwick who at eight that same evening finished eating his well-cooked, daintily-served dinner. Janey Berwick was what her husband's old friends called, with truth, a thoroughly nice woman. After their early marriage she and her husband had had a bitter struggle, but that had only made them come the closer to one another, and now that he was beginning to be really successful, she was determined to make him, so far as lay in her power, comfortable.

She wore to-night her prettiest evening frock, and anyone, seeing them sitting there side by side in front of their cheerful fire in their pleasant sitting-room, would have thought them a pair of engaged lovers, rather than a couple who had been wedded for close on twelve years.

Janey Berwick still looked a young woman, for she had been only nineteen when she had given up a comfortable, even luxurious, home, to throw in her lot with the young man who till two or three months before their wedding had been still a medical student.

He bore more signs than did his wife of the struggle they had gone through. However, that struggle was now a thing of the past, or, at least, so they both had good reason to think.

An intelligent doctor either shares everything or nothing with his wife. Berwick shared everything and now he was engaged in telling her about Jervis Lexton, and how puzzled he was fast becoming over Lexton's curious condition. He also told her how surprised, not to say indignant, he had been to discover, when he had gone to see his patient today, another doctor there, actually prescribing for Lexton-true, only as a friend, but acting, even so, in a most irregular fashion!

"I think I made him feel what I thought of such conduct," he said with satisfaction.

Then suddenly he asked her a question.

"D'you remember that your people took a shooting in Sussex many years ago, when I first knew you, from a man call Gretorex?"

"Of course I do, darling! Anchorford was the name of the place."

She was puzzled at the sudden change in the conversation.

"Well, this young chap I found prescribing for Lexton is Roger Gretorex! I had a sort of feeling I'd seen him before."

"But what an extraordinary thing—I mean, that he should be a doctor."

"I don't see why. Only the old house and that bit of shooting belonged to them, even then. D'you remember Mrs. Gretorex? She was very much the *grande dame* ——"

"Yes, she was in a way, but so really kind. She took a great fancy to me," said Janey Berwick slowly.

"I don't think she approved of me. She thought you ought to do better."

Berwick's wife smiled. It was true that Mrs. Gretorex hadn't much cared for the dour, silent, medical student who was obviously in love with her attractive young friend.

"It all comes back to me. They were fearfully poor; but Mrs. Gretorex was keeping up all her charities in the village just as if she had still been the rich lady of the manor. I thought it splendid of her. What is Roger Gretorex like now? He was such a handsome boy," she concluded, with some curiosity.

Her husband waited a moment, then he answered: "He's still good-looking; I can tell you that much. But I didn't like the look of him. He said that he'd taken over a slum practice, somewhere in Westminster."

"Is he a great friend of Mr. Lexton?"

"He seemed to be, though they're as different as chalk from cheese. The one's a born idler, the other I should say a born worker; though, mind you, Squire Gretorex was a bad man. D'you remember the sort of things we were told about him, Janey? How he had come in for thirty thousand a year when he was twenty-one, and how by the time he was fifty he had run through the whole of his fortune on the turf?"

"I expect Dr. Gretorex takes after his mother," she said with a smile.

Suddenly there came the postman's loud knock, and Berwick, jumping up, went out into the hall.

He came back with only one rather bulky letter, addressed to himself, in a woman's sloping handwriting as yet unknown to him.

He opened the large, square, pale-mauve envelope slowly, deliberately. It contained a note folded in two, and also an enclosure, an envelope on which was written "Prescriptions."

He glanced over the note:

> Dear Dr. Berwick,
> You asked me to send you Dr. Lancaster's prescriptions. I found them just after you left. Jervis is feeling better this afternoon, and the nurse says that if you're busy she doesn't think you need come tomorrow.
>
> Yours sincerely,
>
> Ivy Lexton.

He looked across at his wife. "It's from Mrs. Lexton. She says her husband's better, and that I need not go there tomorrow. That's a comfort!"

Idly he took out what that other envelope contained. Dr. Lancaster's prescriptions might give him a clue as to what the old fellow really thought of Lexton's mysterious condition.

"Hallo!" he exclaimed in a tone of extreme surprise, for what was written on a wide sheet of thin, common paper, folded in eight, ran:

> Friday night.
>
> > My own precious love (for that you are and always will be) —
> > Of course I quite see your point of view. Indeed I absolutely agree in a sense with every word that you have written to me. We have done wrong in allowing ourselves to love one another, and when I say "we" I really mean I Roger Gretorex, not you, Ivy Lexton. You were, you are, the purest and best woman I have ever known.
> > I can swear before God that, had you been even moderately happy, I would have killed myself rather than have disturbed your peace. My only excuse, not for having loved you-of that I am not at all ashamed-but for having let you know that I loved you, is that when we first met you had begun to find how bitter a loveless life can be.
> > You say you feel you ought never to come again to Ferry Place. I bow to your decision, dearest, and I will say that you are right in having come to that decision, even though it causes me agony. Thank you for saying I may still write to you, and that you will sometimes telephone to me.
> >
> > Your devoted
>
> Roger Gretorex.

Berwick read the letter right through. Then he handed it to his wife.

"Janey? I want you to tell me what you think of this! Both of the writer, I mean, and of the woman to whom this letter was written?"

Slowly, with her husband closely watching her, and feeling, it must be admitted, ashamed of what she was doing, Janey Berwick read Roger Gretorex's letter to Ivy Lexton right through.

Then she looked across at her husband, and her face bore an expression that a little surprised him. He had expected it to be filled with the wrath and disgust he felt himself.

"This is written with a man's heart's blood," she said at last. "There must be more in this little Mrs. Lexton than you think, Angus. Surely this letter cannot be in answer to one sent by a silly, frivolous woman?"

"I wonder," he said gloomily, "what their real relations have been. This letter might, of course, mean one of two things."

She was reading the letter once more, slowly and carefully. At last she looked up. "I am inclined to think — —" then she stopped and exclaimed, "I don't know what to think, Angus!"

"What were you going to say just now?" he asked quickly.

"I was going to say that I'm inclined to think that their friendship has not been innocent. That was what I was going to say; but even in these last few moments I've turned right round! Now I would say in all sincerity, my dear, that I think it very probable that there's been nothing but passionate love on his side, and I suppose grateful affection on hers. She evidently doesn't care for her husband; so much is quite clear."

"No one would ever think so, from her way of speaking of him. The only time I've ever seen them together they seemed on the most affectionate terms. He was calling her 'darling' all the time, and she called him 'dear old boy,' and seemed genuinely very much worried about him."

"At any rate she's now made up her mind to do the right thing," said Janey Berwick gravely. "One can't but honour her for that, when one remembers — —"

She smiled, a curious little smile.

"Yes, my dear? Out with it!"

"After all, it is very delightful to be loved," she said softly, "and this poor young chap evidently adores her."

"Now comes a difficult question: what am I to do with this letter? I wonder if I ought to send it back to her — —"

"If I were you, I wouldn't send it back to her. If she's the sort of woman you've described her to be, it's quite likely she'll never discover that she sent it you by mistake."

"Ought I to put it in the fire?"

"I don't think you ought to do that. It doesn't belong to you. You've no right to destroy it. Wait a day or two, dearest, and see what happens. She may ask you if you have got the letter? Then you can give it back to her. I'll keep it if you like, Angus. We'll put it in an envelope and I'll address it to myself. If I keep it in the secret drawer of my old desk over there, only you and I will know where it is."

Chapter seven

A long, long week went by, and it was now the evening of the 16th of November. Nurse Bradfield had been out for an hour after lunch, and while she was out Ivy had "looked after" Jervis. She made a point of doing this at some time of her day, though it was always over-full.

Being both good humoured and good natured, Nurse Bradfield fell in easily with any plan proposed by her patient's wife. She had become very fond of Jervis Lexton, and, though aware of Ivy Lexton's selfishness and innate frivolity and levity, she was yet attracted, in spite of herself, by the younger woman's beauty, and what was in very truth an exceptional charm of manner, and what some of Ivy's friends called her cheeriness.

Nurse Bradfield would have been surprised indeed could she have looked into Ivy Lexton's mind, and seen how often and how anxiously that mind was occupied with herself.

Often the nurse would be touched and gratified by the consideration with which she was treated, and her comfort studied. It was no wonder that she, on her side, never even thought of insisting on her right to a certain amount of rest and exercise. She was no longer a young woman. She had few friends in London, and this day nursing job with a pleasant young couple was an agreeable interlude in her often anxious and hard-working life.

So on this early afternoon Ivy and Jervis had what her patient afterwards weakly described to his nurse as a quiet, nice little time together.

Then Ivy had gone out to a bridge-party, and now she had just come in, leaving herself barely time enough to dress and go out again.

To the young day-maid who hovered, timidly, admiringly, about her, Mrs. Lexton sadly expressed her regret at being in too great a hurry to see Mr. Lexton, even for a minute.

Hurry was the word today. She was hurrying over her dressing as she never hurried before, and, while she made up with feverish haste, there was a strange look on her lovely face. She even noticed that she did not look "quite the thing," as she gazed at herself in the looking-glass, and she tried, but it was a failure, to smile, reassuringly, at herself.

She had turned away from the dressing-table and had just slipped her frock over her head, when there was a knock at the bedroom door, and Nurse Bradfield came in.

"I feel anxious about Mr. Lexton," she said in a worried voice. "I don't like his colour. Will you 'phone for the doctor, Mrs. Lexton? I hate leaving Mr. Lexton, even for a moment!"

Ivy of course murmured a word of assent. Then it was as if her heart bounded in her breast. Had it come at last—her order of release?

She felt a spasm of terror shake her being. Also a sensation of abject fear of hard-faced, cold-mannered Dr. Berwick.

This morning she had discovered the envelope containing the prescriptions which she believed she had sent the doctor a few days ago. And as she stared at it, puzzled, she suddenly remembered—remembered, with a sharp stab of dismay, thrusting Gretorex's letter into an empty envelope which she herself, in the early days of Jervis's illness, acting on Dr. Lancaster's fussy advice, had marked "Prescriptions." Fool, fool that she had been!

There was that in the lovely, sensitive face of her patient's wife that caused the nurse to run forward and put her arms round her.

"Don't be so upset, Mrs. Lexton! We'll have the doctor round in a few minutes. Though he's not my sort, Dr. Berwick is very clever, and maybe he'll think of something to bring him round—quick! But do please now 'phone at once!" And she almost ran out of the room.

But Ivy did not go over to the side of the bed where stood the telephone. Instead, she went and sat down again in front of the pretty dressing-table. She shrank with terror from the thought of sending for Dr. Berwick "all in a hurry, like this."

Oh! What had made her give that large, that dangerous, dose of the-the stuff, to Jervis today? He had felt weak, weak and what he oddly called "spent." So she had mixed him a stiff brandy and soda. And the doing of that had seemed such a good opportunity for . . . Ivy did not end the sentence, even to herself.

55

Again, why wasn't Roger Gretorex in London? What a fool she had been to let him go for a long week-end down to Sussex to his tiresome mother. There was such support in his unquestioning love, in his adoring devotion, especially as he no longer asked her, with pleading, ardent, burning words of longing, to go to that horrid little house in Ferry Place.

At last, slowly, and with dragging steps, she went over to the telephone and rang up the doctor's house.

To her relief it was a woman's voice, kindly, gentle, which answered.

"My husband is away. He won't be back till tomorrow morning. Mr. Lexton less well? I'm so sorry. I'll have a message sent round at once to Dr. Singleton, who always takes over Dr. Berwick's work. He only lives two doors off, and his telephone is unluckily out of order."

Ivy waited for what seemed to the other a very long time.

"Are you sure he'll be able to come at once?" she asked.

There came the slightly impatient answer, "I can't be sure of that, for Dr. Singleton may be out. But he'll come as soon as he can."

"We want someone at once," and the voice sounded so sad, so woeful, that Mrs. Berwick, at the other end of the telephone, felt ashamed of the suspicion she had harboured about young Mrs. Lexton ever since the night she had read Roger Gretorex's love-letter. It was, however, a suspicion she had kept to herself. Even if these two had been lovers, they were so no longer. And in any case it was none of her business.

But what was this Mrs. Lexton was saying?

"There's a doctor living in Duke of Kent Mansion. I think I'd better try and get him, don't you? My husband is so very ill. Nurse is quite frightened!"

Without waiting for Mrs. Berwick's assent, Ivy hung up the receiver.

She felt very much less afraid than she had felt just now. Surely fate was playing into her hands? She told herself that it was really a most fortunate thing that Dr. Berwick happened to be away.

She went out into the hall and listened. But no sounds were coming from the sick man's room.

Timorously she called out, "Nurse!"

She was afraid to open Jervis's bedroom door, for she was determined not to see him. To do so, she told herself, would do him no good, and only make her feel miserable.

The kitchen door, situated some way off, at the end of the long corridor, swung open, and the nurse appeared, a jug of boiling water in her hand.

"I'm coming," she called out, "I'm coming, Mr. Lexton. Is the doctor here already?"

"Dr. Berwick has gone away till tomorrow morning. Shall we try and get the doctor who lives in number 1A, downstairs?"

"Oh, I don't think Dr. Berwick would like us to do that! He was so disagreeable about that nice Dr. Gretorex. Surely Dr. Berwick has someone who takes his patients when he's away? I never heard of such a thing as a doctor leaving his patients unattended! But I've thought of something to give Mr. Lexton that may ease the dreadful pain. He seems a little better now."

"I'm glad of that," said Ivy fervently. And she was glad. It hurt her, made her feel wretched, when she had time to remember it, to think of poor Jervis suffering.

As time had gone on, Nurse Bradfield had liked Dr. Berwick less and less. He had such a short, unpleasant way with him. Also, she was too experienced not to have quickly seen that he was both puzzled and irritated by his patient's lack of reaction to his treatment. Once or twice she had thrown out a feeler about this. But he had rebuffed her, almost rudely, while yet giving her strict instructions never to leave her patient alone, and always to administer herself the food and the medicines prescribed. This had surprised, and even offended her.

Not only had the nurse become fond, in a way, of beautiful Mrs. Lexton, but for Jervis himself she had now almost a tender feeling. He was such a real gentleman, giving as little trouble as he could, and even when in sharp pain invariably patient and good-humoured.

"I suppose you'd like me to stay in to-night?" asked Ivy nervously.

Nurse Bradfield hesitated.

"I don't think you need, really. It isn't as if you could do anything, Mrs. Lexton? I can manage quite well; and if I think it necessary I can always send cook for the doctor in the flat downstairs."

So Ivy went off, with a sensation of intense relief, to a theatre-party, composed of a young married woman of much her own age and two men. Her own special escort was a good-looking bachelor whom she had met since her return to London, and with whom she spent a great deal of what she called her spare time.

She determined to banish Jervis from her mind, and, in quite a short time, she succeeded. After all, he was "a little better," and Nurse Bradfield was kindness itself.

Ivy had abstained from saying to which theatre she was going, and after an amusing evening spent in laughing at a really funny farce, the four went on to supper at the Carlton.

Her new man friend drove her home at almost one in the morning, and she lingered for quite a long while in the deserted hall of the Duke of Kent Mansion, bidding him farewell. When at last he went off she felt quite "good," for she had only allowed him one kiss.

Lightly she ran up the stairs, for the lift stopped working at midnight. But when she reached the landing outside her front door, Ivy Lexton did not at once put her latchkey in the lock. Indeed, she waited for quite a long time. At last, however, she did put the key in the lock, and slowly she turned it.

Then she gave a stifled cry of surprise, for Nurse Bradfield was sitting in the hall, waiting for her.

There was a look of great distress, almost of shame, on the nurse's kind face. She got up, and looked straight into the now terrified eyes of the merry-maker.

"I've bad news for you-very bad news, Mrs. Lexton."

She waited, hoping the other would say something that would imply she understood what that bad news must be.

But Ivy remained silent, staring at Nurse Bradfield with terror-filled, dilated eyes.

"Mr. Lexton took a very serious turn for the worse about half-past ten. I sent at once for the doctor downstairs, but he was out; and-and ———" she did not finish her sentence. "I don't think anything could have saved him. His heart gave way-that's what it was! He looks so young, so boyish, so peaceful."

The tears came into her eyes. "Would you like to see him?"

"Oh no! I—I couldn't!"

The newly-made widow burst into tears, and the older woman led her tenderly to her bedroom, and helped her to undress.

"I'll never forget how kind you were to my poor darling-and to me, too, nurse. I hope to be able to prove my gratitude some day," whispered Ivy, after the other had tucked her up in bed.

Nurse Bradfield was touched. She forgot how selfish she had secretly thought little Mrs. Lexton's conduct had been, in practically insisting on going out this evening. She only remembered thenceforth her pretty ways, her sweet manner to her poor husband, and the easy good nature which always made her willing, when she happened to be at home, to arrange some little treat for her husband's kind nurse.

That night Ivy lay for a long, long while with eyes wide open in the darkness. What had just happened filled her with a kind of awe. She had not known how easy and simple is the passage from life to death.

She reminded herself how very kind, how good a pal, she had always been to poor Jervis, and how happy he had been these last two months, owing to Miles Rushworth.

Dear, delightful, generous Miles Rushworth! The thought of him brought a rush of joy, as well as comfort, in its train.

At last a great peace descended upon her. All the terrors which had assailed her during those infrequent moments when she had been, by some strange chance, alone, during her husband's illness, had vanished as if they had never been.

57

As she looked back she shivered at the thought of how frightened she had sometimes felt. And yet, after all, she knew now that there had been nothing to be really frightened about.

Roger Gretorex had been right as to what he had said, on that evening she still remembered so well. At the time she had thought it horrid of him to imagine such a thing as that-she let what he had suggested stay undefined. No need surely to put it into ugly words, even to herself. All the same, she did bring herself to face the comforting fact that, if rather horrible, it was certainly true. A great many more people are undoubtedly helped out of life than stupid, unimaginative folk suppose. As to those who-well-help them to leave a world which has no further use for them, they certainly, as Roger had declared, "got away with it," often with marvellous success.

True, that disagreeable Dr. Berwick had been puzzled-he had said as much to her. But she had got on much better with him during the last couple of days, since, in fact, he had seen that she really could not endure the sight of poor Jervis's sufferings . . . .

The word "death," which means so much to the great majority of men and women, meant very little to Ivy Lexton. Indeed, she felt, as she lay there in the darkness, that this man who had been her lover-comrade had only gone away out of her life on a long journey —a journey from which, however, he was never to return. The fact that she had planned that journey, that it was owing to her direct action that he had gone from the world he found on the whole so pleasant, would and must, not only remain hidden, but in time be forgotten even by herself.

In a way, she was forgetting it already as she turned to her cloudless, sunny future-to the delightful existence she would henceforth lead, first as the fiancée, and then as the wife, of Miles Rushworth.

Run straight? Of course she would run straight! For one thing, Rushworth wasn't the sort of man with whom it would be safe to run crooked. For all his odd ideas, and to Ivy his ideas as to morality were indeed singular, she realised that he had his weather eye very much open. She would henceforth have to be what to herself she vaguely called "a good woman." But then, how easy it is to be a good woman when one has a hundred thousand a year!

Chapter eight

After a good night of deep, healthy sleep, Ivy Lexton awoke. She sat up in bed and then, all at once, she remembered . . . .

Her first sensation was one of intense, almost painfully acute, relief. True, she would still have, for just a little while, to play a part. But playing a part was to her second nature. Now and again, but very rarely, in moments of suspense, and now and again in moments of panic, there would appear before a pair of astonished eyes another woman altogether to the everyday Ivy.

She slid out of her comfortable warm bed and softly opened the door of her bedroom, to see that the grandfather's clock in the hall marked a quarter past nine.

The kindly, fussy old cook came out of her kitchen, and when she saw the slender figure, clad in diaphanous pale pink ninon trimmed with lace, standing half-in half-out of the door, she hurried down the passage and whispered, "Go back to bed, ma'am! I won't be a minute in getting you a cup of tea. I scarcely slept a wink all night, I was that upset. Mr. Lexton was such a nice young gentleman."

"Thank you very, very much, cook!"

Tears, genuine tears, rose to Ivy's eyes. What cook said was so true-Jervis had been "such a nice young gentleman," especially during this painful illness. It seemed so strange to think of him as gone, for ever, from a world which on the whole had treated him so kindly, and of which he had been so contented a denizen. Ivy did not put the thoughts which haunted her mind in those words, but that was the purport of them.

After she had had her breakfast, she began to feel oddly restless, and so, earlier than was usual with her, she got up and dressed. Nurse Bradfield, it appeared, was still asleep.

The newly-made widow hesitated as to what she should wear. Finally she decided on a pretty black georgette frock she had bought from a friend who had started a profitable little business in French models, some of which she cleverly managed to smuggle over from Paris.

After she had put it on, Ivy looked at the reflection of herself in the long narrow panel of looking-glass set in the wall at right angles from the window. Yes, the dress was charming, and looked just right.

She ran across to a walnut-wood chest, and took out of it the hat she had bought yesterday. For the first time, since she had come into the flat last night, she smiled. The little hat was so chic, really chic! And it made her look so-well, why not say it to herself? —so absolutely lovely.

Slowly, reluctantly, she took off the hat, and then she went into the drawing-room.

The blinds were still drawn down. How strange! Then she remembered why they were drawn down.

She wandered about the room, feeling just a little dazed. Should she telegraph for Roger Gretorex? It was so stupid of his mother to have given up the telephone. No one could be so poor as that; it was just meanness and affectation! But if she wired she knew he would come back at once. She also knew that she could trust him to take off her shoulders all worrying, maybe even unpleasant, arrangements.

And yet the fact that she was now a widow would certainly make Roger "tiresome." So unfortunately certain was this that she felt it better to leave him alone, at any rate for the present. Also she was a little afraid of seeing him just now. After all, owing to his being a doctor, he had such an uncanny knowledge of-of poisons, and of their effect on the human body.

She sat down; then she got up again, and at last she began moving about restlessly.

Suddenly she told herself that she might as well sit down and write to Miles Rushworth. It could be quite a short letter. He would of course remember that in her very last letter she had said that poor Jervis was worse, and that she was feeling anxious.

She wondered how long it takes for a letter to get to South Africa. And then with a sensation of relief came the thought that she could cable. It would be quite natural for her to do that as, after all, her husband had been in Rushworth's employment.

She went over to the writing-table, and, sitting down, drew a telegraph form towards her. She would write it out, and then take it herself to the post office. She didn't feel, somehow, like sending a cable to Rushworth over the telephone. That is the worst of living in a flat. Everything one says may be overheard, especially from the hall.

But instead of taking up a pen, she put her elbows on the table and gazed in front of her.

There had suddenly come over her a most unexpected sensation of loneliness. Oh, if she had one good man friend who wasn't in love with her, and who would help her through the next few days! She did so shrink from—from everything. Laying her head on the table, she began to sob with self-pity.

The door opened, and the nurse came in. Ivy looked up.

"I'm so miserable! So miserable! I don't know what to do!"

"Don't you worry about anything, Mrs. Lexton. Dr. Berwick will be round pretty soon. I telephoned to his house just now, and left a message for him. Mrs. Berwick was shocked to hear our dreadful news. She said she was expecting the doctor back any minute now. I expect Dr. Gretorex will be in some time today, too. Surely he'll see to all the things that have to be done."

"All the things?" Ivy looked timorously at Nurse Bradfield, and shivered.

The other saw her look of dismay. "Poor little thing," she said to herself, "she's not much more than a child, after all."

Aloud she said, "I thought of going out presently. Not for long"—fear had flashed into Ivy's face—"only just for a few minutes."

She added kindly: "I shouldn't try to write, if I were you, Mrs. Lexton. I'd just lie down and have a rest. I don't suppose you've had much sleep?"

Ivy answered plaintively, "I lay awake all night. You see it was such a shock, nurse, such a dreadful shock," and she thought that what she said was true.

In a way it had been a dreadful shock, for Ivy had never come face to face with death. She had been still a pupil at a fashionable school when her father had killed himself.

The nurse led her to the comfortable sofa. "You lie down here."

Ivy obeyed, wondering why she felt as she did feel-so thoroughly upset and unnerved.

She had been lying down perhaps ten minutes when she heard the now familiar knock of Dr. Berwick. She started up, and what natural colour she had left her cheeks. Angrily she told herself that it was stupid to feel frightened. There was nothing to be frightened about.

The door opened, and the doctor strode into the darkened room. He turned a frowning, preoccupied face on the newly-made widow. Then, when his eyes rested on the tear-stained little face, his expression softened.

"I'm more sorry than I can say that I happened to have been away all yesterday, Mrs. Lexton. I only came back this morning."

Ivy began to cry, and again he felt touched by her evident distress.

"Sit down, Mrs. Lexton. Do sit down. I'm afraid you've had a terrible shock."

"A dreadful, dreadful shock!" she sobbed, "I had no idea that Jervis was so ill."

"Last time I was here he was certainly better," he said quickly. "You thought him better too, didn't you?"

"I did. I did indeed."

She was trembling now, and though she was consciously playing a part, her emotion was still genuine.

She sat down on the sofa and the doctor drew up a chair and sat down too, a little to her surprise.

"If you feel up to it," he said, "I want to ask you a few questions. I mean as to what happened yesterday?"

She dabbed her eyes with her handkerchief. "I can't tell you very much, for I was out a great deal yesterday. But nurse never left Jervis, not for one moment. She's been most awfully kind, and——"

He cut her short, brusquely. "I know she's a good old thing. What I want to know is whether Mr. Lexton received any visitor or visitors yesterday?"

"Visitors?" She looked at him in surprise. "Not that I know of. He was far too ill."

In a tone which he strove to make light, he observed, "I thought that your husband might have seen Dr. Gretorex for a few moments."

The colour rushed into her face.

"He can't have seen him. Dr. Gretorex is in the country." Then, a little confusedly, she added, "At least, I'm nearly sure that he is."

"Ah, well, then he can't have come in, of course."

A knock sounded on the door, and Nurse Bradfield came into the room.

Ivy welcomed her presence. Looking up into the kind face, now full of sympathy, she exclaimed:

"Dr. Berwick has been asking me if my husband saw anyone yesterday? But I'm quite sure Jervis wasn't well enough to see anyone."

"Mr. Lexton only had one visitor," said the nurse quickly, defensively, "and that was Dr. Gretorex."

"I thought," said the doctor, turning sharply on Ivy, "that you said just now that Dr. Gretorex was in the country?"

"He was to have been in the country, staying with his mother for a long week-end."

There was no mistaking Ivy's look of surprise. Not that she thought it mattered, one way or the other, whether Roger Gretorex had come in or not yesterday.

"At what time was he here?" asked Dr. Berwick.

The nurse waited a moment. "I suppose it would have been about four o'clock. He didn't mean to see Mr. Lexton."

Said Dr. Berwick grimly to himself, "Oh, didn't he?"

Nurse Bradfield went on, a little nervously: "He asked for Mrs. Lexton, and when he heard that she was coming in soon-you said you wouldn't be out long," and she turned to Ivy—"he said he would come in and wait. After he had been in the drawing-room about ten minutes, he rang for the maid and asked to see me. I told him I thought Mr. Lexton on the whole better, and then he inquired if Mr. Lexton would care to see him. He said he couldn't stay long, as he had a train to catch——"

Dr. Berwick said negligently, "Did you leave them alone together, nurse?"

"Yes, I did, doctor, for I knew they were great friends. Dr. Gretorex thought Mr. Lexton less well than the last time he had seen him. In fact, he saw a great change."

"Did he tell you that?"

She replied quickly, "He told me that he thought him very far from well, and that he was distressed at the change he saw in him."

"You never told me all that," said Ivy plaintively.

"I ought to have done, Mrs. Lexton. But the truth is I was too upset, when Mr. Lexton took a turn for the worse, to remember anything."

"I'm sure seeing Roger Gretorex for a few moments can't have done him any harm," said Ivy gently. "They were great friends."

But as she made that commonplace remark, she flushed again, remembering Roger's highfalutin' letter-what a fool she had been not to destroy it at once!

"So I understood on that occasion when Dr. Gretorex, from my point of view, most improperly began to prescribe for him," said the doctor, in a tone which, even to himself, sounded trenchantly ironic.

Meanwhile Nurse Bradfield, supposing that for the present the doctor had done with her, had turned towards the door.

"I should be obliged, nurse, if you would wait in the dining-room for a few moments. I should like to speak to you on my way out."

"Certainly, Dr. Berwick."

The good woman told herself with a touch of contempt that he could have nothing of any moment to say to her. She had done her duty, and more than her duty as a day nurse, to poor Jervis Lexton.

As she shut the door, Dr. Berwick turned to his late patient's widow.

"In the circumstances," he said, in a slow, emphatic tone, "I am afraid, Mrs. Lexton, that there must be a post-mortem."

"A post-mortem?" repeated Ivy falteringly. "What is a post-mortem, Dr. Berwick?"

She was trying to remember what it was exactly that Roger Gretorex had said about a "post-mortem." Much that he had said, during that conversation which had meant so little to him, and so much to her, was almost terribly present to her mind. But her memory as to that alarming word or expression had become dim.

Ivy Lexton had always remained, until today, most comfortably ignorant of all the terrible, strange, and awful things that now and again occurred outside her own immediate little circle of people and of interests.

The newspaper reports of a really exciting "society case," of the kind which amused and intrigued her special set of friends, amused and intrigued her too; though only if there was nothing going on at the time in her own life of infinitely greater moment. As to what is called, often erroneously, "a murder mystery" she had never felt any interest at all.

Her look of innocent inquiry at once effaced from Dr. Berwick's mind what might have been described as a gossamer suspicion which he had now and again entertained, during the last ten days, with regard to his patient's wife.

He did not answer her question at once. Instead he asked her slowly, "I suppose you have some man relative who can see to everything for you? Though I advise that no arrangements be made today."

"No arrangements?" She looked at him surprised. "Does that mean ———" she waited for a moment, then went on, "that poor Jervis's funeral cannot take place as soon as nurse thought it might?"

"Nurse? What did nurse say?" he asked quickly.

She realised at once that she had made a mistake in mentioning nurse.

Ivy was only clever with regard to those men-they were in the great majority-whom she instinctively knew to be strongly attracted to her lovely self.

"Nurse seemed to think that the funeral could be on Thursday," she answered in a low voice.

"Nothing can be settled till the post-mortem has taken place, Mrs. Lexton. Once the cause of death has been ascertained, the funeral can, of course, take place at once."

Ivy had moved away while he was speaking, and she was now standing by the writing-table, with her back to the window.

Slowly, mechanically, she repeated: "The cause of death?"

Though she uttered the four words in her usual voice, there had suddenly swept over her a sensation of intense terror.

"I'm sure that you feel quite as anxious as I do, Mrs. Lexton, to know what can have brought about your husband's death in so sudden and mysterious a fashion," said Dr. Berwick earnestly. "I have not concealed from you that to me this case, ever since I took charge of Mr. Lexton, presented more than one puzzling feature."

Though, unlike his wife, he felt quite sure that the attractive, silly young creature before him had never returned Roger Gretorex's love, she had certainly been foolishly imprudent. With indulgent contempt he told himself that she was the sort of woman who always likes to have an adoring swain hanging about her.

"I think it more than likely," he said, getting up, and speaking far more lightly than before, "that nothing untoward will be discovered as a result of the post-mortem —which, by the way, simply means an examination. But still, if only for my own satisfaction, and I'm sure that my feelings will be shared by Dr. Lancaster, I should like to be able to put what is the truth, rather than a mere guess, as to the cause of Mr. Lexton's death on the certificate."

Again he had uttered those awful words —*the cause of... death.*

She forced herself to say, with a look of childish appeal, "I daresay you'll think it strange, Dr. Berwick, but this is the first time in my life that I've ever been even in the same house where— —"

She stopped, and he supplied the end of her sentence,

"—there has been a death? That is not so strange as you may think, Mrs. Lexton. Some people go through a long life without coming in contact even with serious illness."

"It's that which makes it all so dreadful," and again she melted into tears.

She was telling herself that if they really found out anything as a result of-what was that strange, terrifying term? —the post-mortem, then this hard-faced man standing there might make a great difference, perhaps all the difference, to her being, well, worried.

Her look of appeal, her tears, did touch the doctor. He asked himself idly what age this lovely little woman could be? She looked so amazingly young. Not a day over twenty! But she must, of course, be much older than that, for Jervis Lexton had talked on one occasion as if they had been married quite a long time.

Ivy felt the wave of kindly feeling, and was reassured.

"I shall be so lonely now," she said plaintively.

"Have you no woman friend who would come and stay with you, Mrs. Lexton? In any case, you ought to communicate with your husband's lawyers. I suppose Mr. Lexton's life was insured?"

"No, Jervis was not insured."

She looked surprised at the question.

"He quarrelled with his lawyer last year," she added forlornly. "And our one really great friend, Miles Rushworth, lives at Liverpool, but he is in South Africa just now."

"You mean the owner of the Rushworth Line?"

"Yes, my husband was in his London office. I'm going to cable to Mr. Rushworth. It's so dreadful to feel I've no one to turn to."

"I should think Dr. Gretorex might be able to help you?"

He uttered the commonplace words in a tone he tried to make matter-of-fact. Still, he threw her a quick look, and he did become aware that the half-question had disturbed her. Though how much he had disturbed her he was never to know.

She turned to the writing-table, and began piling the papers which lay on it to one side, and then there rose before her inner vision a view of Roger Gretorex's surgery as it had looked on that evening when she had been surprised, just for a moment, by his old charwoman. She saw again the jar labelled "ARSENIC" standing on the deal table.

"I'm not quite sure where Dr. Gretorex is just now. Besides, he's so dreadfully busy."

Dr. Berwick reminded himself that the poor little woman had undoubtedly been trying to put an end to Gretorex's infatuation. Gretorex's own letter had proved that. So it was decent of her not to send for him just now.

"I must be going, Mrs. Lexton, for I have a great deal of work to get through this morning."

He took her hand in his, and then he felt startled, for it was icy cold. Poor, pretty little thing! She had evidently had a more serious shock than he had supposed. In her own childish way she must have been really fond of that feckless, yet not unattractive, chap.

True, she had been no more use in the sick-room than an officious, affectionate child would have been! And only this last week he had thought it oddly heartless of her to have been out almost the whole of every day. But he realised, now, that she had never before come in contact with serious illness . . . .

However, there could be no doubt as to her real grief and sense of loss. There were black lines round her long-fringed, violet eyes; marks of tears still stained her roseleaf-tinted cheeks. And-and she was really so lovely that now, when bidding her good-bye, he did hold her hand maybe a thought longer than he need have done.

"Get out of doors all you can," he said feelingly. "Go and walk in Kensington Gardens now, till lunch time. And don't worry about anything! As far as will be possible, I promise to save you all trouble and anxiety."

She gave his strong hand an affectionate squeeze.

"I can't tell you how grateful I am to you, doctor, I shall never forget how awfully kind you've been."

Till a few moments ago she had thought Dr. Berwick very unkind, but Ivy Lexton was dowered with so great a power of self-deception that she really did believe what she had just said.

As the doctor was going quickly through the hall, Nurse Bradfield came out of the dining-room.

"You wanted to see me, Dr. Berwick?"

"Did I? Well, I don't think I need trouble you after all, nurse. Wait a moment, though. I'd just like to have your address. I suppose you are leaving here today?"

Nurse Bradfield was genuinely surprised. She had felt so sure that the doctor thought but poorly of her; and she on her side had no wish to nurse under him again. Still, one never can tell! She took a card out of her handbag, and handed it to him.

"There's going to be a post-mortem," he said suddenly, and then he looked at her hard. Had she had no suspicion of anything being wrong?

Her evident astonishment answered his unspoken question even before she said in a surprised tone: "Have you any doubt yourself, doctor, as to the cause of Mr. Lexton's death?"

He nearly replied: "The greatest doubt! In fact, I don't feel I can sign the death certificate."

But he checked himself. It wouldn't do for her to go and frighten that poor little woman. After all, his suspicions might be-he certainly hoped they were-absolutely unjustified.

And then it was her turn to astonish him.

"I hope Mrs. Lexton won't be put to any great expense," she murmured. "In spite of this lovely flat, and her wonderful clothes, I'm afraid they were very poor. In fact, Mr. Lexton, when he was wandering so much these last two days, talked a lot about money, and seemed to blame himself very much. But I should say that it was she who was extravagant!"

"Extravagant?" said the doctor, surprised. "Is Mrs. Lexton extravagant? I should have thought she had very simple tastes."

Nurse Bradfield smiled to herself. "Men are soft where a pretty face is concerned," she reminded herself tolerantly.

Then aloud she said: "Mrs. Lexton spends a great deal of money over her clothes-and I know that she is a good bit in debt. There was a man here the day before yesterday who said he wouldn't go away till he was paid. But he had to, at last, for she wasn't in till midnight. We must hope that Mr. Lexton was well insured."

"He wasn't insured at all," said the doctor shortly. "I asked Mrs. Lexton, for had he been, she ought at once to have informed the insurance company."

For the first time in his professional life Dr. Berwick went home in what he himself described as "the middle of his round."

Mrs. Berwick saw the motor draw up outside their little house, and running out into the hall she opened the front door.

"Darling!" she cried, "did you forget anything?"

"No, Janey, I forgot nothing. But I've got to arrange for a post-mortem, so I thought it better to come back here, rather than ring up from a call office."

She saw that he was excited and disturbed, and, being a wise woman, she asked him no questions. But she was not surprised when, instead of going straight off to the telephone, he turned into their sitting-room, and shut the door behind him.

"Janey?" he said slowly. "You know that that poor chap Lexton died last night? Mrs. Lexton, as usual, was out. She came in to find him dead."

"How dreadful!"

"He was better, it seems, in the morning-very much better. Then Roger Gretorex came in and sat with him some time alone or so I gather from the nurse."

There followed a long, pregnant silence between the husband and wife. Then there came over Mrs. Berwick's face a look of terrible dismay.

"D'you mean that you suspect ——?" And there was a world of horror in her voice.

"I don't suspect anything," he answered sharply. "And I certainly don't want you to put words into my mouth, or even thoughts into my mind. There's going to be a post-mortem, so we shall soon know part of the truth, at any rate."

She waited a moment, and her voice sank almost to a whisper.

"Then Mrs. Lexton consents to a post-mortem?"

"Her consent was not asked," he said brusquely. "But I'll tell you one thing, Janey. If there's been any foul play, she's not in it. I've thoroughly satisfied myself of that."

"But Roger Gretorex? A doctor? How terrible!"

"I know," he muttered. "But, Janey?"

"Yes, dear?"

"I think it's ninety-nine chances to one against my half-suspicion turning out to be the truth. What with his impudence in prescribing for my patient, and that queer love-letter of his-well, I'm prejudiced against the chap."

"I'm not surprised at that," she breathed.

Indeed, she, Janey Berwick herself, felt strongly prejudiced against Roger Gretorex.

Chapter nine

Roger Gretorex had gone back to his consulting-room after a long morning's round. He loved his work, yet today his heart was not in it, for he was extraordinarily excited, and moved as he had never before felt moved in his twenty-eight years of life.

He had come up early from Sussex by a workman's train, and had found waiting for him an undated and unsigned note in Ivy Lexton's handwriting:

> *I'm not quite sure if you are in London; but I know you will be very sorry to hear that Jervis died suddenly last night.*
>
> *I hardly know what I am doing-the shock has been so great. Nurse says his heart must have given way. I would rather not see anybody for a little while.*

Now that his morning's work was over, he was free to commune with his own thoughts, and to dwell on what the future now held for him —a lifetime of bliss with the woman whom he worshipped, and who had given him the greatest proof of her love a woman can give a man.

His cherished darling was free-free to become, after a decent interval had elapsed, his adored, honoured wife in the face of the world! He thanked God that he had never let his mother know the truth concerning their past relations. He thanked God again that the only time the two had met had been in those early days when he and Ivy had just been friends, and when he, at any rate, had thought that so they would remain.

True, his mother was far too clever, too devoted to him, her only child, not to guess, even then, that he was in love with Ivy. She had even ventured to say a word to him as to the danger of too close a friendship with a married woman. And he had bitterly resented it. He remembered her words, and his answer, "You're wrong, mother. Ivy Lexton is the best and purest woman I have ever known!"

No wonder that, as he had gone in and out of the poor dwellings of his patients this morning, he had asked himself, again and again, how long it would be before he and Ivy could declare their love?

He remembered a war widow in their neighbourhood who had married again within four months of her husband's being killed. Still, the world is very different in peace-time from what it is in war-time. All he would have to consider would be his own mother's sense of what was right and fitting.

Ivy's friends? His sensitive lips curled in disdain. They would scarcely be surprised if she remarried a week after her husband's death!

Then, suddenly, there came over him a feeling which, to such a man as Roger Gretorex, was painfully like shame.

Jervis Lexton had been something of a wastrel and all of a fool, but the young man had also been, according to his lights, a good husband. It was not Jervis's fault that Ivy had never loved him. Her heartless, money-loving mother had forced her into the marriage when she was almost a child. Such was the story she had told Gretorex, and that story he implicitly believed.

He told himself that the only decent thing to do, now, would be to write her a short note of regret and sympathy, as cold and colourless as hers had been.

How he longed, how he ached, to see her! But it was clear she wished to see no one, not even him, the one closest to her, yet.

The long morning of pent-up emotion, and of really hard work, had tired him out-made him feel, too, suddenly very hungry. He got up and took his hat off the peg on the door, intending to snatch a hasty meal at a restaurant in Victoria Street hard by.

Then, just as he was turning towards the door, the telephone bell rang. With a feeling of irritation he took up the receiver.

"Yes?" he called out impatiently.

And then there came over him a thrill of intense joy, for the voice which said in a tremulous tone, "Is that you, darling?" was Ivy Lexton's voice.

She had not called him "darling" once, since her return to London, and that though he knew she often used the endearing term, even to the pet dogs of her women friends.

"Of course it is," he answered tenderly. "How are you, dearest? A little less tired and"—he forced himself to add the word—"unhappy?"

And then he heard her voice again; but now it was full of a kind of cold urgency.

"I've something so dreadfully important to say to you-are you alone in the house?"

"Absolutely alone," he called back reassuringly.

He did not count Mrs. Huntley, the old woman who lived a door or two off, and who "did" for him, as anybody.

"Please don't say my name, and I won't say yours. Telephones are tapped sometimes, and I'm so-so frightened," came the whispered words.

There followed a long pause, and Gretorex suddenly felt filled with an unreasoning sensation of acute apprehension. There had been that in Ivy's tremulous tones which he had never heard there before—a note of horrible fear.

"Are you listening?" came at last the beloved voice, sounding now startlingly near.

"I can hear you perfectly."

"Something so dreadful has happened! I don't know how to tell you. It's so-so strange. You'd never guess what it was!"

He tried to curb his anxiety, his suspense, his impatience.

"What is it that has happened?" he asked quietly.

Again there followed a long unnatural pause. Then, at last, Ivy Lexton breathed the words: "The doctors found out yesterday that poor-you know who I mean-did not die what they call a natural death."

"Not a natural death?" he repeated in a tone of amazement. "What do you mean, darling?"

"They say he died of some kind of poison."

"Poison! D'you mean he committed suicide?" he asked incredulously.

"Oh, no, they don't think that."

Then, in a tone of great relief, she added: "But I suppose he may have done so."

Gretorex felt not only exceedingly surprised, but inexpressibly shocked as well.

"I should be very loth to believe that," he said at last.

"What I really want to tell you is that a dreadful man has been to see me this morning. He's only been gone about half an hour. I was afraid to telephone from my own—" She waited a moment, then uttered the word "house." "I'm speaking from a call office."

"What did the man say? Who was he?" he asked.

"He had to do with the police and he said he was going to see you as soon as he'd had something to eat. I said you generally went to your club to lunch, and that you wouldn't be back before three."

"Why should he want to see me?" Gretorex said wonderingly.

"He seemed to know so much about you. So much"—her voice sank—"about *us*. He asked me such funny questions, darling. Of course I told him—I told him," her voice faltered, "that you were just a great friend of mine and of-you know of whom?"

"So I am. So I was——"

But Roger Gretorex was no fool, and his whole being had become flooded, these last few moments, with an awful sensation of dismay and foreboding.

"Tell me exactly what it was this man asked you, and what you said to him, my pet?"

He tried to make his voice sound confident and reassuring.

"I can't tell you everything over the telephone. It would take too long. He wasn't really disagreeable. In fact, we ended up quite good friends. But he said it was his duty to find out the truth, as that horrible man-you know whom I mean?"

"No," he called back rather sharply, "I have no idea whom you mean! Can't you speak plainly, darling? No one is in the least likely to be listening over the wire."

And then she breathed the one name that she did breathe during that strange, to Gretorex that terrible and ominous, telephone conversation.

"I mean Dr. Berwick, of course. He told them, I suppose, about you."

"Who do you mean by 'them'?"

"The people at Scotland Yard."

"But what could Dr. Berwick tell anybody about me?"

"That you used to come to the flat-that we were friends."

And then, in an imploring voice that was scarcely audible, she murmured: "You won't give me away, dear? You will never let anyone know that——"

Interrupting her he exclaimed, "There's nothing to give away! You and I have only been friends-nothing more."

He felt a thrill of relief when she said, in a more natural tone:

"That's exactly what I said. I mean that's what I told the man who came from Scotland Yard. I think he did believe me at last, but——"

"Yes?" asked Gretorex anxiously. "But what, my dear?"

"I was silly enough to let out that you had been rather fond of me, in a sort of a way."

"I'm sorry you did that. I'm afraid that was a mistake. I mean——"

"I know what you mean! The moment I'd said it I saw what a mistake I'd made! But he spoke as if he already knew such a lot, or at any rate, some part of it."

He said patiently, "What part of it?"

"That even if I didn't care for you, you had been very fond of me."

"I don't see that our private affairs are anyone's business but our own," he said savagely.

She answered despairingly, "Neither do I. But there it is! I know he'll talk about me to you."

Gretorex felt as if he were living through a hideous nightmare. What could, what did, all that Ivy had said, and was saying, mean?

"There's something else I must tell you and warn you about, before I ring off. The man actually asked me, darling, if I'd ever been to see you —I mean alone. Of course I said no, that I had never been alone to see you. Why should I? But I did tell him about the time I came to tea with Rose Arundell, when Captain Chichester came too. The man from Scotland Yard is sure to ask you about that-at least I'm afraid so."

"About my tea-party? Why should he?"

"No, no," she cried shrilly.

Then, in a low tone, she uttered the words, "He'll certainly ask you whether I ever came to see you alone, at Ferry Place. Don't you understand?"

"I hear what you say. But everyone we know is aware that we've been great friends. There's no mystery about it."

"That's what I said. And also that you were so fond of-you know who, and he so fond of you."

To that Gretorex made no answer. In a sense it was true that poor Jervis Lexton had become quite fond of him, and that this was so had made him feel wretched and ashamed.

"Forgive me for having worried you, dear——"

There was something-he would not even to himself use the words-cringing, even abject, in the tone in which she uttered that poor little sentence.

He answered at once, "You could never worry me, my darling! I can't help thinking there's some queer, spiteful enemy of yours, some cruel woman, behind all this?"

She cried hysterically, "It's a spiteful, cruel man! It's Dr. Berwick—I know it is!"

"But why d'you think that, darling?"

Gretorex waited a moment, then asked in almost a whisper, "Was he fond of you? Did he make love to you?"

She was so long in answering his question that, for a moment, he thought they had been cut off. Then he heard the muffled reply, "Not exactly, though of course he liked me. But-but he hated you! I do know that."

"I see," and he thought that he did.

"Dr. Berwick wouldn't sign some kind of a certificate which nurse says a doctor always has to sign when a person dies," she went on. "You know what I mean?"

"Yes."

"That's why they had what is called a post-mortem, and found out my poor sweet had been — —" her voice faltered.

It was, even now, like a blow between the eyes for Gretorex to hear Ivy call Jervis "my poor sweet."

Again she waited a while then he heard her whispered, agitated, half-question:

"I do so wonder what that man will say to you? I feel so horribly nervous."

He said impatiently, "I don't suppose he'll say much. But of course it's the business of the police to get in touch with everyone who can throw even a little light on a mysterious death."

"You'll be very, very careful?"

For the moment he could not think what she meant.

Then, with a painful feeling of self-rebuke and fear, he hastened to reassure her, "Of course I will! Not that there's anything to be careful about."

"I must go home now," and he heard her blow him a kiss.

She hadn't done that for-it seemed an eternity to him.

He hung up the receiver, went across to his writing-table, and sat down. He must think hard, and prepare some sort of story. But even now he could not imagine why his name, his personality, were being brought into this mysterious affair of Jervis Lexton's sudden death.

Jervis Lexton's death caused by poison? And the police already making inquiries? The whole story sounded incredible to Roger Gretorex. He told himself that of course some extraordinary mistake had been made. But whose mistake?

His mind turned at last to Dr. Berwick. He had only seen the man once-and a damned offensive fellow he had seemed to be! So much did Gretorex remember. But Berwick was more than that-he was a blackguard who had made love to a patient's wife.

Poor little Ivy! Poor precious little love! No wonder she had been frightened, made quite unlike her gay, brave self, by the ordeal she had just gone through. How he longed to go and seize her in his arms, to bear her away to some place where they could be just themselves-lovers!

The thought of a crowded restaurant was intolerable. He no longer felt hungry. Besides, the man, he supposed him to be a detective, mentioned by Ivy, would soon be here.

All at once he heard the sounds made by a broom in the passage outside.

He opened the door. "Will you come in here for a moment, Mrs. Huntley?"

The old woman shuffled into the room, and he looked at her fixedly.

"I feel very tired today-too tired to go out."

Taking a two-shilling piece out of his pocket, he handed it to her: "Will you get me some pressed beef or ham? I suppose there's bread and butter in the house? I'm ashamed to bother you, for I know you're in a hurry to get home."

Said Mrs. Huntley, with a rather pathetic laugh, "I'd do a good bit more than that for you, doctor! Why, I'd go to any trouble for you."

"Mrs. Huntley?"

He moved a little nearer to the old woman.

"You've just said that you'd go to any trouble for me — —"

"Ay, and so I would! I'll never forget how good you were to that poor daughter of mine. Why, it's thanks to you that she died easy. I'm not likely to forget that, however long I may live."

"The time has come when you can do something-something very important-for me," he said, wondering if he were being wise or foolish.

"Can I, sir? You've only got to say what it is. I don't mind no trouble."

"I regard you," he said slowly, "as a very superior person, as well as a very trustworthy one, Mrs. Huntley."

She grew red with pleasure at his kind, flattering words, and, troubled as he was, Gretorex's heart went out to her.

69

"All I want you to do," he went on, "is to hold your tongue on my behalf. The time may come when you will be asked what sort of visitors I have received since I came to live here. You may be questioned as to whether any ladies ever came to see me ——"

He waited a moment, feeling acutely uncomfortable at having to ask the old woman to lie for him.

"You will be doing me a great service, Mrs. Huntley, if you will answer that no friends ever come to see me unless they have an appointment. Also that, to the best of your belief, the only time you have ever seen any lady here was when I gave a tea-party some time ago. Do I make myself quite clear?"

"Yes, sir, quite clear."

"And have I your promise?"

"Yes, sir, you have my promise."

He took her withered, work-worn hand in his.

"I'm very grateful to you. This may mean more to me than you will ever know."

"I'll go and get the things for your lunch, sir."

She shut the door behind her, and a moment later, as he saw her pass the window, a hot tide of humiliation seemed to overwhelm him. He had seen, by the expression on her face, that everything there was to know, she knew.

As for Mrs. Huntley, she felt quite sure that Dr. Gretorex, who, though she knew him to be far from well off, had spared neither time nor money in his care of her dying daughter, was about to figure as a corespondent in a divorce case.

Well, in so far as she could help him, she'd do anything. Lie for him? Of course she would! Where's the good of caring for a person if you're not willing to do anything for him or her? Such was Mrs. Huntley's simple philosophy of life. She was a good hater as well as a good lover. In her fashion she loved Gretorex, but she hated Ivy Lexton.

Those who are called "the poor" are seldom deceived in a man's or a woman's real nature and character. They are too close up against the hard realities of life to make many mistakes. It requires no touchstone to teach them the difference between dross and gold.

About three o'clock the telephone bell rang again.

Gretorex hoped for a moment to hear Ivy's voice again, but it was a man who asked, "Can I speak to Dr. Roger Gretorex?"

"My name is Roger Gretorex."

"I have a matter of business to discuss with you, Dr. Gretorex; and I'm telephoning to know if I may come along now, as you are in?"

"Pray do so. But may I ask your name? And would you mind telling me your business?" he called back.

"My name is Orpington. As to my business, it would take too long to explain. But I will be with you in a very few minutes."

Mechanically Gretorex began to tidy his consulting-room. For the first time in his life he felt horribly afraid, he knew not of what, but that made his dread of the coming inquisition all the sharper, the fuller of suspense.

His mother had managed to keep one conservatory going, and though he had given away a good many of the flowers he had brought up with him this morning, there was still a lovely nosegay on his writing-table. And the sight of these fragrant blossoms recalled poignantly to her son's mind the woman who had gathered them for him. Was he going to bring sorrow, and what to her would be worse than sorrow—shame—on her honoured name?

Chapter ten

As Inspector Orpington, of the Criminal Investigation Department, Scotland Yard, entered dusty, poverty-stricken Ferry Place, he made up his mind that he would be, so far as was possible in the circumstances, frank with the man he was on his way to see with regard to Jervis Lexton's death.

Like many an Englishman of his type, he had his own clear, if unexpressed, philosophy of life. He preferred the straight to the tortuous way, and that, it may incidentally be observed, is true of all the really successful men in his peculiar line of work.

Such men naturally suffer from the defects of their qualities. Inspector Orpington had no belief in what he called to himself the French methods of criminal investigation. For one thing, he was convinced, and backed his conviction from experience, that in the vast majority of cases there is seldom anything mysterious, or out of the way, even in the best-planned and most intelligent type of crime.

With regard to the case concerning which he had just been ordered to make certain preliminary inquiries, the story he had been able to piece together was even now, from his point of view, a straightforward story of illicit love leading to a cold-blooded and cruel murder. He had already interviewed the dead man's two regular medical attendants, his trained nurse, and last, but by no means least, his tearful, hysterical, and singularly attractive young widow.

Ivy Lexton remained, in Inspector Orpington's mind, the one point of doubt and mystery, if indeed "mystery" you could call it, in the affair.

He had found it very difficult to make up his mind as to whether Mrs. Lexton was entirely innocent regarding the events which had led to Lexton's death. He had detected certain flaws in the story she had appeared, in spite of her agitation, so willing to tell. But he had been naturally impressed by the firm conviction expressed by the two doctors who had attended Jervis Lexton. They had both declared that their patient's wife had been not only innocent, but quite unsuspicious, of the sinister tragedy which had undoubtedly been enacted during the fortnight which had preceded her husband's death.

Dr. Berwick had said brusquely: "Why, the woman was never there! She was out morning, noon, and night. I myself only saw her three times, each time only for a few minutes, and only once with her husband."

Orpington had also been struck by the liking both the nurse and the cook showed for Lexton's widow; and that though they both admitted she was selfish and pleasure-loving.

But what weighed the scale most of all in favour of Ivy's complete innocence was the fact that the life of Jervis Lexton had not been insured, and that with her husband apparently disappeared the poor, pretty little woman's only source of income.

Long experience had convinced Inspector Orpington that there are only two outstanding motives for secret murder-money, and the passion called love. As he considered the story in all its bearings, it seemed plain to him that, whereas it had been very much to Ivy Lexton's interest to keep her husband alive, this young man, Roger Gretorex, had undoubtedly had a strong motive for compassing his death. Mrs. Lexton, in the course of the long examination and cross-examination to which she had been submitted this morning, had admitted, albeit with a certain reluctance, that Roger Gretorex not only passionately loved her, but had also at various times pestered her with unwelcome attentions.

Everyone interested in the detection of crime is aware that persons arrested on a charge of murder are always solemnly warned that anything said by them may be used in evidence against them. But probably few people know that the giving of any such warning is left to the discretion of the C.I.D. men who are engaged in those preliminary inquiries which, in the majority of cases, do end by bringing a murderer to justice. Certain rules are laid down for their guidance; but even so a great deal is left to the ordering of their own consciences, to what each individual considers it fair or unfair to ask of one who may be actually suspected of having committed the crime under investigation.

Orpington's object was to get at the truth. It was his considered opinion that the guilty are painfully alive to their danger, and will go to any length to protect themselves. In their case the plainest warning is wasted. As to an innocent witness, he believed the best way to put him or her at ease is to be reasonably frank.

He felt sure that, in Roger Gretorex, he would find one both forewarned and forearmed. What he desired to know, as a result of his coming interview with the young doctor, was how far Mrs. Lexton had told the truth as to her relations with the man who, owing to his passion for herself, had almost certainly poisoned her husband.

Slowly he walked, with the sergeant he had brought with him, down the now deserted, airless little street. What a contrast to the broad avenue in which stood the fine block of flats known as Duke of Kent Mansion! It was difficult to believe that the woman with whom he had spent over an hour this morning, in the shadowed drawing-room where everything spelt not only comfort, but affluence and luxury, could have been on terms of close intimacy with a man who lived in Ferry Place.

Before he had time to ring the bell, the narrow front door of the tiny two-storied house opened, and the person he had come to see and, he felt sure, to convict of the most hideous and cruel form of murder known to civilised man, stood before him.

What a fine young chap! And what a haughty, sombre, defiant countenance!

Yet the voice in which Gretorex uttered the commonplace words, "Will you come in?" was a deep, pleasant, cultivated voice.

The doctor led his two visitors into his consulting-room, a room which, though poorly furnished, was yet, as the inspector quickly noted, that of a man accustomed to the amenities of life. For one thing he noticed the lovely bunch of fragrant hot-house flowers standing in a glass on the writing-table. He felt what he very seldom did feel—surprised.

As the three men sat down, Gretorex full in what light came in through his one window, the inspector observed:

"My name, doctor, as I told you over the telephone, is Orpington, and I am attached to the Criminal Investigation Department of Scotland Yard. I have come to ask you certain questions concerning the death of a gentleman who was at one time, I understand, a patient of yours."

"If you will tell me his name, I will look up his case," said Gretorex quickly.

"His name was Jervis Lexton, and his death took place last Tuesday in Flat 9 of Duke of Kent Mansion, Kensington."

"Jervis Lexton was never a patient of mine," the young man answered firmly; and then he hesitated, and finally added, "He was a friend —I suppose I might even say a great friend."

"Are you already aware of the circumstances concerning Mr. Jervis Lexton's death, Dr. Gretorex?"

And then Roger Gretorex told the first of the lies he felt it incumbent on him to tell during this, to him, terrible interview.

"I've been in the country for nearly a week, and I only learnt on my return here, this morning, of Mr. Lexton's death. I am as yet unaware of the circumstances to which I presume I owe your visit."

He waited a moment, then told the inspector what was indeed the truth:

"I was exceedingly surprised to learn of his death, for I had seen him just before leaving town. Though I thought him far less well than the last time I had been with him, there was nothing to indicate the seriousness of his condition."

"Yet you told the nurse that you were dismayed by the charge in his appearance?"

"I daresay I did. She thought him distinctly better, I do remember that, and I disagreed with her."

"You did not ask to see Mr. Lexton, Dr. Gretorex. The nurse tells me your call was on Mrs. Lexton. As that lady was out, Nurse Bradfield, I understand, suggested you should see her patient, as she thought it would cheer him up."

"That is so, and I was not with him for more than ten minutes."

"You were, I think, alone with him during that time?"

"Yes, I was."

"You went down to the country immediately after seeing him?"

"Yes. I went to my home in the country the same afternoon, and, as I told you just now, I only came back this morning."

"Mr. Jervis Lexton died during the evening of the day you saw him-that is, on Tuesday, the 16th of November. His regular medical attendant, Dr. Berwick, was not satisfied as to the cause of death. A post-mortem was held on the Thursday, and revealed the fact that Lexton's death was due to a large dose of arsenic administered some hours before death. According to Nurse Bradfield, you, Dr. Gretorex, were the last person, apart from herself and, I believe, the cook, who saw him alive. That is why I am here."

Gretorex stared at the speaker in silence; and, gradually, all the colour ebbed from his face.

In spite of himself the inspector felt sorry for the young man. He told himself that Roger Gretorex evidently saw the game was up. Still, the doctor looked the sort of chap who would put up a fight for it.

Inspector Orpington made an almost imperceptible sign to the sergeant he had brought with him, and the man at once quietly left the room.

Orpington got up and looked out of the window until he saw his sergeant in the street outside. Then he turned and said to Gretorex:

"I sent my sergeant out of the room, doctor, because I am obliged now to ask you a question which I thought you would prefer to have put to you privately. You were, I understand, a friend of Mrs. Lexton's as well as a friend of her husband?"

"I was on terms of friendship with them both," and his face turned deeply red.

"But you saw much more of Mrs. Lexton than you did of her husband?"

This was a bow drawn at a venture, and it brought down the quarry.

"I sometimes escorted Mrs. Lexton to a picture gallery, and now and again we went to a theatre together. But — —" he waited a moment, and the colour ebbed from his face. Though what he was going to say was true, he hated saying it —"Mr. and Mrs. Lexton always seemed on the best of terms together."

"So I understand. But I am not seeking information as to the relations of Mr. and Mrs. Lexton. What I wish to suggest, without offence, is that you, Dr. Gretorex, would have liked to have been on closer terms of friendship with Mrs. Lexton than she thought it right to allow? I will be frank with you-Mrs. Lexton has admitted as much."

A burning flush again rose to Gretorex's dark face. Poor Ivy! Poor, foolish little darling! He did not feel the slightest feeling of anger with her. He only felt a choking sensation of dismay. Whatever had possessed her to say such a thing?

He answered, speaking quietly, passionlessly, "Mrs. Lexton is a very attractive woman, and a beautiful woman. It is difficult to be with her without feeling inclined to-well — —" and as he hesitated, the older man smiled.

"To make love to her? I absolutely agree, Dr. Gretorex. Though she was naturally very much upset when I saw her this morning, I thought Mrs. Lexton one of the most engaging, as well as one of the best-looking, young ladies I had ever come across."

Poor Gretorex! He would have liked to have struck Inspector Orpington across the face, and yet his own words had called up the look that had so grossly offended him on the other's countenance, and had also provoked his remark.

"Do you admit, Dr. Gretorex, that you were very much attracted to this lady?"

"You put me in a difficult position; but I admit that perhaps I did say one or two foolish things to her."

He was wondering, with a feeling of agonising anxiety, whether Ivy had kept his letters.

"Did Mrs. Lexton ever by chance come here, to 6 Ferry Place?"

"She came to tea on one occasion, but not alone, of course. A friend of hers, a widow called Mrs. Arundell, and a man friend of Mrs. Arundell's, came with her."

And then Roger Gretorex leant forward:

"I do hope that you will believe me when I tell you that any-well, feeling of attraction, was entirely on my side. When I did, I admit very foolishly, once try to tell her——"

He stopped, and the other interjected, not unkindly, "How much she attracted you?"

Gretorex nodded, and then he gasped out the lying words—"She made me feel at once she was not that kind of woman."

"I suppose," said the inspector with a twinkle in his eyes, "that Mrs. Lexton used that very expression."

Gretorex tried to smile back.

"Well, yes, I believe she did. It happened a long time ago, in fact when I first made the Lextons' acquaintance."

Now this observation gave the direct lie to Ivy Lexton's statement, which Orpington honestly believed had been extracted from her against her will.

"I suppose that you can suggest no reason why this man, Jervis Lexton, should have wished to take his own life?"

"No, none at all. He had just obtained an excellent job."

"You can throw no light either, I presume, as to how the arsenic which undoubtedly caused his death can have been administered to him?"

"Not only can I throw no light on it, but I find it almost impossible to believe what my reason tells me is true-your assertion that his death was directly due to the administration of arsenic."

The speaker's voice was strong, assured. At last he was on firm ground.

"I take it there is a surgery attached to this house, and that you make up your own medicines?"

The inspector asked that vital question in a very quiet tone, but Gretorex realised its purport as he answered, "I do-for the most part."

"I should like to see the surgery."

"By all means."

Roger Gretorex got up. Then he placed his back against the door.

Instantly Inspector Orpington, though he was a brave man, and had been in more than one very tight corner, felt a cold tremor run through him. Was this fine-looking young chap going to whip out a revolver and kill, not only himself, but also the man whose unpleasant duty it had been to show him that the game he had been so mad as to play was up?

But he need not have been afraid.

"Look here! Before I take you into my surgery, where you will find a jar of arsenic as likely as not on an open shelf-for I am a careless chap, and no one has access to the place but myself and my old charwoman—I want to say something to you. I don't suppose you will believe me, but I wish to tell you, here and now, that I have no more idea of how poor Lexton got at the arsenic which caused his death-if it did cause it-than you have, and that the one thing of which I am quite sure is that it did not come out of my surgery."

Chapter Eleven

Instead of doing what he ought to have done-that is, to have sought at once the best legal aid in his power-Roger Gretorex made up his mind to go back to Sussex, if only for a few hours.

Ivy's words of agonised fear now found an echo in his own heart. His mother must hear the very few and simple facts concerning Jervis Lexton's death from himself.

On his way to the station he saw two newspaper placards, and he felt as if it was at him that they shouted the ominous words:

**Kensington
Poisoning
Mystery.**

**Well-known
Clubman
Poisoned.**

He bought an evening paper in the station, and then, when he unfolded it, he felt a sharp stab of anger and disgust. In the centre of the front page was a charming portrait of Ivy-Ivy looking her sweetest and most seductive self. Above and below the photograph was printed a series of paragraphs dealing with the joyous life the young couple had led in the care-free existence which centres round the idler members of the fashionable night-clubs. It was also stated that, on the very night of Mr. Lexton's unexpected death, Mrs. Lexton was supping at the Savoy with "a smart theatre-party."

In the grateful darkness of a late November afternoon, Roger Gretorex walked the two miles which separated the little station from Anchorford, the village which he still felt part of the very warp and woof of his life, though he owned practically no land there. All that his father had been able to keep was the manor house, and the little portion of the park which had surrounded the dwelling-house of the owners of Anchorford from the days of Domesday Book.

Now and again Gretorex, as he hurried through the narrow lanes, would tell himself that the inexplicable mystery attaching to Jervis Lexton's death by poison was bound to be cleared up, and probably in some quite simple way—a way that he himself was now too excited and too anxious to think out for himself.

Then there would come a sudden sensation of doubt, of despondency. Like Ivy, but with far more cause, Roger Gretorex began to feel as if a net were closing round him.

At last he turned into the long avenue which led to Anchorford House, and his heart leapt when he saw the long Elizabethan front, now bright with twinkling lights.

He rang the front door bell, and then he schooled himself to wait patiently for old Bolton, who, once his father's head groom, now acted as general factotum and odd-job man.

But when, all at once, the door opened, it was his mother, tall, upright, grey-haired, who stood there, her face full of eager welcome.

"I knew it was you, my dearest! I don't believe in presentiments, but I have been thinking of you all today, even more than usual."

His face gave no answering smile. He looked very grave, and yet how young he seemed to her, standing there; how strong, how finely drawn and carved, was his now serious face!

"I wish you'd wired, Roger. Enid was coming in to late supper; but I'll put her off——"

"You needn't do that, mother. It's true I've come down to tell you of something rather unpleasant that's just happened to me. But the telling of it won't take long. Please don't put off Enid. In fact I shall be glad to see her, and I may have to go back to town by the last train."

He followed her across the wide hall which formed the centre of the old house, and so into a lobby which led to the charming sitting-room which had always been associated in his mind with his mother. They both sat down there. But he waited a moment before he began his story and then in the telling of it he chose his words with painful care.

"A very odd thing has happened, mother, and I felt I should like to tell you about it at once."

"What is it that has happened, Roger?"

As he said nothing, she went on quietly, in a matter-of-fact tone: "Whatever it is, I know quite well that you have not been to blame in any way."

"Well, no, I don't think I have been to blame. And yet, well, mother, I've not been ——" and then he stopped dead.

For the first time in his life he felt afraid. The extraordinary story he had come to tell suddenly took on gigantic proportions. Until today, though he had felt discomfort, and something akin to shame, sometimes, when with Jervis Lexton, Roger Gretorex and Fear had never met.

"You remember," he said at last, "my friend Ivy Lexton? She came down here for a week-end last winter."

"I remember Mrs. Lexton very well," answered Mrs. Gretorex in a tone of studious detachment.

As her son had uttered the name of the woman he called his friend, a feeling of fear coupled with a sensation of painful jealousy filled the mother's heart. Remember the beautiful woman she had instantly known, without his telling her so, that Roger loved? There had scarcely been a day in the last few months when she had not remembered, with a sensation of discomfort, lovely Ivy Lexton.

"Jervis Lexton, Ivy's husband, fell ill about three weeks ago ——"

And then again Gretorex felt as if he could not go on.

"What has happened is put as clearly, here, as anything I can tell you!" he exclaimed at last, and he handed her the evening paper containing Ivy's photograph.

She took the paper from his hand, and she was in such haste to see what it was that her son did not dare to tell her himself, that she did not wait to put on her spectacles.

Holding the sheet right under her reading lamp, she read the ominous paragraphs headed "A Kensington Poisoning Mystery" right through.

"Well," she said at last, "and in what way, Roger, does this concern you? Were you acting as Mr. Lexton's medical attendant?"

He answered at once, "I'm glad to say I was not. In fact I only saw the poor chap twice during the whole course of his illness. He was being looked after by a very good doctor, a man called Berwick."

She said again, "Then in what way does this horrible story concern you, my dear?"

There followed a long pause, and all at once a certain suspicion rushed into Mrs. Gretorex's mind.

"Is it possible," she said at last, in a very low voice, "that your friend Mrs. Lexton is suspected of having poisoned her husband?"

Roger Gretorex leapt to his feet.

"Good God-no, mother! Whatever made you think of such a thing?"

"I don't know. Forgive me, Roger."

For the first time in her life she felt that her son was looking at her with something like-oh, no, not hatred, but anger, furious anger, in his blazing eyes.

He repeated the cruel question: "Whatever made such a monstrous idea come into your mind?"

She faltered, "It was foolish of me."

"More than foolish-and very unlike you, mother," he said harshly.

Then he moved his chair closer to hers, and stretching out his hand, he took hers.

"Ivy was the best of wives to Jervis Lexton," he said in a low voice. "Lexton ran through a large fortune, and then, instead of trying to get a job, simply idled about, and lived on his friends. He was a complete wastrel."

"Then isn't what the paper says true?" she asked in bewilderment. "I mean about his having joined the firm of Miles Rushworth? I thought the Rushworths were shipping millionaires?"

"So they are. And it's quite true that Lexton had just got a job in the Rushworths' London office. He was well connected, and had a lot of good-natured friends who were always trying to get him something to do. However ——" and then he quoted the familiar Latin tag concerning ill words of the dead.

She gazed across at him. His dark face, now convulsed with feeling, was partly illumined by the lamp which stood on a low table between them.

"Is it conceivable, my son ——"

Then she, like him, stopped short, afraid to utter the words she was going to say.

"Yes, mother?"

His voice had suddenly become listless. He had dropped her hand, and was lying back in his chair. He was feeling spent, worn out.

"Have you any reason to suppose, my boy, that you are in danger of being accused of having poisoned Jervis Lexton?"

He straightened himself, got up, and then gazed down into her pale but still calm face, and she saw that he looked, if surprised, yet unutterably relieved.

"Yes, mother! That is what I came down to tell you. But what made you hit on the truth?"

Should she tell him the reason why that frightful thought had come into her mind? After a moment of indecision, she decided that she ought to do so.

"Can't you guess why that fearful suspicion came into my mind, Roger?"

His eyes fell before her sad, steady, questioning gaze.

She went on slowly, "I said a word to you the evening of the day you brought Mrs. Lexton down here. I suppose you didn't take my advice?"

"There are certain things about which a man must judge for himself, mother. And with regard to my friendship for Mrs. Lexton I judged for myself."

He sat down again and covered his eyes with his right hand. The words he had just uttered had brought Ivy vividly before him.

"Now tell me everything, Roger."

"There's very little to tell," said Gretorex, raising his head. "I feel sure, quite sure, mother, that there's some perfectly natural explanation of what now seems so mysterious."

"If, as I hope, you have come down to consult with me as to what is the best thing to do, then I trust that you will tell me the whole truth. After all, I am your mother, my darling."

Her voice rose in entreaty.

"Whom should you trust, if you do not trust me?"

He felt very much moved, and, to her surprise, he came and knelt down by her.

She put her arms round him. "Now tell me everything," she whispered.

And he did tell her almost everything. But he did not tell her, and he never told anyone, of his telephone talk with Ivy Lexton.

His mother was quick to see the flaw in his apparently frank account of all that had happened that morning.

"How did you first hear of Mr. Lexton's death?" she asked. "You were there, I note from the date given in this paper, on the afternoon of the day he died. You must in fact have gone straight to the station, from your unfortunate call on the poor man."

"I did, mother."

"Then how, and when, did you hear of his death, Roger?"

He got up and went across to the chair where he had been sitting.

"I found a note from Ivy when I arrived at Ferry Place this morning. She knew I was away, and she sent me the note to await me on my return. It was written, evidently, some days ago."

"I hope you have kept her note."

He shook his head. "No, mother, I didn't keep it. There was really nothing in it-simply the bare statement that Jervis Lexton was dead. She had had an awful shock, and she said she didn't want to see anyone."

"Then you've not seen Mrs. Lexton since her husband's death?"

"No, I have not seen her."

There trembled on the poor mother's lips a further question —"Or had any further communication with her?" But she feared he might be tempted to tell her a lie, so she refrained from asking that, to her, important question.

Instead she said, "Though you have not put it into words, you feel sure that the man from Scotland Yard suspects you poisoned Jervis Lexton so that his wife would be free to marry you?"

"That is certainly what the inspector had in his mind, when he questioned me as to my acquaintance with her."

"Forgive me for asking you the question, Roger. I suppose you would marry Mrs. Lexton, if you had the chance?"

He said at once, "I'd give my soul to marry her, mother. I love her-love her more, I think, than man ever loved woman."

She gave him a searching look. "Does she love you?"

He hesitated, painfully. "I've seen very little of her lately. I know she felt we were not doing right in seeing as much as we were seeing of each other."

And then he sighed, a long, long sigh.

"Try to love her, mother. She is free now, and she is all my life. Please, please try to love her for my sake."

"I will, my darling boy."

Mrs. Gretorex was ashamed of the hatred-she acknowledged to herself that it had been hatred-of Ivy Lexton which had filled her heart. She now told herself that this woman whom her boy adored must have some good in her.

There came the sound of the front door opening.

"Here, I think, is Enid Dent," exclaimed Mrs. Gretorex.

Roger jumped up from his chair, and went forward to meet the girl who, as he knew deep in his heart, loved him.

Was it because he had known that his mother eagerly desired him to marry Enid, or was it simply because he knew her too well? Be that as it may, it had only taken three meetings with Ivy Lexton, the wife of another man, to blot Enid out from his heart.

To-day, the most terrible day of his life, the sight of her honest, thoughtful face brought comfort. For one thing, it was such an infinite relief to know that in Enid Dent his mother would have an entirely trustworthy, devoted support and stay, during days which he feared must be anxious and painful days, terrible days to remember, though he had no doubt at all as to the ultimate result of any inquiry into the facts surrounding Lexton's death.

As for Enid Dent, she had loved Roger Gretorex with a silent, unswerving devotion since she had first known what love meant. Though he himself was scarcely aware of it, his whole manner had changed during the last few months, and while this caused her sharp anguish, which she had successfully hidden from those about her, it had never occurred to her, strangely enough, that that alteration had come about because of another woman.

Now, gazing from the mother to the son, she understood at once that they were both in deep trouble.

"I'm afraid I've come too soon," she said.

"I'm glad you came early, my dear. We're going to have supper in a few minutes, for Roger has to go back to town to-night."

Old Bolton hobbled into the room.

"Rosie Holt says you promised to see her some time today, ma'am. She's in the kitchen. Shall I show her into the drawing-room?"

Mrs. Gretorex made a great effort over herself.

"Yes, please do, Bolton," she said quietly, "and I'll come and see her."

Roger turned to Enid:

"I wonder if you'd take a short turn before supper? I don't get nearly enough exercise in London."

"Of course I will."

They went into the hall, and she hurried on her hat and coat. It was fully a year since she had last taken even a short walk with Roger Gretorex.

Once they were in the open air, in the kindly darkness, he drew her arm through his.

"Enid, I want to tell you something."

He spoke almost in a whisper-as if he were afraid he might be overheard.

"Yes, Roger?" and she slightly pressed his arm.

"I'm in trouble," he said sombrely; "in great trouble, my dear. What makes it worse is the knowledge of how unhappy it is going to make my mother."

And then at once, for though she was young she was no fool-your country-bred girl often knows a great deal more of real life than your town-bred girl-Enid Dent said to herself that Roger's trouble was connected with a woman.

"Tell me all about it," she said quietly, and she stiffened herself to bear a blow.

"I will tell you all about it. But I'm afraid you will be very much shocked."

To that she made no answer. No doubt some London girl was bringing a breach of promise action against Roger. That was the sort of trouble Enid Dent visualised.

"Things are never so bad when one talks them over," she said, and tried to smile in the dark night. "Nothing could make me feel any different to you, Roger. Why, you're my oldest friend!"

They were walking away from the house, down a broad path where they had often played when he was a boy of twelve and she a little girl of five.

"No talking can make any difference to my trouble," and there came a harsh note in his voice.

They walked along in silence, and then he gently shook himself free of her arm.

"I've reason to believe that in the next few days — —"

He stopped short. The ignominy, the horror of what might be going to happen to him, overwhelmed him.

"Yes, Roger? What is it that you think is going to happen? Tell me."

He would have been surprised, indeed, if she had suddenly uttered aloud the words that she was saying in her heart, "Don't you see the agony I am in? It's cruel, cruel to keep me in suspense!"

"I think it possible, perhaps I ought to say likely, that I may be arrested on a charge of murder, within the next few days." He uttered the dread words quietly enough. "And that though I assure you, Enid, that I am absolutely innocent — —"

She cut across his words, "You needn't have troubled to tell me that, Roger."

"Though I'm absolutely innocent," he repeated, "yet I'm beginning to realise that appearances are very much against me. I've felt all this afternoon as if I were living through a frightful nightmare, and I'm always expecting to wake up and find it was only a dream, after all."

Enid knew that this man she loved had a violent temper. She supposed that he had had the kind of quarrel with another man in which one of the two strikes out.

"I've been wondering, during the last few minutes, whether you would be able to come up to London with my mother? It would be such a comfort to know you were with her, if this thing really happens."

"Of course I will!" she exclaimed.

He went on: "You've always been like a daughter to her, haven't you? And I know that, next to me, she loves you best in the world."

"I think she does," she whispered in a strangled voice, for she was now near to tears. "But a long way after you, Roger."

"Well, yes," he answered, in a matter-of-fact tone; "no doubt a long way after me. But still she loves you dearly, and she trusts you utterly, as I do."

"I'll stay with her all through the trouble-if the trouble comes. I promise you that, Roger."

"It's not that I have any doubt as to the outcome. The man whose death is being, I feel sure, put down to my account, almost certainly committed suicide. There's no other solution possible."

"Who was the man?" she asked diffidently.

"An acquaintance rather than a friend of mine, called Jervis Lexton. He fell ill-that I have to admit is a mysterious point about the whole business-about a fortnight ago. He died, rather suddenly, last week, on the 16th. A post-mortem revealed the cause of death to have been a virulent poison-arsenic. I saw him alone a few hours before he died, and I have a jar of arsenic in my surgery. There you have the story in a nutshell."

He spoke in an awkward, constrained tone.

"Are you really going back to-night?" she asked. "Can't you stay till tomorrow morning? It would be such a comfort to Mrs. Gretorex."

"I'm afraid I must go back. You see, I've a lot of patients, and it isn't fair to put all that work on another doctor."

"I see."

"I wonder if you and my mother can come to town tomorrow? She'd be wretched, staying on here in suspense, waiting for news of what, after all, may never happen."

They were turning now towards the house, and as they emerged from under the trees they both noticed that the front door was open. Through it a shaft of bright light fell on the stone-paved courtyard, and Gretorex suddenly became aware that, in the shadow, a motor with hooded lights was drawn up.

"Who can that be at this time of the evening?" he said, surprised.

They walked swiftly across the wide lawn, and so on to the stone pavement. Then, as they passed through the open door, they heard Mrs. Gretorex's voice and the unfamiliar voice of a man in the great hall.

"I think I hear my son coming in. In any case, I assure you he won't be long."

Mrs. Gretorex uttered the words in a matter-of-fact yet anxious tone, as if she feared the person she spoke to might not believe her.

Roger followed Enid through the lobby which separated the front door from the hall, and then he saw his mother standing with a tall, slight man whom Roger knew to be the Inspector of Police at Lynchester, the county town hard by. They had met two months back in connection with a local poaching affray.

"May I speak with you for a few moments in private, Dr. Gretorex?"

A look of great relief had come over the inspector's face; he was aware in what high regard Mrs. Gretorex was held throughout the neighbourhood. He had also noticed the young lady who had just come in, and knew her for the only daughter of a local magistrate. So he was anxious to get through the unpleasant business which had brought him to-night to Anchorford Hall, as quietly and quickly as possible.

"I'm quite at your service. We'll go into the smoking-room, but — —"

Gretorex turned right round and began rapidly walking towards the front door.

As a matter of fact, the door had been left open, and he wished to close it.

But the inspector believed his lawful prey intended to escape into the darkness, and a hundred suspicious, angry thoughts flashed through his mind.

What a thing it would be to have to search the downs and woods all this coming night! 'Twould be like looking for a needle in a stack of hay.

He strode past Mrs. Gretorex, and seized Roger with no gentle hand by the collar.

"I'm surprised, sir, at your trying to get away. I didn't expect such a thing from you!"

Gretorex wrenched himself free.

"I don't know what you mean!" he exclaimed angrily.

"Oh, yes, you do. You were making for that door."

"I was making for the door to shut it."

He was shaking with anger, and the two glared at each other for a moment in silence.

Then the inspector took a step forward, and laid his hand on the young man's arm.

"I arrest you," he said, in a voice that was not quite steady, "on the charge of having murdered Jervis Lexton on the 16th of this month."

Roger Gretorex stood still. Then he asked:

"May I speak to my mother in private for a moment?"

"No," said the inspector quickly. "I cannot allow you to do that, Dr. Gretorex. I'm sorry, but from now on you are my prisoner."

"May I make a statement to you now? I suppose there is no objection to my telling you that I'm absolutely innocent?"

The older man hesitated.

"I should advise you," he said, not unkindly, "to make no statement. You are, of course, aware that anything you say may be used against you in evidence. I need hardly tell you that every facility will be given you to procure legal advice."

"And what is going to happen to me now?"

"You will go with me to Lynchester, and you will be kept there in a police cell till you are conveyed to London tomorrow. Once there, as you probably are aware, Dr. Gretorex, you will be taken to the police station of the district where the alleged murder was committed, and in due course you will be charged."

Meanwhile the inspector was watching his prisoner closely. He was remembering that during the brief telephone conversation with Scotland Yard, which had led to his presence here, he had been reminded how near Anchorford was to the sea, and he had been warned that he might find his bird flown.

What a fool he would look if, after having actually arrested him, this man effected even a temporary escape!

"May I shake hands with my mother and-and with my friends?"

"I will take it on myself to allow you to do that, Dr. Gretorex," was the cold reply. "Then, I'm afraid, we must be getting on."

"Won't you allow my son to have some supper before you take him away?" asked Mrs. Gretorex. For the first time her voice was not quite steady. "Won't you both have supper here? It's quite ready."

"No, ma'am, I'm afraid I can't do that. But I promise you your son shall have something to eat, as good as I can get him at this time of night, when we reach Lynchester."

The inspector's voice had become kindly, even respectful, to his prisoner's mother. He felt very sorry for her.

But for Roger Gretorex he was not at all sorry. He had been given to understand, quite unofficially of course, that there was a married woman in the case, and that she provided a strong enough motive to hang a dozen times over the fine young fellow now standing by his side.

"What I would advise you to do, ma'am-advising you as a private person, I mean-would be to go up to London tomorrow morning, and get in touch with a good solicitor. Dr. Gretorex will be allowed to see his lawyer alone as much as he can reasonably require. At least that is the usual procedure."

Roger Gretorex held out his hand. Something seemed to warn him that it would be wiser for him to remain standing exactly where he was standing now. He felt that the inspector was watching him intently.

Mrs. Gretorex took a step forward. She shook hands quietly, unemotionally, with her son.

And then something very unexpected happened-unexpected, that is, by every one of the four people there.

Enid Dent approached Roger a little timidly. Had he not, a few moments ago, called her his friend? When she was close to him, she looked up into his face, for he was far taller than she. And then, all at once, he bent forward and, putting his arms round her, he kissed her good-bye.

Chapter Twelve

As Ivy stepped down out of the telephone box, after her conversation with Roger Gretorex, she felt, though partially relieved, yet at the same time agitated and still terribly frightened. She was, indeed, so much affected that she did not even notice the admiring glance thrown at her by a man in the next box.

Her interview that morning with Inspector Orpington and his subordinate-for he had brought with him a sergeant-had made her feel sick with fear. True that, after she had answered with apparent frankness the first probing questions put to her, she had felt, as she almost always did feel with any man with whom life brought her into temporary contact, that the inspector was beginning to like her and to sympathise with her. But, even so, she had experienced this morning what she had never experienced before-not only a sensation of abject fear, but also as if she were becoming entangled in a horrible, close-meshed net.

During a brief visit to Paris, in the old days when she and Jervis still had plenty of money to burn, she had gone with a gay party to the Grand Guignol. There she had seen acted a terrifying little play which showed the walls of a room closing in on a man. That was exactly how she had felt during the long examination and cross-examination she had endured this morning.

One of the things that had made her feel so dreadfully frightened was that the two men from Scotland Yard had not begun their investigations by seeing her, the widow of the dead man. They had first interviewed Nurse Bradfield, and then the cook.

While this had been going on, Ivy had waited in the drawing-room, sick with terror and suspense, wondering what the two women were saying about her. At long last, the strangers had come into the drawing-room, looking very grave indeed.

And now, as she walked back to Duke of Kent Mansion, choosing instinctively a roundabout way, Ivy kept living over again that strange, even she had realised momentous, interview.

The inspector had gone straight to the point. When had she, Mrs. Jervis Lexton herself, last been in the company of her husband before his unexpected death? After an imperceptible pause, during which she was wondering fearfully if Nurse Bradfield had remembered all that had happened on that sinister last afternoon, she had answered the question truthfully. She said that she had been with Jervis after luncheon, while the nurse had gone out for a short time.

When Ivy had made this admission, there had come a look of alert questioning on the inspector's face, for Nurse Bradfield had not mentioned that fact, which indeed she had forgotten. And then it was, on seeing the sudden change of countenance on the part of her inquisitor, that Mrs. Jervis Lexton had gently volunteered the statement that, after she herself had gone out, the sick man had had another visitor that afternoon, a friend of her own and her husband's, a young man named Roger Gretorex, who was a doctor.

She had allowed, and consciously allowed, herself to look embarrassed, as she made what sounded like an admission. As she had intended should be the case, the inspector had at once run after that hare. But she had not bargained for what had followed immediately-insistent questioning as to her own and her husband's relations with the man who had been, with the exception of the cook and the nurse, the last person to see Jervis Lexton alive.

How long had they known Dr. Gretorex? Did they see much of him? What had been her own relations with him? When, for instance, had she herself last seen him before the death of Jervis Lexton?

At last, when she was beginning to feel as if the meshes of the net were becoming smaller and smaller, he had "got out of her," so Ivy put it to herself, that Roger Gretorex cared for her far more than a bachelor ought to care for the wife of a friend.

Nevertheless, everything would now have been "quite all right" from Ivy's point of view if it had stopped there. But to her dismay and surprise, Inspector Orpington suddenly began on quite another tack.

In spite of the fact, which he assured her he accepted as true, that she had rejected with indignation Dr. Gretorex's advances, he suggested that it was odd that her own and her husband's friendship with the young man had gone on. He "presumed" that Lexton had known nothing of Gretorex's unwelcome attentions to Mrs. Lexton? Ivy had reluctantly admitted that that was so. And, as he pressed her, with one quick, probing question after another, she saw, with a clear, affrighted, inward vision, that what she had intended should be a molehill was growing into a mountain.

At last had come the most alarming query of all—had she ever been to see Dr. Gretorex at 6 Ferry Place?

All the questions put to her she had answered with apparent ease and frankness. And, as to the last, she explained that she had gone to Dr. Gretorex's house with a great friend of hers, a lady who had then been a widow, a Mrs. Arundell, but who had married again, and was now in India. They had been accompanied by a young man who was a friend of Mrs. Arundell.

As to going out with Roger Gretorex, she had done so only occasionally, and never since he had confessed he loved her. No, never since her husband's illness.

How deeply thankful was Ivy Lexton that she had really seen so little of Roger Gretorex of late!

And then, all at once, the inspector had said something which had made, as she put it to herself, her heart stand still.

"I suppose there is a surgery attached to the house in Ferry Place?" he had remarked, speaking his thought aloud. And it had been those words, as to the probable existence of a surgery, that had suddenly made up her mind for her as to the line she would take concerning Roger Gretorex and their relations to one another.

Did Ivy Lexton then realise the full import of what she had done? Most certainly not. Subconsciously she was aware that her avowals, her timorous admissions as to his passion for her lovely self, could do Gretorex no good. But her only object had been to shift, at any cost, suspicion from herself.

There had been an interval, perhaps as long as a quarter of an hour, when she had been alone with Inspector Orpington. He had sent away his sergeant into the dining-room next door. At the time she had not known why.

Then he had spoken to her kindly, yet in a very solemn, searching tone, adjuring her to be frank, and to tell him of any knowledge, or even suspicion, she might harbour in her mind. But though every word he said added to her secret terror, that terror which was at once tangible and vague, for she knew nothing of the law, she had been wary, and very clever, in her answers.

Then the other man had come back, and to her surprise and horror she found she was expected to sign a statement.

"You had better read it over," the inspector had said quietly.

And Ivy had read it over, hardly realising what it was she was reading, but having the wit to know that this man from Scotland Yard had played fair by her.

Though in a sense Ivy had said nothing of any importance, apart from that fatal admission of Roger Gretorex's love for her, Orpington had left the flat well satisfied. He believed he now had the threads of what had seemed at first such a mystery, all clutched up into his hands. Incidentally, at the end of that long searching inquisition he had reconstituted every moment of the last day of the dead man's life.

But as he had got up to leave, he had suddenly returned to the fact that Mrs. Lexton had been with her husband alone on that last afternoon of his life. That the inspector evidently attached importance to this fact brought back all Ivy's terrors. But her remarkable powers of dissimulation stood her in good stead, and she again gave a pathetic little account of those few last minutes with her husband.

"I don't quite know how long it was. Time went by quickly, for I thought he was better; and we had a little chat, making up our minds where we would go when he was well enough to have a change."

"Did he have anything to drink —a dose of medicine while you were with him, Mrs. Lexton?"

"Oh, no! Nurse was not out long enough for that."

And then it was that Orpington made his one mistake. Not that it made any difference at all in the long run. But, unconsciously, he had been affected by Ivy's soft, feminine charm, as well as by her fragile loveliness.

"Of course we shall let you know the result of our investigations as soon as I have concluded my inquiries. As for Dr. Gretorex, I shall go and see him as soon as I have had something to eat."

See Roger? Roger, who was so truthful, so incapable of telling even a white lie?

The knowledge that Gretorex was going to be subjected to a searching examination made her turn faint with fear. Had she been guilty of folly, and worse than folly, in admitting, nay, in volunteering the information, that Roger loved her? Within herself she debated that question. If Orpington had suspected the truth, then, of course, she had been wise. But had he-had he?

In any case, the warning of Gretorex had seemed the only thing to do, and on the whole she now felt strengthened, comforted, by his unquestioning faith.

As at last she went up in the lift of the Duke of Kent Mansion, she heard quick, light steps running up the stairs, and she shivered with apprehension. But it was only a telegraph boy, and as they arrived together at the door of the flat, she asked quickly, "Is the name Lexton?"

"Yes, ma'am, 'Mrs. Lexton,'" and he handed her the telegram.

In her bedroom she tore open the buff envelope and looked first at the signature:

> Just read with great concern result post-mortem. Have cabled John Oram solicitor instructing him to afford you all help financial and other on my behalf. Sister dangerously ill or would return at once myself. Please keep me acquainted with any developments. Deepest sympathy.
>
> Miles Rushworth.

She burst into hysterical tears of relief. Nothing, surely, could happen to her now that Rushworth had come to her help?

Always Ivy Lexton had been sheltered, guarded, lifted over the rough places of life by menmen who had been conquered, pressed into her service, by that alluring quality which means so much more than beauty. But not one of the many men to whom she had cause to be grateful in her life had been in the powerful position of Miles Rushworth, as regarded either character or wealth.

She lay down on the comfortable couch which stood at right angles to her pretty bed. It was the first time she had ever done so, for she was a strong young woman, in spite of the air of delicacy which added so much to her charm in the eyes of many people, women as well as men. But she felt tired-dreadfully, consciously tired, today.

She closed her eyes and, deliberately, she lived over again Rushworth's last long, passionate embrace on the yacht. It was as if she heard spoken aloud his ardent, broken-hearted words, "*If only you were free!*"

Well? She was free now, even at what she was beginning to realise might be a fearful cost. Even so, it could only be a question of months, perhaps of weeks, before she became Rushworth's wife.

She opened her eyes and smiled for the first time that day, a radiant, secretly confident smile. Leaping off the couch she read through Rushworth's long telegram again.

John Oram? What a curious name. Being a solicitor, he must be on the telephone. She would ring him up immediately after she had had lunch, and ask him to come and see her.

Going into the hall, she called out, in almost a joyous voice, "Nurse? Here I am! I'm so sorry to have kept you waiting."

85

Nurse Bradfield came slowly down the corridor. The events of the last few days had aged her, and Ivy was struck by her sad, bewildered expression. She secretly wondered why Nurse Bradfield looked so old and unlike herself? Nurse Bradfield, lucky woman, had nothing to be afraid of.

Ivy Lexton never knew all she owed to the woman who had tended Jervis Lexton through his last illness. When Inspector Orpington had done with the nurse, he had formed, albeit unconsciously, a very definite view of the dead man's widow. Thus, even before he had seen Ivy, he had accepted Nurse Bradfield's view of young Mrs. Lexton's nature and way of life. That is, he regarded her as selfish, feather-headed, and extravagant; but good-natured, easy-going, and quite incapable of planning and of executing such a crime as that which had brought about her husband's death.

That Jervis Lexton had died as the result of a foul crime on the part of some man or woman who had a strong motive for wishing him to be obliterated had appeared plain to the man in charge of the case, even before he had interviewed any of the people concerned with it.

But if Ivy, unknowingly, had reason to be grateful to Nurse Bradfield, Nurse Bradfield just now had cause to be very grateful to Ivy. It meant a great deal to her that she could stay on here, in this luxurious flat, living in quietude and comfort, instead of going back to the hostel which was her only "home" between her cases.

She had already learnt, and great was her dismay thereat, that she would become an important witness for the Crown, should the mystery be so far cleared up as to bring about a trial for murder. Small wonder that today she felt too upset and too disturbed to eat, and she watched, with surprise, Ivy's evident enjoyment of the good luncheon put before them.

The nurse was the more secretly astonished at the newly made widow's look of cheerfulness because she was well aware that "little Mrs. Lexton" was most uncomfortably short of money.

All that morning, and especially during the latter half of that morning, there had come a procession of tradespeople to the flat requesting immediate payment of their accounts. Some of them had been interviewed by the cook, others by Nurse Bradfield herself. As for Ivy, she had absolutely refused to see any of them. "I have no money at all just now," she had observed sadly. "But of course everybody will be paid in time."

Nurse Bradfield had even begun to wonder if she would ever be repaid a certain ten pounds which she had lent Mrs. Lexton a few days before. But she was not as much troubled by that thought as some of Ivy Lexton's fairly well-to-do friends might have been. She even told herself that, after all, she was now receiving far more than ten pounds' worth of comfort and quiet.

As if something of what she was thinking flashed from the nurse's mind to hers, Ivy said suddenly, "I shall have plenty of money soon, Nurse. And the moment I've got anything I'll give you back that money you were kind enough to lend me."

There was a tone of real sincerity in her voice, and Nurse Bradfield felt reassured.

"I only want it back," she said quietly, "when you can really give it me conveniently, Mrs. Lexton. Of course ten pounds is a good deal of money to me. But now that I know poor Mr. Lexton was not insured, I realise that things must be very difficult for you."

"It's going to be quite all right," exclaimed Ivy impulsively.

Oh! what a difference to life Rushworth's cable had made! She felt almost hysterical with joy and relief.

And then, as there came a ring at the bell, she said quickly to the maid who was waiting at table, "Do tell whoever it is that I shall be able to pay up everything soon—I hope even within the next few days."

But this time the visitor was not an anxious tradesman. He was a tall, thin, elderly man, with a keen, shrewd face, who gave his name as "Mr. Oram."

After a few moments spent by him in the hall, he was shown into the drawing-room, there to wait for the lady concerning whom he already felt a keen curiosity.

Chapter Thirteen

John Oram was an old-fashioned solicitor of very high standing. His firm had always managed all the private business of the Rushworth family, and he was a personal friend of the client from whom he had received a long and explicit cable about two hours ago. The receipt of that cable, and above all the way it had been worded, had induced Mr. Oram to come himself to Duke of Kent Mansion, instead of sending one of his clerks. He felt intensely curious to see this newly made widow in whom Miles Rushworth evidently took so intimate and anxious an interest.

Rushworth's cable to John Oram had been nearly three times the length of his cable to Ivy; and the purport of it had been that the solicitor was to help Mrs. Lexton in every way in his power. The last words of the cable had run: "Find out from Mrs. Lexton the name of her bankers, and place two thousand pounds to her credit."

After reading the cable, Mr. Oram had sent for his head clerk, an acute, clever man named Alfred Finch, who was some twenty years younger than himself.

"Can you tell me anything of some people of the name of Lexton, who live in Duke of Kent Mansion? I gather there's some sort of legal trouble afoot."

The answer had been immediate, and had filled him with both surprise and dismay.

"Yes, sir, I know all there is to be known. It's not very much, yet. A Mr. Jervis Lexton died some days ago in one of the Duke of Kent Mansion flats. And, as the result of a post-mortem, it has been discovered that death was occasioned through the administration of a large dose of arsenic."

The speaker waited a moment. His curiosity was considerably whetted, for he had seen a look of astonishment, almost of horror, come over his employer's usually impassive face.

Alfred Finch went on, speaking in a more serious tone:

"This Mr. Jervis Lexton must have been a man of means, for you may remember, sir, that he drew up the lease of a flat in Duke of Kent Mansion for the Misses Rushworth about eighteen months ago."

"Aye, aye, I do remember that. I think the rent of their flat was four hundred a year, and the two ladies had to pay a considerable premium on going in. As you say, the Lextons must be well-to-do."

Mr. Finch allowed himself to smile.

"There's only one of them now, sir-the dead man's widow. She's said to be very attractive, and well known in smart society."

"I see. That will do."

It was no wonder that John Oram, while waiting in the drawing-room of the flat for Ivy to join him, gazed about him with a good deal of interest. Then, all at once, he recognised a fine picture which he knew to be the property of the Misses Rushworth, his clients, and Miles Rushworth's cousins. In a moment what had appeared a mystery was to his mind cleared up. There must be, there was, of course, some sort of connection between the Rushworths and the Lextons; and the rich, precise, old-fashioned maiden ladies, who, he now remembered, were wintering abroad, had lent their flat to these family connections.

That would explain everything-Miles Rushworth's urgent cable, as also his evident anxiety that everything should be done to help and succour Mrs. Lexton in her distress.

Just as he came to this satisfactory explanation of what had puzzled and disturbed him, the door of the drawing-room opened, and Ivy walked in.

She held out her little hand. "Mr. Oram?" she cried eagerly, "I'm so glad to see you! I had a cable just before lunch from Mr. Rushworth, telling me that you were going to help me. Everything is so dreadful, so extraordinary, that I feel utterly bewildered, as well as miserable ——" and then tears strangled her voice.

For a moment her visitor said nothing. He was amazed at her exceeding loveliness, puzzled also, for he was very observant, by the expression which now lit up the beautiful face before him. Though tears were running down her cheeks, it was such a happy expression.

"Won't you sit down?"

Her tone was quite subdued now; the hysterical excitement which had been there had died out of her voice.

He obeyed her silently, and there shot over Ivy Lexton a quick feeling of misgiving. Mr. Oram looked so grave, so stern, and he was gazing at her with so curiously close a scrutiny.

"It's very kind of you to have come so soon," she said nervously.

"I am anxious to help you in every way possible, Mrs. Lexton," he answered quietly.

Though the old solicitor was exceedingly impressed by Ivy's beauty, instead of being attracted, he felt, if anything, slightly repelled, by her appearance.

For one thing, he was sufficiently old-fashioned to feel really surprised, and even shocked, by her "make-up."

Ivy had made up more than usual this morning, and before coming into the drawing-room just now she had used her lipstick quite recklessly. So it was that while Mr. Oram asked her certain questions, each one of which was to the point, and allowed for but very little prevarication on her part, he avoided looking straight at her.

How astounding, he said to himself with dismay, that such a woman should be a friend of Miles Rushworth! A direct question had shown him that she had no knowledge of, or even a bowing acquaintance with, the Misses Rushworth.

At last he said rather coldly, "I take it you are in possession of very little money?"

"Very little," she answered, almost in a whisper.

"At the request of Mr. Miles Rushworth, I have a sum of money to place at your disposal. As a matter of fact, it is a considerable sum-two thousand pounds. If you will tell me who are your bankers, I——"

And then Ivy, keeping the joy she felt out of her voice, interrupted him:

"I have not got a banking account, Mr. Oram. I had one many years ago, before my husband lost all his money, but I have not had one for over three years. And oh! it's been so inconvenient."

A kinder look came into the lawyer's grave face.

"In that case, Mrs. Lexton, I advise you to open an account at the local branch of the Birmingham Bank. It is close here, in Kensington High Street. Mr. Rushworth informed me in his cable that you would probably stay on in this flat for the next few weeks."

"I should like to do that," she said in a low tone.

"Your husband, I understand, was a great friend of Mr. Rushworth?"

"Yes, my husband was working in Mr. Rushworth's office when he fell ill."

"Was he indeed?"

That the Lextons could be what the sender of the cable had called "my closest friends" had surprised the solicitor. He had believed himself acquainted with all Miles Rushworth's intimate circle.

Ivy had come across a good many lawyers in her life, and she had always found them bright, cheery, and pleasant. All of them, to a man, had admired her, and made her feel that they did so.

Very, very different was this lawyer's attitude. She realised that he did not approve of her, and she even suspected that he regretted his client's interest in her. That was quite enough for Ivy, and she began to long intensely for Mr. Oram to go away. She had already made up her mind that he was "horrid," and she was sorry indeed that such a man should be Miles Rushworth's representative.

"I will pay in the cheque to the Birmingham Bank tomorrow morning, Mrs. Lexton," said the solicitor. "I will call for you, if I may, at eleven, for you will have to come too, in order that the manager may register your signature."

At last he got up, and then he said suddenly: "Have you yet seen anyone from the police?"

"Yes, I saw a gentleman from Scotland Yard this morning."

"I trust your legal adviser was present."

"I have no legal adviser," and she looked at him surprised.

"I'm sorry for that. I had hoped to learn that you had a solicitor, and that he had been present. However, I don't suppose it will make any odds. I presume you told the gentleman from Scotland Yard everything that it was within your power to tell him, concerning the mysterious circumstances surrounding Mr. Lexton's death?"

"Yes, I did," she said falteringly.

It seemed to her that he was looking at her with such a hard, cold look on his bloodless face. She even had a queer feeling that this Mr. Oram could see right through her, and she felt a touch of deadly terror.

But Ivy's fears were quite unfounded. The solicitor's view of Ivy Lexton was very much what "the gentleman from Scotland Yard's" had been. But whereas Inspector Orpington had liked and pitied her, Rushworth's lawyer already regretted that, if only as a matter of common humanity, he must now secure for her the best legal advice in his power.

John Oram had the faults of his qualities. His life's work had brought him in contact with more than one skilful adventuress. But against such a woman, when she came across his path, the dice were already loaded.

Thus he had never had much trouble with the kind of girl who infatuates a foolish "elder son," and then, maybe, tries to extract an enormous sum out of him by a threat of a breach of promise case. More difficult to deal with he had found, in his long career as a family solicitor, the sort of woman blackmailer who has letters in her possession. But, even in regard to that type of woman, Mr. Oram, with the law on his side, invariably came out of the duel triumphant.

He had never had to do, even remotely, with a case of murder, and the last thing that would have occurred to his mind was that this lovely young fribble of a woman-for such was his old-fashioned expression-could be a secret poisoner.

"I think you must authorise me to instruct counsel to represent you at the inquest which I understand is about to be held."

"What is counsel?" asked Ivy.

She felt surprised and uneasy. Was this disagreeable old man going to run up what she knew was called "a lawyer's bill" which she would have to pay out of Rushworth's munificent gift?

Mr. Oram looked at her with scarce concealed contempt.

"A counsel," he replied drily, "is any member of the Bar. But naturally some are better than others, and, with your permission, I will obtain for you the services of a gentleman who is thoroughly experienced in cases of this kind."

The next morning Mr. Oram arrived at his office early, and, after glancing over his letters, he had just made out a cheque for two thousand pounds to "the order of Mrs. Ivy Lexton," when a card was brought into his private room. But before he looked at the card he had already fully made up his mind that he could see no one, however important their business might be, till his return from Kensington.

Already the solicitor and his head clerk, Alfred Finch, had gone into the question of who should represent Mrs. Lexton at the inquest, and at the various other proceedings which were likely to take place in connection with Jervis Lexton's mysterious death. Money, as the saying is, being no object, they had selected as her counsel one known to them to be by far the soundest man for that sort of watching brief.

The old lawyer was sorry indeed that Miles Rushworth had brought him in touch with what he termed to himself "this very unpleasant business."

His feeling was not shared by his head clerk. Alfred Finch was already keenly interested in the Lexton case. He was an intelligent man, keen about his work whatever it might be, and he already had managed to make certain pertinent inquiries. Indeed, he very much startled Mr. Oram by a remark he made towards the end of their discussion.

"They do say, sir, that Scotland Yard as good as know already who poisoned Mr. Lexton. I think it quite probable that you will see the news of an arrest on the newspaper placards on your way to Duke of Kent Mansion."

"What sort of person has been, or is to be, arrested, Finch? Have you discovered that?"

"Well, sir, I haven't yet got hold of the man's name. But I gather he's a gentleman, and one who was described to me as—" he coughed discreetly "—a beau of Mrs. Lexton. Mrs. Lexton seems to have been a bit of a flyer, sir. She was out every night dancing at what they call a smart night-club, or in some big hotel, during the days when her unfortunate husband was being slowly done to death by this friend of hers."

"Have you heard anything serious against Mrs. Lexton's character?"

Mr. Oram was very old-fashioned. The term "night-club" signified to him something vaguely terrible, and utterly disreputable.

"Oh, no, sir, there's nothing against her. On the contrary, the story goes that, though the man under suspicion was crazy about her, she only flirted with him, so to speak. Mrs. Lexton, it seems, gave him away, quite unknowingly, to the C.I.D. inspector who is in charge of the case."

Finch smiled, "They say it's likely to be the most important case of the kind there's been at the Old Bailey for many a long day. The public are about ready for another murder mystery."

"Not much mystery about it, if your information is correct, Finch," observed Mr. Oram grimly.

"It's Mrs. Lexton-they say she is such a very pretty, smart little lady-who will provide the mystery and the sensation, sir. She'll be the principal witness for the Crown."

Mr. Oram felt very much disturbed on hearing this piece of information.

"I do not regard myself as being in any sense Mrs. Lexton's legal representative," he said stiffly. "With regard to this lady, I am simply acting as Mr. Miles Rushworth's solicitor."

And now, just as he was reaching out for his hat and coat, feeling more perturbed than he would have cared to acknowledge, a client for whom he had a great regard called to see him. Though John Oram was not the kind of man who changes his mind lightly when he saw whose name was engraved on the card which had been brought in to him, the lawyer at once made up his mind that he must spare time for this visitor.

For one thing, her business must be serious, for she lived in the country, and this was the first time she had ever called on him without first making an appointment. Further, she was a widowed lady he had known since he was quite a young man, and for whom he had a very high esteem, and, it might almost be said, affection. But he had despised her husband, and he did not really like her son-though the son had none of the faults which had brought his father to ruin. Lastly, Mr. Oram was willing to see this client because she was a woman of few words. She would tell him at once why she wished to see him, and then she would go away.

"Show Mrs. Gretorex in," he said quickly.

"There is a young lady with her, sir."

"A young lady?"

Did that mean that Roger Gretorex was thinking of getting married? If so, unless the girl had money, he would be doing a very foolish and improvident thing. Mr. Oram did not really think that this was at all likely to be the reason for Mrs. Gretorex's unexpected visit; but a solicitor is apt to consider every possibility.

However, Mr. Oram's old friend and client came unaccompanied through the baize door of his private room. Mrs. Gretorex had left Enid in the waiting-room, for there were certain things which she knew she would have to say, and which she felt she could only say when alone with the solicitor.

As she looked at her old lawyer's stern face, though the expression on it was just a little softer than usual, even her high courage faltered.

"Perhaps you know, Mr. Oram," she said in a low voice, "what it is that has brought me here this morning?"

"No," he said, surprised, "I have no idea at all, Mrs. Gretorex——"

He could see she was very much disturbed, and he drew forward a chair. After all, it wouldn't hurt that frivolous little widow to wait for an extra half-hour or so for the two thousand pounds Miles Rushworth was so rashly presenting to her free and for nothing. Mr. Oram's knowledge of human nature told him that probably a very great deal more money was coming Ivy's way from the same source as this money came from.

Mrs. Gretorex bent a little forward. She fixed her sunken eyes, for she had not slept at all the night before, on the lawyer's face.

"Roger has been arrested on the charge of having murdered a man called Jervis Lexton———"

"Roger arrested on a charge of murder? God bless my soul!"

He took off his eyeglasses and began cleaning them mechanically with a small piece of washleather which he kept for that purpose.

Here was indeed a complication! And a very troublesome as well as a painful complication, from his point of view. His own connection with the Gretorex family was hereditary. His grandfather had been, not only the lawyer, but the very close friend and trustee, of Mrs. Gretorex's father-in-law. As for the rich Rushworths, they were in Mr. Oram's estimation mere upstarts compared to the ancient, if now impoverished, county family.

"If you don't mind," he said suddenly, "I'll send for Finch. In a case of this sort two heads are better than one. Also Finch can take notes of any information you can give me about the matter."

Mrs. Gretorex would much rather have told her story to this good old friend alone. But she saw the sense of his suggestion, and they both waited in silence till the head clerk came in.

Mrs. Gretorex rose and shook hands with Mr. Finch. She was well acquainted with him, and she had always liked him.

"May I tell Finch what you have just told me?" Mr. Oram asked.

She bent her head, overwhelmed with a passion of agony and shame.

"Mrs. Gretorex has brought bad news, Finch. Her son has just been arrested on the charge of having caused the death, I presume by the administration of arsenic, of Mr. Jervis Lexton. I take it"—and he looked very straight into the younger man's face—"that you had no notion of this fact, when you told me, this morning, that you had heard that an arrest was about to be effected in connection with the Lexton affair?"

Alfred Finch prided himself on his self-control, and wise lack of emotion, where anything connected with business was concerned. But his face was full of dismay as he answered instantly, "No name at all was mentioned, sir. I was simply told that an arrest was imminent."

He turned to Mrs. Gretorex. "When was it that Mr. Roger was arrested?" He had known "Mr. Roger" from childhood.

Tears welled up to her tired eyes. "Last evening," she answered.

"I wish he'd sent for us at once," Finch exclaimed. "It's always important to get one's blow in first, and especially over a matter of this kind."

"My son was arrested at Anchorford House. I came up by the night train, as the police inspector from Lynchester said he would be brought to town the first thing this morning. I suppose he is in London by now."

Finch looked at his employer.

"In that case, don't you think, sir, that I'd better go off at once and try to find Dr. Gretorex? Let me see. Where would he be charged?"

Mentally he answered his own question. Then he observed, "I hope he made no statement to the police?"

"He wished to make a statement, but the inspector advised him not to do so."

"You think, Finch, that you'd better go off now, instantly?"

"I'm sure of it, sir. Even now, I fear I shall be too late to stop his saying something he'd best keep to himself."

"I feel quite sure he has nothing to hide," said Mrs. Gretorex rather stiffly. But neither of the two men made any comment on that.

Mr. Oram was the first to break the silence.

"Very well, Finch. You go off," he said. "Start at once! And of course no expense is to be spared?"

He glanced at his client, and she quickly nodded.

"Meanwhile, I'll make rough notes of any information that Mrs. Gretorex is good enough to give me. But I don't suppose she really knows very much."

And then in a serious tone he asked her, "Were you yourself acquainted with Mr. and Mrs. Lexton?"

He put the question just as the other man was leaving the room, and Mrs. Gretorex saw Finch stay his steps. It was clear that he wished to hear her answer.

"I've never seen Mr. Lexton; but Mrs. Lexton spent a week-end at Anchorford last winter."

Both men noticed the somewhat embarrassed way in which Roger Gretorex's mother answered that question.

At last, reluctantly, Finch shut the door. How useful it would be, sometimes, to find oneself in two places at once!

Being the manner of woman she was, Mrs. Gretorex did not try to conceal anything of what was in her heart from her old and trusted friend.

"I am absolutely certain, Mr. Oram, that Roger had nothing to do with Mr. Lexton's death. On the other hand, it would be dishonest to conceal from you my conviction that he is in terrible danger."

"What makes you think that, if you are certain he is innocent?"

"Because," answered Mrs. Gretorex in a low tone, "he loves this woman, Ivy Lexton, desperately. He admitted as much to me last night, before we supposed there was any fear of an immediate arrest, but after he had already had an interview with someone from Scotland Yard — —"

"Roger in love with a married woman. That's the last thing I should have expected to hear!"

Mr. Oram got up. "I have a bit of business I must attend to this morning, Mrs. Gretorex. But I suggest that you wait here till a telephone message comes through from Finch."

As they shook hands, "I beg you, I implore you," she said in a stifled voice, "to try and believe Roger innocent."

Mr. Oram said to himself, "I will-until he is proved guilty." Aloud he exclaimed:

"Of course I believe him innocent! But, Mrs. Gretorex, I have something very serious to say to you; that is, I feel that this is not the kind of case of which I have the necessary experience, and I doubt if I should be able to afford your son the kind of legal assistance which he needs."

He saw a look of terror and of fear flash over her face.

"Don't desert me in my extremity!" she exclaimed. "You know as well as I do that I haven't a single man relation in the world. You, Mr. Oram, are my only hope." And he saw that tears were rolling down her cheeks.

"If you feel that, Mrs. Gretorex, then be assured that I shall do my best for Roger."

Chapter Fourteen

While that, to both of them, woeful conversation was going on between the mother of Roger Gretorex and the old lawyer, Ivy Lexton sat in her drawing-room, waiting impatiently for John Oram, and-his cheque.

She felt quite differently from what she had felt the day before, and happier from every point of view. For fear, that most haunting of secret house-mates, had gone from her. Indeed, after seeing Mr. Oram, she had spent the rest of the afternoon at the establishment of the dressmaker who was just then the fashion in her set. Whilst there she had bought four black frocks "off the peg," and she had also ordered a splendid fur coat.

No wonder that she was now waiting feverishly for the old lawyer to call and take her across to the bank. Two thousand pounds? What an enormous lot of money! It was the first time Ivy had had even a quarter of such a sum absolutely at her disposal. In the old days, when Jervis was still a man of means, she had never had a regular allowance. She had simply run up bills, and Jervis, grumbling good-naturedly, had paid them.

But the moments, the minutes, the quarters of an hour slipped by, and Mr. Oram dallied. What could have happened? She had become uncomfortably aware yesterday that Miles Rushworth's solicitor did not like her, and that he thought Rushworth's interest in her strange and inexplicable, so she began to feel thoroughly "rattled," as she expressed it to herself.

At last she heard the lift stop outside the flat. What did that portend? The longed-for coming of Mr. Oram with his bountiful cheque, or more trouble for her, for poor little Ivy?

Then she gave a gasp-but it was a gasp of joy, for she had heard the lawyer's frigid voice inquiring whether she were in. Before the maid could open the door of the drawing-room she had opened it herself and exclaimed, "Is it Mr. Oram?"

She was too full of instinctive tact when dealing with any man to utter even a light word of reproach, though the solicitor was over an hour later than he had said he would be.

Mr. Oram walked into the drawing-room, and then, very deliberately, he shut the door behind him.

Again there came over Ivy a sick feeling of fear. He looked stern, forbidding, and as a certain kind of man looks when he is the bearer of bad news.

"I'm sorry I'm late," he said abruptly, "but I couldn't help myself. I've brought the cheque, and we will proceed in a few moments to the bank. But first I would like to tell you, Mrs. Lexton, that circumstances have arisen that will make it impossible for me to act as your lawyer with regard to any proceedings that may arise in connection with your husband's death."

He cleared his throat, and then went on: "As I cannot act for you, I will find you a first-class man, who will probably have far more time to devote to your affairs than I should have been able to do."

She looked at him, wondering what this really meant, and a tide of dismay welled up in her heart.

"But Mr. Rushworth," she began falteringly, "again told me, in a cable that I received only this morning, that you would do everything you could for me, Mr. Oram?"

She had not meant to tell anyone of that long, intimately-worded cable, the first in which Rushworth had allowed something of his intense exultation at the knowledge that she was now free to pierce through the measured words. It seemed to her impossible that anyone could disregard the wishes of so important and, above all, so wealthy a man as Miles Rushworth. To Ivy the sound of money talking drowned every other sound in life. But this, to her discomfiture, was not the case with John Oram.

"I know that," and this time he spoke more kindly. "And I'm sorry I shall not be able to do what Mr. Rushworth very naturally hoped I could do. But I have discovered ——" and then he stopped for what seemed to her a long time.

He was wondering whether she was yet aware that Roger Gretorex had been arrested on the charge of having murdered her husband. Already the fact was billed in all the early editions of the evening papers.

"The truth is," he began again, and in a colder tone, "not only I, but my father before me, and my grandfather before him, acted in a legal capacity for the Gretorex family."

The colour rushed into Ivy's face. She said defensively, "But need that make any difference, Mr. Oram?"

"Well, yes, I'm sorry to say that it will, Mrs. Lexton. Roger Gretorex, as you are no doubt aware, was arrested last night on a charge of having poisoned Mr. Jervis Lexton. He has put his interests in my hands. It would not be to your advantage were you to employ the same solicitor as the man who is accused of having murdered your husband. I am sure," he cleared his throat, "you are aware of what Dr. Gretorex's motive is supposed to have been, assuming that he is guilty of that of which he is accused?"

Ivy looked so frightened that for a moment he thought she was going to faint.

Then she hadn't known of Gretorex's arrest? Even John Oram, who was already strongly prejudiced against her, could not doubt that the horror and distress with which she heard his news were genuine.

She sank down into a chair.

"But this is terrible-terrible!" she moaned.

"It is terrible, Mrs. Lexton. And, incidentally, you see, now, how I am situated? When I came here to see you yesterday, I naturally did not associate my friend and client, Dr. Roger Gretorex, with the strange and mysterious circumstances surrounding your husband's death. I have not yet seen a copy of the statement you appear to have made to the inspector who came to see you from Scotland Yard; but I gather that you made certain admissions that were very detrimental to my client."

"The man pressed me so! I didn't want to hurt Roger," she exclaimed, and thought she spoke the truth.

Twenty minutes later, as the two came out of the bank, Mr. Oram said quietly:

"With your permission, Mrs. Lexton, I am going to put you in touch with an old friend of mine, a most able lawyer named Paxton-Smith. He will not only watch your interests in a general sense, but you can trust him to give you the soundest advice. In your place, I would make a point of being frank with him concerning everything connected with your husband's life as well as with his death."

It was strange what a feeling of repugnance, almost of horror, this beautiful girl-for she looked a girl-inspired in him. But that, so he told himself, for he tried to be fair-minded, was no doubt owing to the way Roger Gretorex's mother had spoken of Ivy Lexton that morning.

"Tell Mr. Paxton-Smith, as far you know it, the truth, the whole truth, and nothing but the truth," he went on. "Many ladies, when in conference with their legal adviser, are tempted to hold something back. There can be no greater mistake. You can be absolutely sure of Mr. Paxton-Smith's discretion; and unless he knows everything you can tell him, it will be impossible for him to advise you adequately."

She was gazing at him with affrighted eyes. Tell the truth, the whole truth, and nothing but the truth? Why, she couldn't even begin to think of doing that! But, even so, the old lawyer's words impressed her. Why, oh! why, had she been tempted to tell the man from Scotland Yard that half-truth as to Roger and his love for her? By now, when it had become clear to her that no one suspected her, she had almost forgotten what had brought about that dangerous admission.

"You are, I understand, going to be the chief witness for the Crown," said Mr. Oram solemnly.

"I didn't know that! What does being that mean?" faltered Ivy.

"It means," he said drily, "that the prosecution is counting on you to aid them in proving that Roger Gretorex became that most despicable of human beings, a slow, secret poisoner, in order that you might be free to become his wife."

She unconsciously stayed her steps, and was staring up at him as if hypnotised by his words. He looked down fixedly into her face. What lay hidden behind those lovely eyes, that exquisite little mouth, now spoilt, according to his taste, by a smear of scarlet paint?

"Only God knows the secrets of all hearts, Mrs. Lexton. I have not asked you, and I do not propose to ask you, if you believe that unhappy young man to be guilty of the fearful crime of which he is accused, and for which he is about to stand on trial for his life. But if there is any doubt in your mind, and, far more, if you believe him innocent, I beg you, earnestly, to consider and weigh every word you utter from now on."

But, even as he made that appeal, moved out of his usual cautious self by his real regard for Roger Gretorex and his intense pity for Roger's mother, he felt convinced that Ivy Lexton would, in all circumstances and contingencies, only consider herself and what was to her own advantage.

How amazing that such a man as was Miles Rushworth should be moved to passion by such a frivolous, mindless, selfish woman! But that such was the case John Oram had far too much knowledge of human nature to doubt, even for a moment. He was, indeed, by now as sure as was Ivy herself that, in due course, Mrs. Jervis Lexton would become Mrs. Miles Rushworth.

Suddenly Ivy said something which very much surprised her companion, and made him dislike her even more than he already disliked her.

"Are you going to cable everything that has happened to Mr. Rushworth?" she asked in a frightened tone.

"Mr. Rushworth will learn precisely what the Cape Town newspapers choose to publish, and what you choose to cable to him. He has not asked me to communicate with him, and I am not proposing to do so."

He held out his hand. "And now I must say good-bye, Mrs. Lexton. I will try to arrange that Mr. Paxton-Smith shall ring you up before lunch. He will then make an appointment to see you. I should like, if I may, to give you one word of advice. It is this. Refuse, however great the temptation, to disclose anything that concerns your husband's death to anyone, excepting, of course, to Mr. Paxton-Smith."

"Then shan't I see you again?" she asked.

Though deep in her heart she was glad to be seeing the last of Mr. Oram, she knew him to be her only link, in London, with Miles Rushworth.

"Should Mr. Rushworth cable me instructions to do so, I shall of course transmit to you any money or any messages he may choose to send through me. But, apart from that, it is clear that in your own interest Roger Gretorex's legal adviser should have no more communication with you."

That same afternoon Philip Paxton-Smith had his first interview with Ivy Lexton. Unlike John Oram, he took an instant fancy to the prettiest client and most attractive little woman, so he told himself, that a Providence which was apt to be kind in that way to the shrewd and popular solicitor had ever sent his way.

So it was that, after a very few moments, Ivy found herself chatting to him almost happily.

He listened with unaffected, indeed absorbed, interest to her sentimental half-true, half-false, account of her first meeting with Roger Gretorex. Of how the young man had "fallen for her" at once, and how she had seen coming, and tried to stave off, his declaration of passionate love.

She also managed to convey to her new friend's sympathetic ears what manner of man she now desired Jervis Lexton to be supposed to have been. Easy-going, good-tempered, devoted to her, and yet entirely selfish, frightfully extravagant, and, when they were not out together enjoying a good time, a great deal at his club.

"Poor lonely little woman," said the lawyer to himself. "The real wonder is that she remained as straight as she did."

Paxton-Smith and his partner did a very different class of business from that associated with the firm of which John Oram was now senior partner. They were constantly associated with what are loosely called "society cases," and Paxton-Smith himself, something of a gay bachelor, was seen a good deal in that section of the London world which seems to live for pleasure. He was well liked by men. As for women, well, he liked women-and they liked him too.

During his first interview with Ivy Lexton, after he had, as he believed, won her entire confidence, he cleverly led her to give an almost verbatim report of the conversation which she had had with Inspector Orpington. And though once or twice he shook his head when he heard what she had admitted, he was able to do to her what he failed to do to himself, that is, make her believe that, on the whole, she had been wise rather than unwise in her dealings with the man in whose charge had been the preliminary inquiries concerning her husband's death.

Philip Paxton-Smith was both a clever man and a clever lawyer. But "this dear little woman," as he already called her to himself, was more than a match for him. How amazed would he have been could some entity outside himself have been able to convince him, at the end of the two and a half hours that he spent with Ivy Lexton that afternoon, that she had, as a matter of fact, so completely deceived him as to make him believe her everything she was not!

True, he had begun by thinking her just a little stupid; but he had ended by realising that she was far more intelligent than many of the women with whom he was in contact. That, naturally, had made him like her all the more, for there is nothing more tiresome or annoying to any good lawyer than having to deal with a dull and obstinate client.

As for Ivy, she was happier after Paxton-Smith had left her than she had felt since the terrible moment when the card of Inspector Orpington had first been brought in to her.

Not only did the genial lawyer inspire her with confidence, but she was naturally pleased and relieved to feel that he believed everything she told him. It was such a comfort, such a moral support, to feel that he "liked" her, and that he was going to do his very best to help her through what even she now realised was going to be a dangerous and anxious time.

By the morning following the day of Ivy's first memorable interview with her lawyer, it was obvious to all those concerned with the case that what was already called "The Lexton Mystery" was going to develop into a *cause célèbre*.

Already the personality of Jervis Lexton's young widow was becoming of moment, indeed of absorbing interest, to hundreds of thousands of newspaper readers. And as the dark, early winter days slipped by, men and women engaged in wordy combat as to whether she was the sweet, wholly innocent, guileless woman portrayed by her admirers, or a typical example of the selfish, heartless, extravagant little minx old-fashioned folk are wont to describe the modern girl and young woman.

Very soon her exquisite face became as familiar to the public as those of the more popular actresses. She, not Roger Gretorex, emerged as the central figure of this drama of love and death; this if only because she was, to the mind of everyone interested in the story, the one point of mystery.

Had she loved in secret the good-looking young doctor who had almost certainly slowly, craftily, done to death the man who was now described as having been his best friend? Or was it, as she was said to aver, the truth that Gretorex had adored her with no touch of encouragement on her part?

Here and there some were found ready to whisper that perhaps "Ivy" had been "in it." But they were a small minority of the vast public interested in such a story, and, for the most part, they kept their view to themselves. It is a dangerous thing to libel the living-especially a woman blessed with as many ardent champions as was Jervis Lexton's widow.

And Ivy herself? For a little while Ivy remained unaware of the amazing interest which was already being taken in her past thoughts, past secret emotions, and past way of life.

She went through many anxious, troubled solitary hours till, all at once, those acquaintances, both men and women, who become friends at a moment's notice, crowded round her, pleased and excited to be associated with so terrible and mysterious an affair.

Their new mission in life, so they pretended to themselves and others, was to try to cheer up poor pretty little Ivy in her solitude. It must be admitted that these, for the most part, young friends, succeeded in their laudable object to an extent that sometimes amazed Paxton-Smith.

Those giddy, good-natured, carelessly heartless men and women all took so absolutely for granted the fact that Roger Gretorex had committed murder for love of Ivy Lexton. Some of the men about her indeed hinted with a half-smile that they could well understand the poor chap's motive.

One of them, the well-to-do idle bachelor who had been about with her so much this last autumn, and who was acting as her cavalier at the theatre and supper party on the evening of Jervis's death, actually said to her, "I wouldn't back myself not to have done the same thing in his place! After all, 'opportunity makes the crime.'"

But, if comforted, she had also been stung by that well-worn saying; for she knew, better than anyone in the whole world just now, how great is the awful truth embodied in those trite words.

The women who gathered round Ivy Lexton during those days were not all inspired by morbid curiosity and excitement. Especially was Lady Flora Desmond very kind to her.

Lady Flora thought she understood something of what Mrs. Lexton must be feeling because she herself had gone through such a terrible agony when her husband had died. Lady Flora was a real support to Ivy during those long days of waiting for the day when she would be compelled to appear as chief witness for the Crown at the trial of Roger Gretorex.

True, this kind friend wanted to take her away to her country cottage, but Ivy refused with quiet obstinacy. She knew that she would go melancholy mad were she left with no one to talk to except one affectionate, sympathising woman friend.

Mrs. Jervis Lexton had plenty of good excuses for remaining in London, for, during the comparatively short time which elapsed between Gretorex's arrest and the opening of his trial, there took place the long-drawn-out legal formalities of which the public are only aware to an extent which whets, without satisfying, curiosity.

But at last everything was "in order"; so Paxton-Smith put it to the woman to whom he found himself devoting far more thought, as well as time, than he had ever done before to any client, however charming, in his successful legal career.

The shrewd solicitor sometimes felt something like angry contempt for the foolish, selfish, talkative men and women who buzzed round the young widow during these, to him, anxious and tiring days. He supposed himself, naturally enough, to be just now her only real stand-by in life.

How amazed, how piqued, he would have been, had some tricksy spirit whispered in his ear the news that every morning, and sometimes in the evening too, Ivy received a long cable of sympathy, support, and even, as the days went on, of disguised passion!

Of that passion of love which can assume so infinite a variety of shapes and disguises, Ivy Lexton had had many an exciting experience, but none so satisfying as that conveyed thousands of miles, and in a shadowy form, from the man for whom, as she now dimly realised, she had run at any rate the risk of a shameful and horrible death.

Ivy, for once, was quite alone, lying down in the drawing-room, reading a magazine, one evening, when suddenly the door opened.

"Mrs. Gretorex wishes to see you, madam," said the maid in a nervous tone.

Ivy leapt up from the sofa, and by the shaded light of the reading lamp which had stood close to her elbow, she saw a tall, spectral-looking figure advancing into the room.

But it was a firm and very clear voice that exclaimed: "I did not write and ask you to receive me, Mrs. Lexton, as I feared you might say 'No.' I'm not acting on Mr. Oram's advice in thus coming to see you, but I know he doubts, as I do too, if you are really aware in what deadly danger my son now stands?"

"Do sit down," murmured Ivy.

She felt a surge of angry fear of Roger Gretorex's mother, but she had quickly made up her mind to be what she called "sweet" to her unwelcome visitor. When, always against her will, the thought of Gretorex forced itself on her mind, there was coupled with it the terrifying perception that by now he must be well aware of who it was who had brought about the death of Jervis Lexton.

"Appearances," said Mrs. Gretorex in a low, quiet voice, "are very much against Roger. His counsel is thinking, we understand, of putting forward a theory that your husband committed suicide. I have come to ask you if you can advance anything to add even a tinge of probability to that theory? Was there insanity in Mr. Lexton's family? Did he, above all, say, even once, that he might be tempted to take his life?"

These clear, passionless questions gave Ivy no opportunity for the display of her special gifts. She asked herself nervously what she ought to say in answer to these definite queries.

Would it be to her interest to allow it to be thought that she, at any rate, believed it possible that Jervis had done away with himself? Then she decided that, no, it would not pay her to accept what everyone who had ever come in contact with her husband, including Nurse Bradfield, and the two doctors who had been attending him, would know to be impossible. So:

"I never heard him say anything of that sort," she answered regretfully, "except in fun, of course." She added, as an afterthought, "But I know how much Jervis hated to be poor, Mrs. Gretorex."

The older woman threw an imperceptible look round the luxurious room.

"But he wasn't poor," she said quickly. "He had just got, or so we understand, a good new post."

"I know he had. That's one of the things that makes it all so dreadful— —"

And then Mrs. Gretorex, who was herself a very honest woman, felt impelled to ask what was perhaps a dangerous question.

"I need hardly ask you what you think? Whatever be the truth, you do not believe, Mrs. Lexton, that my son poisoned your husband?"

Ivy did not answer for what seemed to Mrs. Gretorex a long, long time. Then she exclaimed, twisting her fingers together:

"It's no good asking me that sort of thing, because I honestly don't know what to think. It's all so strange!"

"But surely you know Roger to be innocent?"

Ivy let her eyes drop.

"Of course, I want to think that," she said in a low tone.

"You want to think it, Mrs. Lexton? D'you mean that you have any doubt about it?"

Again Ivy twisted her fingers together.

"It's all so strange," she repeated falteringly. "And it's so unfortunate that Dr. Gretorex was the last one to see my husband alone on the day he died."

Mrs. Gretorex got up.

"I see," she said in a dull tone. "Then you are half inclined to believe that Roger did do this terrible thing-for love, I suppose, of you?"

And there flashed a look of awful condemnation over the mother's worn face.

"Please don't say that, Mrs. Gretorex! I never said that I thought poor Roger really did it!" cried Ivy hysterically. "Perhaps Jervis did commit suicide, but, as nurse says, if he did poison himself, where did he get the stuff to do it with? Also Roger was so fearfully gone on me. It's all so very, very strange!"

Oh, why had Mrs. Gretorex come here, just to torture her and frighten her? It was too cruel!

Then Roger Gretorex's mother did make to the woman who stood before her, this woman whom her son loved to his undoing, a desperate appeal, though she worded what she had to say quietly enough.

"I understand that you're going to be the principal witness for the Crown at my son's trial?"

Ivy began to cry.

"Yes," she sobbed. "Isn't it dreadful-dreadful? As if I hadn't gone through enough without having to go through that too!"

"On what you say," went on Mrs. Gretorex firmly, "may depend Roger's life or death. After all, you and he were dear friends?"

She uttered that last sentence in a tone she strove to make conciliatory.

Ivy stopped crying. Then Roger hadn't given her away, even to a very little extent, to his mother? It was a great relief to know that.

"I implore you to guard your tongue when you are in the witness-box," went on Mrs. Gretorex.

"I will! I will indeed ——"

"Can you think of no natural explanation with regard to the utterly mysterious thing which happened?"

Her eyes were fixed imploringly on the beautiful little face of this frivolous-Mrs. Gretorex believed mindless-woman, whom Roger still loved so desperately.

"I've thought, and thought, and thought ——" whispered Ivy.

And then for the fourth time during this brief interview she uttered the words, "It's all so strange."

As, a few minutes later, she walked down Kensington High Street, still full of bustling, happy people on shopping intent, Roger Gretorex's mother was in an agony of doubt, wondering whether she had done well or ill in thus forcing herself on Mrs. Jervis Lexton.

Again and again there echoed in her ear the silly, vulgar little phrase: "Roger was so fearfully gone on me."

Gone on her? Alas, that had been, that was still, only too true. Even now his one thought seemed to be how to spare Ivy pain, and, above all, disgrace.

She stepped up into a crowded omnibus at the corner of Chapel Street, and for a while she had to stand. Then a girl gave up her seat to her, and heavily she sat down.

Who, looking however closely at Mrs. Gretorex sitting there, her worn face calm and still, would have thought her other than an old-fashioned, highly bred lady, leading the placid life of her fortunate class, that class which even now is financially secure, and seems to be so far apart from and above the sordid ills and anxieties of ordinary humanity?

Yet there can be little doubt that Roger Gretorex's mother was the most miserable and the most unhappy woman of the many miserable and unhappy women in London that night. To the anguish, which was now her perpetual lot, was added a feeling that she had done, if anything, harm, in forcing herself on Mrs. Lexton.

"I've done no good!" she exclaimed as she walked into the sitting-room of the lodgings in Ebury Street where she and Enid Dent had taken refuge, after spending two or three days with a kind friend who, they had soon discovered though no word had been said, considered Roger almost certainly guilty.

The girl looked dismayed, for it had been at her suggestion that Mrs. Gretorex had gone to Duke of Kent Mansion.

Enid Dent now felt convinced that Ivy Lexton held the key to the mystery of Jervis Lexton's death. She had never seen this woman whom she now knew that Roger loved, but she had formed a fairly clear and true impression of Ivy's nature and character. Hatred, as well as love, has sometimes the power of tearing asunder the most skilfully woven web of lies.

And then there began for them all what seemed an interminable time of waiting. And all those nearly concerned with the case, apart from Ivy herself, felt almost a sense of relief when the winter day at last dawned which was to see Roger Gretorex stand his trial at the Old Bailey.

Chapter Fifteen

During the night which preceded the day when Ivy Lexton was to appear as chief witness for the Crown, she lay awake, hour after hour, dreading with an awful dread the ordeal that lay before her.

Her chattering, excited circle of friends had all unwittingly terrified her with their accounts of how Gretorex's counsel, Sir Joseph Molloy, was apt to deal with a witness. And in the watches of the night, Ivy, shivering, saw herself faced by that ruthless cross-examiner.

What was this formidable advocate going to say to her, to get out of her, by what one of her admirers had laughingly called "his exercise of the Third Degree?"

For the first time the widow of Jervis Lexton realised how insincere and how shallow were the sympathy and the cloying flattery with which she was now surrounded. Only two human beings seemed really sorry at the thought of what was going to happen to her tomorrow-Lady Flora Desmond and Philip Paxton-Smith.

The concern manifested by her solicitor made Ivy feel sick with apprehension. He had spent hours with her trying to teach her what she had to say; that is, what to admit, what to deny, during her cross-examination.

It was plain, dreadfully plain, to her, that Paxton-Smith was very much afraid of how the great Sir Joseph Molloy would treat her when he had her in his power.

Again and again, during that long winter night, she asked herself with terror whether Sir Joseph could have found out anything with regard to her past relations with Roger Gretorex.

She knew Gretorex far too well to suppose, even for a moment, that he had given her away. But the short interview with Roger's mother, though she, Ivy, had appeared to come out of it so well, had left a frightening impression. And she shivered as she recalled the terrible expression which had come over Mrs. Gretorex's face when making to her the appeal which she had rejected with words implying that she, too, believed the man who loved her had been guilty of a terrible crime.

Ivy even asked herself with a kind of angry resentment, in the darkness of the night, why Roger Gretorex had not done this thing of which he stood accused?

Her own set, the men and women round her, all seemed to think it natural, in a sense, that he should have done it. And yet, though he had had many opportunities of ridding himself of Jervis Lexton, in the days when he had been so much with them, and though the only bar at one moment which had stood in the way of his happiness had been the life of Jervis Lexton, the thought of doing such a thing had evidently never even occurred to his mind!

Looking back, Ivy knew that there had been a time last winter when, had she then become a widow, she would have married Gretorex. She had been-how curious to remember that time now, though it was less than a year ago-infatuated with the splendid-looking young man who loved her with so intense and passionate a devotion.

She remembered, also, how reckless she had been in those old days. Anyone but Jervis would have suspected the truth. Thank God, she hadn't known Miles Rushworth, even slightly, during those mad weeks of what she had called her love for Roger Gretorex. Rushworth would have guessed, nay more, he would have known, what was going on.

Had Roger's mother suspected the truth? Almost certainly, yes. If Mrs. Gretorex thought it would help Roger, she would of course tell the famous advocate who was now fighting for her son's life what she believed had been the real relations between her son and the woman who was to be the chief witness against him.

Always it was to Sir Joseph Molloy, the man whose name she had never heard till, say, a fortnight ago, that Ivy's thoughts turned with dread, during those endless hours of darkness when she tossed this way and that through the long night.

Nurse Bradfield had had a terrible time in the witness-box. Indeed, she had confessed to Ivy last evening that Sir Joseph could have made her say black was white and wrong right! He had dwelt with sinister insistence on the short time that she, Mrs. Lexton, had been left alone with Mr. Lexton on that fatal last afternoon; nay, more, he had almost gone so far as to imply that, had Nurse Bradfield been faithful to her trust and had not gone out for those few minutes, Jervis Lexton might be alive today. Also he had called her "Woman!" She had even appealed to the Judge to protect her-not that that had done her much good.

The nurse's account of the ordeal she had been through filled Ivy with such foreboding that she would have done anything, even gone back to the old black days when she and Jervis lived in those poverty-stricken Pimlico lodgings, if she could thereby have wiped out all that had happened since.

When at last there came the morning, she got up, pale and really ill. Then she waited, in an extremity of nervous fear, till, at last, there came the moment when Mr. Paxton-Smith, looking, so she told herself, like an undertaker, and not at all like his usual jovial self, called in his car to take her to the Old Bailey.

During their long drive in the crowded streets the lawyer remained almost entirely silent. He had explained and made her rehearse yesterday, carefully and kindly, everything she must say and refrain from saying.

When passing the Piccadilly end of Bond Street, for the chauffeur, chauffeur-like, had taken them the longest way, a sob escaped Ivy. There had risen before her a vision of care-free, happy nights, spent in dancing, and in what old-fashioned people would have called riotous living, within a few yards of where the car was now being held up in the traffic.

After they had gone on again, her frightened eyes caught glimpses of the newspaper placards. On each one was blazoned forth her now notorious name:

Lexton Mystery.
Lexton Murder.
Nurse in the Box.

Though she was singularly unimaginative, Ivy shuddered as she told herself that, in a couple of hours from now, maybe there would be the words, "Mrs. Lexton in the Box," or, worse by far, "Mrs. Lexton Cross-examined."

At last, after what seemed both to Paxton-Smith and to his client a long drive, the car drew up by a side door of the great frowning building called by that name of dread to every evildoer the Old Bailey.

What an awesome, and in some ways superb, spectacle is the scene presented by every British trial for murder! And if this is always true, even in the humblest country town Assize Court, how much more tense and awe-inspiring is what takes place in the court-house of the Old Bailey, when the prisoner in the dock is the central figure in a murder mystery which has suddenly become world-famous. Especially is this true when the accused man is putting up a struggle, not only for his life, but what to some men really does mean more than life-his honour.

Since the war there has appeared in London a new world of idle, luxury-loving human beings who live for pleasure, and who, if their income is fluctuating and uncertain, yet mysteriously appear always plentifully provided with ready money to burn on what they call "fun."

To the eyes of those composing this new world, lovely Ivy Lexton, and good-humoured, popular Jervis Lexton, had been familiar figures, especially during the years when they were merrily engaged in running through their capital. All these people regarded the trial of Roger Gretorex as a spectacle produced and staked for their special benefit, and while the more enterprising and fortunate among them attended each day the exciting proceedings at the Old Bailey, the others all read with avid interest the full accounts of the trial which appeared every morning in whatever happened to be their favourite daily paper.

Although the case was called the Lexton Mystery, none of the hundreds of thousands of Roger Gretorex's fellow-countrymen and countrywomen, who were following each detail of the story as unfolded now day by day in Court, considered that there was very much mystery about it. What was of tense interest, and what formed the real enigma, was the latest variant of the eternal triangle-the story of the relations of the three, wife, husband, and lover.

One doubt remained in many a mind. That doubt concerned the relations of Ivy Lexton and of Roger Gretorex. To what extent, if any, had that beautiful young woman been involved in her lover's guilt? Was it true that her own feelings, with regard to the young man who had slowly done a husband to death so that a wife should be free, had been simply those which it was known she was going into the witness-box to swear they had been? Had they really been feelings of kindly and indifferent, not to say tepid, friendship?

Another question which is always being asked by every student of human nature was asked in this case-that is, whether a certain kind of exalted passion, the passionate love of a man for a woman which leads to crime, can exist without even a touch of secret encouragement?

The more worldly-wise shook their heads, and said that, whatever romantic poets and novelists may aver, such entirely unrequited passion on the part of an intelligent, educated man is impossible. Surely, before such a man as Roger Gretorex had set out to do that awful thing, he must, at any rate, have had some cause to believe that Ivy Lexton, when widowed, would become his wife?

There was yet another point which made this judicial drama appear, to use a phrase sometimes used in such a connection, "a full-dress trial." Justice may be blind, yet she can see the glitter of gold. No money had been spared on either side. Indeed, judging by the array of counsel engaged, there must have been limitless wealth available for the defence. And, in a sense, there was, for Mrs. Gretorex had thrown all the fortune that remained to her into the struggle for her son's life.

And now, on the fourth day, was approaching the great moment of Roger Gretorex's trial for murder. The highest peak of the fever chart of this drama, which was being watched not only by those who were present in Court, but by hundreds of thousands of English-speaking people all over the world, was now about to be reached.

There came a peculiar rustle through the Court, followed by a moment of complete silence, as Ivy Lexton stepped, with short, dainty steps into the witness-box, and faced what appeared to her a myriad world of eyes fixed on her pale countenance. In accordance with a strong hint given yesterday by her solicitor, Ivy had not made up her face at all today.

Paxton-Smith, as the tense moments flew by, felt full of admiration for his beautiful client.

Ivy even remembered everything that he had advised with regard to her behaviour when in the witness-box, including certain things she might well have been pardoned for forgetting. One of these had been that, when answering counsel for the Crown, she should hold her head well up.

This she obviously tried to do, and when, as more than once happened, she threw what looked like a child-like glance of fear and supplication at the kind, if grave, face of the inquisitor whose only desire was to learn the truth and nothing but the truth, a thrill of sympathy went through her great, silent audience.

Again, when the flawless oval of her face appeared framed in the tiny little pull-on black hat, and her star-like eyes for a moment looked wild, many a man, watching her, told himself that he could well understand, indeed almost sympathise with, any crime being committed by one who loved her, and who longed, as only lovers long, to have the exquisite creature standing there at bay entirely his own.

But one curious thing was observed by those who note such things. This was that not once did Ivy Lexton glance at the prisoner in the dock, during the long examination-inchief.

As for Gretorex, he on his side crossed his arms and stared straight before him as if with unseeing eyes, during the whole of the time the woman he had loved with so devoted and trusting a love, remained in the witness-box.

Sir Jonathan Wright, the leading counsel for the Crown, to whom fate had assigned Ivy Lexton as his principal witness, was very gentle with her, moved, no doubt, by her evident, shrinking fear. But all those present in Court were struck by the clear way she answered the questions concerning her early married life, the loss of Jervis's fortune, and his final, successful, effort, to find work.

It was not until she was questioned as to her relations-her "friendship," as counsel put it-with the prisoner that Ivy's voice for the first time became inaudible, and that the Judge had to admonish her to speak louder.

But at once she responded with pathetic submission to the flick of the whip.

"I am sorry to have to press the question, Mrs. Lexton"—and the distinguished man on whom had fallen the, to him, painful duty of conducting the prosecution did feel really sorry for this lovely, pathetic-looking, young creature—"but I put to you, and most solemnly, the question: What were your real relations to and with Dr. Gretorex?"

"We were great friends. All three of us were great friends. My husband, too," she answered, in a tone which, if clear, yet quivered with pain.

"Were your husband and Dr. Gretorex friends before you ever met Dr. Gretorex?"

Then came a whispered, "I don't know."

"Eh, what?"

The Judge, Mr. Justice Mayhew, was old, but none the less keen and clear as regarded his mind, though he was slightly deaf.

"She does not know, my lord," said Sir Jonathan emphatically.

Then he turned back to his witness.

"Do you think they were already acquainted?"

"I really don't know." And then, perhaps because she saw she was creating a less good impression than had been the case with regard to her other answers, "I think not," she said firmly.

As the examination went on, it became clear that Ivy Lexton was painfully anxious to say all that was good of Roger Gretorex. More than once she managed to bring into one of her answers to a short question the fact that he had been kind to her-very, very kind.

And those who listened breathlessly to Ivy's artless story of how the prisoner in the dock had come to love her, were moved by her apparent surprise and gratitude that he should have been "so kind" to her.

With quivering lips, again and again, in no wise checked by the man who was taking her, step by step, through the story of these last few months, she said a good word for the now tragic lover with whom she had been on those terms-peculiar, and yet how usual nowadays-when a beautiful young married woman, while enchanted to take all she can from a man, will yet give nothing in exchange.

And with every word she uttered, with every apparently spontaneous admission, Ivy threw a secret thought over the sea to Miles Rushworth, and of what he would think tomorrow of what she said, and left unsaid, today.

How strangely drawn out appeared that first portion of her ordeal, to Ivy herself, and to the man now on trial for his life! Not so to those who listened, with ever-increasing curiosity and excitement, to her admissions, omissions, and equivocations.

But it was generally agreed that, as a matter of fact, the murdered man's wife had very little to reveal, after all. Even the most mindless and stupid of those present knew that the jury only had to look at her, standing there in the witness-box, and then to look at the prisoner in the dock, to know what must have been that young man's motive for the crime of which he stood accused.

Ivy was so helpless-looking, so fragile, so appealing, as well as so exceedingly lovely. She seemed, indeed, to some of those watching her, like some poor little delicate furry creature caught in a cruel steel trap.

Had she flirted dangerously, heartlessly, with Roger Gretorex? Even that seemed doubtful to some of those listening to her low-toned replies to counsel for the Crown.

There were women now watching her intently who had come into Court that day with the strongest prejudice against Ivy Lexton. Yet they were conquered by what appeared to be her effortless, youthful charm, as also by her evident suffering. And then her many pitiful little efforts to say the best she could say for this man who had loved her moved her own sex, in some cases, to tears.

Many a woman there told herself that the witness now in the box had once loved the prisoner in the dock, even though she had not known it then, and though she would deny it, no doubt, even to herself, now.

At last came the moment which Ivy had visualised hundreds of times in the last few days-the moment, that is, when Sir Joseph Molloy rose to begin his cross-examination of the chief witness for the Crown.

The silence that there had been before was as a loud noise to the silence there was now. But, as always happens, three or four people coughed nervously, and were angrily hushed by those about them.

What was Sir Joseph going to do? One thing certainly. It would be nothing less than his bare duty to try to prove to the jury that, because she had taken everything, and given nothing, the beautiful wife of Jervis Lexton had goaded this young man, Roger Gretorex, to the frenzy which leads to crime.

Not long ago Sir Joseph had caused two juries to disagree over what, to the plain man, had been a clear case of murder. That simply because he had been able to prove that the prisoner in the dock, who was a far from prepossessing type of bucolic lover, had been rendered jealous to madness by the foolish girl whom he had killed, and this though his act had been clearly premeditated. That had been a very different case from the Lexton case, and one not nearly so exciting to those in Court. Still, there were many present today who remembered the terrible cross-examination of the poor dead girl's mother. It had been the way Sir Joseph had dealt with the trembling woman, the admissions he had forced out of her, which had saved his client's life.

Chapter Sixteen

But even in a court of law, where everything, in spite of what the more ignorant section of the public may think, is arranged and prearranged, the unexpected sometimes does happen.

To the amazement of everybody present, Sir Joseph Molloy was almost as kindly, as courteous, as careful of hurting her feelings, in his cross-examination of Ivy Lexton, as his good friend Sir Jonathan Wright had been during the examination-inchief. Indeed Sir Joseph, as a famous descriptive writer declared the next morning, was positively dove-like in his gentleness. When cross-examining Mrs. Jervis Lexton, his object seemed to be simply that of proving that Roger Gretorex, in everyday life, had been a considerate, chivalrous, and extremely unselfish friend. And that had already been freely admitted by the leading counsel for the Crown.

True, there came a moment when Sir Joseph, who found it painfully difficult to play the rôle he had faithfully promised Roger Gretorex to play, pressed Ivy just a little hard as to what form of words the prisoner had used on the last occasion he had made love to her.

The witness broke down, for the first time, over that probing question, and it was sobbing that she asked: "Must I answer that?"

The Judge explained to her, kindly enough, "Yes, prisoner's counsel is entitled to an answer to that question. But if you cannot remember the exact form of words which were used on that occasion, you are entitled to say so."

And then she replied, uttering the words very clearly this time: "I can only remember that he said he loved me, and that were I free he hoped I would become his wife."

Now those were the last words Sir Joseph had intended Ivy Lexton to utter in answer to his question. And the knowledge that this was so caused a murmur of-was it amusement? —to run through the Court. The public much enjoy hearing a witness score off counsel.

"And what did you answer to that?" he asked sharply.

And then, as Ivy again began sobbing, shrugging his great shoulders he signified that his cross-examination of the principal witness for the Crown was over.

Some of those present in Court were cruel enough to regret that Sir Joseph had not been up to his usual form. What would not such people have given to have heard what had passed at an interview the great advocate had had, only yesterday, with the man now standing rigid in the dock!

Sir Joseph Molloy always insisted on seeing any man or woman whom he was about to defend on a charge of murder and, at his final interview with Gretorex, the prisoner had begun by begging him most earnestly to refrain from cross-examining Ivy Lexton.

But as to that, his counsel had refused to be guided by the accused man's wishes.

"Do you expect me to put the hangman's rope round your neck?" he had asked harshly.

Even so, he had promised that he would be very gentle with her. And gentle he had been, all the more gentle, perhaps, because, at the very end of that painful, curious interview, Gretorex had said to him, gazing right into his eyes:

"Treat Mrs. Lexton as you yourself would treat the woman you love, or your own cherished sister, were she in the witness-box and you her cross-examiner."

So it was that, to his bitter regret, Sir Joseph Molloy had behaved, with regard to Ivy, in a way quite foreign to his nature. What he had longed to do was to turn this lovely little creature inside out, and to apply to her, in his own inimitable, almost affectionately feline, manner, that awful Third Degree before which even the innocent trembled.

After a great deal of anxious thought, he had made up his mind to plead, on his client's behalf, a fit of temporary insanity. He hoped, that is, to persuade the jury that, by some extraordinary combination of circumstances, Jervis Lexton had been suffering in very truth from some commonplace digestive disorder up to that last day when Gretorex, driven mad by jealousy and love, had done the awful deed. Not, that is, as the slow poisoner goes to work, but as a man takes out a knife to stab his rival to the heart.

105

That had been, roughly speaking, the line Sir Joseph had intended to take before he had seen his client. But to do that he would have had to play with Ivy Lexton as a powerful cat plays with a young mouse, and that course of action had been absolutely forbidden by the man whom he now believed innocent, even though reason whispered that he must be guilty.

Then was it all over-the ordeal she had so dreaded at an end? Ivy felt suddenly as if everything were whirling round her, and indeed she nearly fainted. But she made an effort to pull herself together, and to those who saw her leave the witness-box the expression on her white face appeared deeply pathetic.

"Bravo! You did splendidly! I'm proud of you," whispered Paxton-Smith.

And then he asked, "Would you like to stay on in Court, or shall I take you home?"

He hoped she would say "Home."

For a moment she looked undecided, then, "I think I would like to stay," she murmured.

Now that her part was done, and with her legal adviser's "Bravo!" pounding in her ears, she felt she would prefer to be here rather than alone in the flat. Indeed, when Paxton-Smith had found her a comfortable seat among her friends, she began to feel a curious sense of detachment, as if the drama of the trial being played out before her scarcely concerned her personally at all.

This strange feeling was really the measure of her profound relief at having, so to speak, weathered the storm of what everyone had told her would be such an awful experience. Why, it hadn't been really terrible at all! There had been moments of her examination-not of her cross-examination —which in a sense Ivy had almost enjoyed. She had been able to make herself out, to the great company of people about her, what she believed herself to be —a sweet-natured, unselfish little woman, whom everybody loved . . . .

The appearance of Dr. Berwick in the witness-box gave her a momentary sensation of unease. He was clear, unemotional, and not in the least nervous.

There was a little tiff between him and counsel when he told the story of how he had come in one day, and found the prisoner prescribing for his, Dr. Berwick's, patient. It was put to him as a fact that Gretorex had not made out any form of prescription and that when he was "caught" apparently doing so, he had only been writing down the name of an ordinary gargle, to be found made up in every chemist's shop. Also, at the time he had written down the name of that proprietary preparation, Gretorex was under the impression that, Dr. Lancaster having had an accident, the sick man had no one attending him, at any rate at that moment.

Even so, Dr. Berwick's evidence was regarded by all those present as very damaging to the prisoner, and Sir Joseph could do nothing with him, save to denounce him angrily for not having insisted at once, as soon as he became uneasy, on a second opinion.

And then Roger Gretorex's famous counsel flung by far the greatest sensation of the trial on the Court.

In a quiet, toneless voice he observed, as if he was stating the most natural thing in the world, "I do not call any evidence."

There ran an excited murmur through the, till now, still audience. Everyone had fully expected that the prisoner would give evidence on his own behalf and, to the great majority of those there, the fact that Gretorex had refused to go into the witness-box, not only signed his own death-warrant, but proved conclusively that Sir Joseph regarded his client as guilty.

At first Ivy did not understand what it was that had happened. Then two or three of the friends by whom she was surrounded excitedly explained the exact meaning of Sir Joseph's apparently casual remark.

She, the woman in the case, said nothing in answer to these eager, wordy explanations. Indeed, she seemed hardly to take in all that was being told her. But inwardly she was feeling, oh! so thankful, so intensely thankful, that Roger Gretorex had refused to give evidence. She had been so horribly afraid that when in the witness-box her one-time lover might, unwittingly, give her away.

It was of Miles Rushworth that she was thinking, ever thinking, deep in what she called her heart. He had been to her the only audience that mattered, while she had been examined and cross-examined as to her relations with the prisoner.

"And now," whispered someone just behind her, "comes the closing speech for the Crown."

Ivy was not particularly interested in the closing speech for the Crown. And, truth to tell, neither was anyone else in Court, excepting, it must be hoped, the jury.

Sir Jonathan sat down at the end of-was it twenty minutes, or only a quarter of an hour?

There was a short moment of breathing space, and then all prepared to give their best attention while Sir Joseph Molloy started what was afterwards described as "his great speech for the defence."

But though it may have been a great speech, it was a very short speech, for the famous advocate knew that the only hope of saving Gretorex from the gallows would be to make the kind of appeal to the jury which is always made in France with regard to what is called there a *crime passionnel*.

The fact that Sir Joseph had not elected to call any evidence gave him, as all those instructed in the law who listened to him were well aware, the last word. And he made the most of his privilege.

More than once during the course of what was simply a noble panegyric of Roger Gretorex, the prisoner went from deathly pale to very red. He would have given many of his few remaining days of life to close his powerful advocate's mouth. Also, what was the use of it all? Gretorex knew as well as did the Judge that the fact that he was high-minded, chivalrous, the best of sons to a widowed mother, and a man whose money affairs were in perfect order, had nothing to do with the question as to whether he had committed the murder for which he was being tried. Neither, for the matter of that, would the fact that he had adored the wife of Jervis Lexton, and had gone temporarily mad for love of her, save him from the gallows.

One man, on whom by accident the prisoner's eyes were fixed for a moment, actually shrugged his shoulders, when Sir Joseph brought in a swift allusion to the fact that one of the prisoner's great-uncles had died in a lunatic asylum.

Now the Judge desired-indeed they all desired-to finish the case that day.

"Do you wish to stay on for the summing-up and for the verdict?" whispered Paxton-Smith to his client.

Again he hoped that Ivy would-well? have the decency to rise and say, "No, I will go home, now."

But instead of saying "No," she whispered, "Yes, I think I should like to do that."

And then, in slow, impressive tones, the Judge began his summing-up.

Though Mr. Justice Mayhew took what seemed to be a considerable time, his was one of the shortest addresses to a jury ever delivered in an important trial for murder at the Old Bailey. The story he had to recapitulate was, in a sense, so very ordinary. It had been unfolded, in all its stark simplicity, by a tiny handful of witnesses, including of course the most important of them all, the young wife of the murdered man.

Even so, speaking himself with impressive clarity, the Judge went over the now well-known tale step by step. And finally his lordship directed the jury that the fact that a man has been what is loosely called "driven mad" by love does not mean that he is not capable of keeping command over his faculties. Why, at the very time this was supposed to have happened to the prisoner, he was in charge of a large medical practice, and carrying out all the responsible, anxious duties attached to such a practice in an admirable manner!

"We have here the not uncommon case of a strong man's infatuation for a beautiful woman who gives him little, if any, encouragement," he observed.

And there was a murmur of disapproval when one of Ivy's women friends gave a sudden little cackle of laughter, to the shocked surprise of everyone in Court.

The Judge brushed aside with relentless logic any effect that might have been produced on the jury by Sir Joseph Molloy's moving account of Gretorex as a wise, unselfish physician, a devoted son, and within the possible limit a generous landlord. No doubt all that was true. But the whole history of crime was there to prove that a person could be all these excellent things, while being also a cruel, callous, secret murderer.

In this case, assuming Gretorex was guilty, the man who had been slowly done to death had been the secret poisoner's own familiar friend, his boon-companion in many a party of careless pleasure. Further, the man before them, the prisoner in the dock, had not even dared to go into the witness-box. The Judge pointed out in solemn, measured tones that he had the right to comment, and comment most seriously, on that omission.

As the afternoon wore itself away, every one became very weary. Even Ivy began to wish that she had gone away when Paxton-Smith had last suggested that she should do so.

She stole a glance at Roger Gretorex. He was looking straight at the Judge, with a thoughtful, measuring glance. He looked far more himself, his reserved, intelligent self, than he had done when Sir Joseph was engaged in making that dramatic, useless appeal to the jury.

Ivy Lexton gazed at the prisoner in the dock with a strange feeling at her heart. In a sense she was still proud of this man who had been her devout, adoring lover. He looked so brave, so cool, so completely self-possessed. The majority of those who now and again glanced his way to see how he was "taking it" thought him revoltingly callous.

And, at the same moment that Ivy was doing so, Roger's mother stole a look at him. Her heart was full of such agony that she felt as if merciful death might suddenly intervene and end it all for her. And her agony was shared, one is tempted to say, almost to the full, by the girl who sat beside her.

At last the summing up was over. The prisoner was taken below, and then began the waiting for the verdict.

To many of those in Court the jury seemed to be away a long, long time. Yet as a matter of fact, it was only a bare half-hour before all those who had gone out to stretch their legs, and talk over for the hundredth time the only real point of mystery in the story, came swarming back into the Court.

Slowly, almost in a leisurely way, the nine jurymen and the three jurywomen filed in. Some of those present noticed that not a single juror looked at the prisoner, who had been brought back to the dock and now stood at ease between two warders.

Although the verdict was a foregone conclusion, every human being there looked strained, anxious; and Ivy Lexton again felt sick and faint. For the first time since she stepped into the witness-box no one was looking at her, for everyone was looking at the jury.

Everything being now ready, the Judge returned to the bench, all those who were seated in Court rising to their feet.

The Judge, having bowed to the Court, seated himself, and so, apparently, did everyone else there, except the three men, the prisoner and his custodians, standing in the dock.

Then the Clerk of the Court asked the fateful question:

"Members of the jury, have you agreed upon your verdict?"

There was a pause, but at last the foreman of the jury, a nervous, intelligent-looking man, who was evidently intensely relieved that his responsible task was now over, answered in a clear tone, "We have."

"Do you find the prisoner, Roger Kingston Gretorex, guilty or not guilty of the wilful murder of Jervis Lexton?"

There was a scarcely perceptible wait, and then came the one word—"Guilty."

And it was as if there swept a great sigh through the now lighted Court, followed by a sudden buzz of talk.

But this was instantly quelled when the ushers cried sternly, "Silence!"

All eyes were now fixed on the prisoner. He was standing far more stiffly to attention than he had done a moment ago, as the clear tones of the Clerk of the Court rang out:

"Roger Kingston Gretorex, you stand convicted of wilful murder. Have you anything to say for yourself why the Court should not give you judgment according to law?"

"Only that I am innocent."

The five words were uttered in a cool, firm tone.

It was the second time during the whole course of the trial that anyone there had heard Roger Gretorex's voice.

Ivy felt better now, and she watched everything that went on with eager, excited interest.

Sitting near the Judge was a young man to whom no one had before paid any special attention. But now every eye was fixed on him, for it was he who lifted a square of black cloth, and placed it, with careful deliberation, on the Judge's wig.

Then solemn, slow, emphatic tones of admonition fell on the heavy air. They were not cruel words, for the Judge felt deeply sorry for the young man before him. He had heard, only last evening at a dinner-party, something of the quiet, kindly, useful life that Mrs. Gretorex and her son had both led since the death of the husband and father who had caused their financial ruin.

And then came the awful words —

"Roger Kingston Gretorex, the jury, after a careful and patient hearing, have found you guilty of the wilful murder of Jervis Lexton. The sentence of the Court upon you is that you be taken from here to a lawful prison, and from there to a place of execution; and that you be there hanged by the neck until you be dead; and that your body be buried within the precincts of the prison in which you shall have been last confined after your conviction; and may the Lord have mercy on your soul."

As Ivy Lexton, supported by a number of her friends and acquaintances, left the Old Bailey by a back way, she chanced in the passage to meet Mrs. Gretorex face to face. The eyes of the two women crossed-and a stab of horrible pain flashed across the worn, yet even now calm, face of Roger Gretorex's mother.

Chapter Seventeen

"I took Mrs. Gretorex a nice cup of tea at seven o'clock, for I heard her moving about even before then. But the poor lady only just sipped it. She said her throat seemed swollen, so she couldn't swallow. But she's up now, and I do wish, miss, you'd go in and try and persuade her to have just a little bit of breakfast. Me and my husband-well-we both fairly broke down and cried last night, when we thought of how we'd feel if it was our boy that was going to be hanged by the neck till he was dead."

"I hope she doesn't let her mind dwell on that," Enid's pale face went a shade paler, as she looked into the kind, pitying eyes of Mrs. Gretorex's landlady.

"How can she help hearing those awful words a-ringing in her ears? Why they rings in mine, ever since yesterday! I'm sorry I did stay till the end. A friend warned me, so she did. She says to me, 'Maria, you'll enjoy every bit of it up to the jury coming back. But if I was you I'd leave the Court before the Judge puts on his black cap.' I wish I'd done that now!"

As Enid advanced into the sitting-room, and saw Mrs. Gretorex's figure leaning back in the deep grandfather's chair, she thought for one moment-and to her it was a blessed moment-that her dear old friend was dead, that she had died, literally, of a broken heart, so rigid was the lonely looking figure, so calm and white the face, so pale the lips.

But Roger Gretorex's mother was not dead, and hearing Enid's footsteps, she opened her eyes.

"I want you to have something to eat, Mrs. Gretorex. Mr. Oram told me yesterday that he thought you might be allowed to see Roger today. You must keep up your strength."

"I will," said the other quietly. "But it's an odd thing, Enid, when that kind soul brought in my cup of tea this morning I found I couldn't swallow. Perhaps I can now. At any rate I'll try."

Enid came up a little closer to the big chair.

"I wonder if you would think it strange if I went and had a talk with Mr. Finch?" she said a little nervously.

"With Mr. Finch?" Mrs. Gretorex looked surprised.

"From something he said the other day, I gathered that he has some theory which is not shared by Mr. Oram. I should like to know what it is. Somehow I feel that there must be something we could do——"

There was such a fervour of revolt, of anguish, in the steady voice, that the older woman for one moment forgot her own agony.

She felt deeply moved; even she had not realised how much Enid cared. The girl had kept an entire curb over her feeling during the terrible days that the two had sat next to one another in Court.

She got up from her chair, and came close up to Enid Dent.

"I feel as if there was nothing left, for me at any rate, to do but to endure."

"I feel," cried the girl, "as if there was a great deal left to do! Mr. Oram is an old man, Mrs. Gretorex, and though he's been so awfully good to us, I've had the feeling——" then she stopped.

"I know," replied Mrs. Gretorex in a low voice. "I realise, too, that he believes that Roger did that awful thing."

"But Mr. Finch," said Enid eagerly, "knows that Roger is innocent! Would you mind my going and seeing him? He's always at the office long before Mr. Oram arrives there in the morning."

"You can do exactly what you think best. I trust you entirely; so, I know, does Roger."

Twenty minutes later Enid Dent was sitting in the rather drab-looking waiting-room, lined with steel-bound boxes, where she had spent, during the last few weeks, many dreary, anxious minutes. But this time she had not long to wait, for Mr. Oram's head clerk soon appeared, a look of surprise on his face.

"I'm afraid you'll think I've come very early," she said nervously. "But the truth is, Mr. Finch, I wanted to have a short talk with you. And I was anxious to see you before Mr. Oram arrived here this morning."

"You come up now, at once, to Mr. Oram's room, Miss Dent. He won't be here today, at all."

A feeling of relief swept over Enid Dent. She had a regard for Mr. Oram, but she was also rather afraid of him. And she resented keenly a fact which had become at once apparent to her-that he was convinced, even if most unwillingly, of his client's guilt.

Enid had a direct, honest nature, as have so many people who yet do not wear their hearts upon their sleeves. So it was that when the two were together in Mr. Oram's room, she began without any preamble:

"From something you said the other day, Mr. Finch, I understood that you believe there's some as yet quite unsuspected mystery behind this story of Jervis Lexton's death. If I am right, will you tell me what it is you do think? Also whether anything can be done to bring the truth to light before —" And then once more she repeated that word "before," which may mean so very much or so very little in life.

Alfred Finch felt and looked uncomfortable. To make a remark in a casual way is very different from being pinned down, and asked what it is exactly that you meant by saying what you did. But the girl was looking at him with such anxious, appealing eyes, and, after all, if he was a fool, he was being a fool in good company, that of the great Sir Joseph Molloy himself.

Mr. Oram's head clerk and the famous counsel had become friends over the Lexton case, and what Mr. Finch was about to expound to Enid Dent as his own theory was really Sir Joseph Molloy's theory. Not, as he intended carefully to explain, as to what had certainly happened, but as to what might conceivably have happened, to provide an explanation of what seemed inexplicable-how, that is, Jervis Lexton had come by his death.

"You may be aware," he began a little nervously, "that there is a section of the public, including whom I may call our most noted amateur criminologists, who are convinced that we needn't go further than Mrs. Lexton herself. Their view is that, apart from Mr. Roger, no one else, except the lady who is now his widow, can have had the slightest motive for getting rid of poor Lexton. Now I don't share that view at all!"

"Neither do I," said Enid quickly. "We all know that Mrs. Lexton had every reason for wanting her husband to remain alive."

"But what I do believe," and a queer expression came over Alfred Finch's shrewd face, "is that Mrs. Lexton knows a good deal more than she admitted yesterday in the witness-box. I can't help suspecting that there is some man, a stranger to the case, but well known to her, who had some vital interest in compassing Jervis Lexton's death. Far stranger things happen in real life than any novelist would dare to put in a story, Miss Dent. Men, aye, and women too, are more unscrupulous than any ordinary person would imagine. Even Mr. Oram would agree to that. If we can find among Mrs. Lexton's admirers-and she has a goodish few-some wealthy man who is in love with her, *and who has easy access to any form of arsenic*, we might have something like new evidence to offer when the case comes up on appeal."

"But if that is true," said Enid quickly, "then the nurse must have known that Mr. Lexton had some other visitor within a few hours of his death-and the parlourmaid who gave evidence as to admitting Dr. Gretorex the afternoon before Mr. Lexton died must have known it too."

Alfred Finch looked straight into the girl's now flushed, anxious face.

"What is it," he asked impressively, "that rules the whole world today?"

And, as he saw she looked bewildered, he snapped out the one word, "Money! What Mrs. Lexton and her lot call 'the ready.'"

What did he mean? In what way could money have played a part in this sinister business? His next words enlightened her.

"Money can do anything nowadays, for everybody wants money, and spends money as they never did before. Believe me, Miss Dent, no one, in these days, is incorruptible."

"What a terrible thing to say-even to think!" exclaimed Enid.

"It may be terrible, but it's the truth, Miss Dent! And it's particularly true when one considers the people who were mixed up in this affair. All women, and poor themselves, mark you. I don't mean to imply for a moment that they meant to connive at murder. My view is that their mouths, maybe, were shut with gold before they had any idea what it was that they were going to be asked to stay 'mum' about. But then? Well, then, they wisely, in their own interest, continued to keep their mouths shut!"

"I see," said Enid slowly.

"I was very much struck by the demeanour of that Nurse Bradfield in the witness-box," he went on eagerly. "Sir Joseph reduced her to a drivelling state of terror. Now, why was that? You remember, maybe, how he pressed her as to who else came to the flat besides Mr. Roger; and how at last she had to admit that several ladies and gentlemen came there, and that often she really didn't know who they were! Now, isn't that a singular thing? We have the master of the house lying ill-not ill enough to have a night nurse, but still, ill enough to have a nurse all day. And yet a lot of people come and go-to lunch, to play bridge, and to take Mrs. Lexton out in the evening! Now that, to me, sounds very odd, not to say suspicious."

"I quite agree that it does seem strange and heartless," said Enid in a troubled tone. "But I liked Nurse Bradfield. I thought her a truthful woman, though it was plain she was awfully frightened of Sir Joseph."

"I never can understand why an honest witness should feel frightened when in the witness-box," exclaimed Mr. Finch in a tone of contempt.

"Oh, I can understand it so well!" cried the girl. "I know I should be terrified, especially if Sir Joseph were cross-examining me as he cross-examined that poor woman."

"Well, be that as it may, Miss Dent, my point is that it came out very clearly that a certain number of men, all friends and admirers of that pretty little lady, came in and out of the flat during the poor chap's illness."

"And you actually think that Mrs. Lexton——" and while she was seeking for the right word he broke in with:

"If my theory is correct, I am inclined to think that Mrs. Lexton must have a shrewd suspicion as to who the man was who did that terrible thing-and I shan't be at all surprised if she makes what is commonly called a good marriage before the year is out!"

"But what an awful thing-to allow an innocent man——"

Again he cut across her words: "She's a thoroughly selfish woman, and only thinks of herself. But capable of murder?" he shook his head. "Oh no, Miss Dent! The folk who are inclined to think that of her know but little about human nature. I don't claim to know more of the set Mrs. Lexton lives in than one can gather from the newspapers, and perhaps I ought to say from proceedings in the Bankruptcy Court. But, though they'll do almost anything for money, those sort of people stop short at murder, believe me."

"Still, you do think it possible that Mrs. Lexton may be shielding a murderer?"

Mr. Finch hesitated. "That's it exactly. I think she may be shielding a murderer. How did she strike you in the witness-box?"

"I thought her very clever," said Enid Dent slowly. "Her one object was to produce a good impression, and she succeeded."

Instinctively Mr. Finch lowered his voice.

"I watched her very carefully, and listened even more carefully, while she was in the witness-box, and I made up my mind that she believes Dr. Gretorex to be an innocent man. Did I say believe? I think she knows he is innocent."

"I think another thing," said Enid, and she, too, allowed her voice to drop.

"What's that, Miss Dent?" Mr. Finch bent forward.

"I feel quite sure"—and suddenly her pale face became red—"that Roger suspects who did it. I think that's why he wouldn't give evidence."

"God bless my soul," exclaimed Mr. Finch, "I never thought of that! You may be right, after all. But if it's true, well, then he's——"

"Very quixotic?"
"No, Miss Dent. Saving your presence, I was going to say he's a damn fool."

Chapter Eighteen

That same morning, the morning after the conclusion of Gretorex's trial, Ivy awoke late. For a moment she remembered nothing, for she had gone through a very terrible strain the previous day, a greater strain than she herself had been aware of, at the time.

And then, all at once she remembered-remembered everything, and a sense of something akin to ecstasy flooded her heart. She flung her white arms above her head and stretched herself out luxuriously. Then-for it was very cold-she snuggled down into bed again.

How marvellous to know that her ordeal was over. All over-all over! That from now on she need never see any of the people who had been connected with this awful episode in her life. Perhaps, though, she would make an exception as to Paxton-Smith, for he had been so awfully kind to her, and he admired her so much! His description of how brave and plucky she had been in the witness-box would surely delight Miles Rushworth. Yes, Paxton-Smith should remain her friend.

Meanwhile she would follow his advice. She would go away, that is, to the country for a few days, to the delightful cottage near Brighton belonging to Lady Flora Desmond. She could not go today, unluckily, for Lady Flora had lent the cottage to some tiresome people. But they would be leaving soon, and then she would go down there and have a thorough rest.

Ivy felt she wanted what some of her friends called "a rest cure," after all she had gone through.

All at once there came a knock on the bedroom door—a knock, and a quick whispered conversation outside. Something, too, very like a giggle.

She called out sharply "Come in," and the day maid came in with a broad grin on her young face.

"Cook thought maybe that you'd like to see the paper she takes in, ma'am. There's such a beautiful picture of you in it!"

And on the pink silk eiderdown the maid put down two picture papers, the one that Ivy always glanced at every day, and another paper.

Why, yes-there was the picture, and a very good one, too. Ivy had been snapped by a Press photographer just as she had stood on the doorstep of Duke of Kent Mansion, a moment before she got into Paxton-Smith's car. She gazed with pleasure at all the details of her becoming costume. What a good thing that she had bought that charming little model hat just before poor Jervis's death. She had soon discovered that what is called "mourning headgear" is apt to be singularly unbecoming.

"It does look nice, ma'am, don't it? Cook says as how you looked bewitching while you was giving evidence," ventured the girl.

"I wasn't thinking of how I was looking," said Ivy.

And indeed this was the truth. As she had stood up there, the target of all eyes, she had only thought of her coming cross-examination by Sir Joseph Molloy.

And then the girl made a mistake, and she knew that she had done so as soon as she had said the words.

"It does seem sad about that poor Dr. Gretorex, don't it?" she exclaimed.

For at once Ivy burst into tears-angry, frightened tears. It was too bad, too bad, when she herself had succeeded this morning in entirely banishing Roger from her mind, that he should be thus stupidly, cruelly, thrust into it again.

"Oh, ma'am, I'm so sorry! Please forgive me!" And the tactless young woman almost ran out of the room.

Nurse Bradfield came in to see what was the matter. She looked wan and worn. Unlike Ivy, she had not slept the previous night; unlike Ivy, the face of Roger Gretorex, especially his expression as he had uttered, in answer to the awful question, the quiet words, "Only that I am innocent," rang in her ears.

She had felt then, and she still felt now, a most painful sensation of doubt.

Was it possible, was it conceivable, that Gretorex was innocent after all, and that her patient had secretly done himself to death?

Every nurse comes across strange and most unexpected happenings in the course of her work. And Nurse Bradfield, though in a sense she had had an uneventful career, had yet been more than once very much startled and surprised by the astonishing things people will sometimes do.

She sat down, now, on the bed, and put her arms round the slender figure, still shaken by angry, frightened sobs.

"I know how you're feeling, Mrs. Lexton," she whispered. "I, too, can't get Dr. Gretorex out of my mind. But there's still a chance, you know, that something may be found out, even now. I mean between now and his appeal. Mrs. Berwick told me last night that she knows some great friends of Sir Joseph Molloy, and that he honestly does believe Dr. Gretorex to be innocent. She says that Sir Joseph is going to leave no stone unturned to try to prove his innocence. He's in a terrible state about it all, and he was very distressed at Dr. Gretorex refusing to give evidence on his own behalf."

"But you think he did it, don't you, nurse?"

Ivy lifted her tear-stained eyes and gazed at the older woman.

"I did think so," muttered Nurse Bradfield. "And even now I can't see any other explanation. You and I know quite well that Mr. Lexton was not the sort of man to do away with himself."

"Of course he wasn't!" exclaimed Ivy, with a touch of indignation.

The nurse sighed. "Such extraordinary things do happen in life," she observed.

"What is it Sir Joseph Molloy thinks he can find out? Did Mrs. Berwick tell you that?" asked Ivy.

She put the question in a careless tone, but she really wanted to know; indeed she was very, very anxious to discover what it was that Sir Joseph Molloy meant to do.

"What he says he means to find out," said the nurse, "is whether there wasn't some other person in the world who had a motive for getting rid of Mr. Lexton, besides Dr. Gretorex. He's got a sort of an idea that there must have been someone else-someone who's not been thought of yet-someone whose name didn't appear in the case."

And then was heard a hesitating knock on the door, and the maid came in again, looking very much subdued.

On the silver salver lay what had become Ivy's daily cable from South Africa.

She saw a curious look flash over Nurse Bradfield's face. As a matter of fact, those daily cables were a source of much interest and speculation to the household, now composed, apart from Ivy, of three women. It was the more mysterious as Mrs. Lexton never left those thick telegrams lying about. The daily cable always disappeared within a comparatively short time of her receipt of the buff-coloured envelope.

Ivy did not open the envelope. She put it on a little table by the side of her bed, and went on talking and listening.

"Everyone in Court admired the way you gave your evidence, Mrs. Lexton. Mr. Paxton-Smith told me you were the best witness he had ever had. Indeed, he said that you were just perfection! Not too shy, and not too bold. So clear, too! Every word you said could be heard, even where I was sitting."

And then the speaker added, with considerable heat, "Some of the people there seemed to me like hyenas! Blood-blood-blood-that's what they wanted, the horrid ghouls! Why, there was a man just behind me who said he hoped that Sir Joseph would make mincemeat of you ——"

"I know that some of them wanted that," murmured Ivy.

"The story goes," went on Nurse Bradfield, "that Dr. Gretorex begged Sir Joseph to leave you alone."

"I wonder if he did?"

That had not occurred to Ivy. But now, of course, she knew this to be almost certainly the reason Sir Joseph had been so-so unlike what everyone had expected him to be.

And then there did come over her a little glimmer of gratitude. Yes, Roger certainly loved her. No one would ever care for her as he cared. She remembered, now, his having once said that he would go through any torture in order to save her a moment's pain. Well? Poor Roger hadn't really gone through torture exactly-that sort of thing has been given up long ago, luckily. Still, it was very touching that, even in his own time of danger, he had thought of her and of her reputation.

After Nurse Bradfield had left the room, and after Ivy's light breakfast had been brought in and arranged on the bed-table, she broke open Rushworth's cable.

> My sister died yesterday. Sailing for home the day after tomorrow. Will keep you advised by wireless of exact date of my return. I have been thinking of you night and day.

Rushworth coming back now, almost at once? Small wonder that a feeling of ecstasy flooded Ivy Lexton's whole being. She had gone through a terrible ordeal, but that which was already in sight would make up for everything.

She jumped out of bed and locked her door. Then she went over to the fireplace, and watched the flimsy sheets curl up and become thin and black in the flames. After the first, she had always burnt each of Rushworth's cables as soon as she had read it through. Somehow it seemed to her safer to do so.

Unlocking the door, she rang for the maid to put on her bath, for she wanted to go out and telegraph to Miles Rushworth.

It was half-past ten when Ivy came back to the flat.

"There's a young lady to see you in the drawing-room, ma'am," said the maid.

Ivy walked into the room smiling, for she expected to see waiting for her one of the many women belonging to her old, idle, easy life. Why shouldn't they go out together shopping, and then come back to lunch?

But the smile froze on her face, for it was a stranger who rose and confronted her. Certainly a stranger, and yet somehow she had a disturbing feeling that she had seen her visitor before, and in disagreeable circumstances.

Then all at once, with a feeling of sharp annoyance, she realised that this was the girl who had been sitting with Mrs. Gretorex during the concluding hours of Roger's trial yesterday. And when she, Ivy, and Roger's mother had met face to face in a corridor of the Old Bailey, the stranger had been there too.

"I hope you'll forgive my coming in this way without having first asked if you would see me," said Enid Dent. "But the matter is very urgent, Mrs. Lexton, and the time is short, very short, between now and Roger Gretorex's appeal, otherwise I feel sure Mrs. Gretorex would have come herself. Unfortunately, she is ill today."

As Ivy still said nothing, only looked at her with an expression of fear, and yes, of dislike, on her lovely face, Enid exclaimed desperately, "I am sure you would do anything to help Roger Gretorex, Mrs. Lexton?"

And then Ivy did what all through her life she had often done, when in doubt. She burst into tears.

"Of course, I'd do anything," she sobbed, "anything I could do! But what can I do? I've gone through such an awful time. No one knows what I've gone through, or how miserable I've been. No one thinks of me!" she ended hysterically. "I feel as if I hadn't a friend in the world——"

Enid went up close to her, and touched her on the arm.

"I'm so sorry," she said in a troubled tone. "I know how terrible it must have been for you yesterday."

She felt ashamed of what she had been led to believe by Mr. Finch an hour ago. It seemed incredible to her that the poor little creature before her, now trembling with emotion, could have acted the cruel part Alfred Finch and Sir Joseph believed she was acting, shielding the real murderer of her husband, and condemning an innocent man to a frightful death.

Ivy saw that she had made a good impression, and she became gradually calm.

Her one object was to get rid of this tiresome girl quietly. It had been stupid, very stupid, of the maid to allow a stranger to come in and wait, without knowing anything of her business. After all, this girl didn't look in the least like one of her, Ivy's, smart friends. Enid looked, to her critic's practised eyes, a country bumpkin dressed in a plain and by no means expensive, if well-cut, coat and skirt.

"I suppose," she said politely, "that you're poor Mrs. Gretorex's companion?"

"Yes," answered Enid, "I am her companion. I've known her all my life; and I'm very, very sorry for her." And then her voice, too, broke.

"What is it that Mrs. Gretorex thinks I can do?" asked Ivy in a timorous voice.

As the girl, who was struggling with her tears, answered nothing to this: "Of course I'd do anything if I thought it could be of any good," she concluded.

And then, suddenly, she had an inspiration.

"People seem to forget all about poor Jervis," she said in a hurt tone. "After all, he was my husband, and I was very fond of him, Miss — —?"

"Dent," said the other quietly. "My name is Enid Dent."

And then she moved a little farther away from the still fur-clad little figure, for those words, uttered in so pathetic a tone, had suddenly brought Roger before Enid Dent. Roger, God help him, had loved, perhaps still loved, this woman.

"Well, Miss Dent, no one ever thinks now about poor Jervis, do they?"

That had been a remark made to Ivy by Paxton-Smith a few days ago, and she had been struck by the truth of it.

Enid felt a tremor of discomfort flash across her burdened heart. It was quite true that though his mysterious death had formed the subject of a great and searching inquiry, none of them, now, gave any thought to Jervis Lexton, the unfortunate young man who had certainly been poisoned by someone masquerading as a friend.

"I do know how you must feel about that," she said in a low voice. "But it's only natural for Mrs. Gretorex, and the friends of Roger Gretorex, to be thinking of him rather than of your husband, Mrs. Lexton. You see, we who have known Roger all his life, are absolutely convinced that he is innocent."

And then Ivy, whose nerves were on edge, suddenly made, in her own immediate interest, a mistake.

"Everyone *I* see," she said quickly, defensively, "feels quite sure that Roger Gretorex did do it. You must know that, Miss Dent, though of course I wouldn't say so to his mother."

"Does that mean that you" —Enid Dent took a step forward, and the other instinctively stepped back as she met the accusing look in the girl's eyes —"yourself are convinced of his guilt, Mrs. Lexton?"

"I don't think you have a right to ask me such a question!" She uttered the rebuke lightly, pettishly.

Why, oh! why, didn't this tiresome, disagreeable girl go away? She had no business here. Besides, she was only a paid companion. Ivy had a great contempt for any woman earning her own living in a quiet, hum-drum way.

A tide of anger was rising up in her heart, making her what she seldom was, really angry.

"It's a hideous misfortune for me that I ever met Roger Gretorex!" she exclaimed. "And yet you heard what I said in the witness-box? I did try, indeed I did, to help Dr. Gretorex. What is more — —"

Enid had moved away again. She was standing still now, a look of despair on her face.

" —Mr. Paxton-Smith told me I oughtn't to say a word, and I promised him that I wouldn't say a word to anyone ever, unless he was there too!"

Anger is very catching, as most of us know, and wrath had also risen up in Enid Dent's heart. How agonising it was to know that it was this cruel, foolish, selfish, silly woman who had stolen the man she, Enid, loved, and who, she believed in her heart, had loved her, before some malign fate had thrown him in Mrs. Lexton's way.

So it was that, when she saw Ivy begin sidling towards the door, with a quick movement she flung herself across the room and stood with her back against it, barring the way.

"Mrs. Lexton?"

She uttered the other's name calmly, though she was now shaking all over.

"Yes, Miss Dent? I'm sure no good can come of our going on talking— —"

"Not only do I believe, but certain people, whose opinion you no doubt would value far more than mine, believe too, that you know Roger Gretorex to be innocent!" cried Enid. "They are convinced that you are well aware who it was who craftily, cruelly, secretly poisoned your husband. I warn you here and now, that if that is true, the truth is going to be discovered!"

She stopped, ashamed of, and frightened at, her own emotion. She felt now, as if it were someone else who had uttered that passionate warning.

Ivy Lexton suddenly gave a stifled cry. Tottering forward she sank down on a chair, and, moaning, covered her face with her hands.

All at once, she could not have said why, perhaps it was a glimpse she caught of Ivy Lexton's convulsed face, there flashed into the girl's mind a certain dread suspicion; and much that had seemed inexplicable suddenly became clear.

Ivy slipped off the chair on to the floor, and lay there quite still.

Enid Dent opened the door.

"I am afraid," she said quietly to the maid who had been in the hall obviously listening to what was going on inside the drawing-room, "that Mrs. Lexton has fainted."

As the scared-looking young woman went to call Nurse Bradfield, who was then packing, for she was about to go on to a new case, Enid left the flat and, without waiting for the lift, she ran down the stairs.

Hailing a taxicab she threw the driver her address in Ebury Street. She felt extraordinarily excited, carried out of herself. Consciously she longed for the man who was driving her to go faster-faster! At last he drew up; she paid him off, put the latchkey in the lock, and then, shaking with excitement, she walked straight into the room where Mrs. Gretorex was still lying back in the big arm-chair.

"I think I know now," she said in a stifled voice, "who poisoned Jervis Lexton, and you and I, Mrs. Gretorex, must try and think of a way in which we can get proof, proof-proof!"

Mrs. Gretorex looked up at the girl.

"Who is it you now suspect?" she asked slowly, "of having poisoned Jervis Lexton?"

Enid hesitated for a moment, then she said in a low voice, "His wife."

"I have felt almost sure, from the first, that Ivy Lexton poisoned her husband," said Mrs. Gretorex quietly.

Then she rose and, coming quite close up to the girl, she added: "What is more, I am convinced that Roger knows the truth now. That is the real reason why he begged Sir Joseph Molloy to be very careful as to what questions he put to Mrs. Lexton in his cross-examination."

Mrs. Gretorex took Enid's hand.

"You and I believe this terrible thing of Ivy Lexton. But it can do Roger no good to say what we believe. It would, even, probably, do him harm."

"Does Mr. Oram know that you think her guilty?"

"Yes," said Roger's mother, and she sighed. "I told him just before the trial opened. He begged me most earnestly to put any idea of the kind out of my mind, as he felt convinced I was wrong. He pointed out to me that there was not what he called an iota of evidence connecting Mrs. Lexton with the crime. In fact, I saw that I dropped very very much in his estimation as a sensible woman when I told him of my more than suspicion, of my absolute conviction, that Mrs. Lexton had had some all-powerful motive for wishing her husband dead."

"Surely we can discover what that was?"

Mrs. Gretorex shook her head. "She certainly did not wish to marry Roger-of that I feel quite sure. I hoped against hope that something might come out while Sir Joseph Molloy cross-examined her. But, of course, nothing did come out, and it is my conviction, Enid, that nothing ever will."

That same day the fact that Roger Gretorex had made up his mind not to appeal appeared in the late editions of the evening papers. "It will only prolong the agony for my mother," he had said to Mr. Oram. "And as for me, I am sufficiently a coward to long for it to be all over."

And so they all-those who loved Roger, and she who feared him, together with the myriads of men and women who regarded him as a callous murderer, and who hoped that he would finally confess his crime-waited for the end.

Chapter Nineteen

And now there were but two days-to be accurate, but two nights-to the date fixed for Roger Gretorex's execution. All those to whom the matter was of grave moment had given up hope, and, to the great relief of each member of what may be described as the outside circle of those concerned in the still mysterious story, there was something stoic in the resignation and self-control of both the mother and the son.

But Enid Dent showed many signs of the strain and agony she was enduring, and Sir Joseph Molloy felt quite unlike his powerful, jovial self. Even against his better judgment he still felt convinced that an awful miscarriage of justice was going to be enacted. His conviction actually affected the nerves of Sir Edward Law, the Home Secretary, who happened, unfortunately for himself, to be one of Sir Joseph's oldest friends.

Sir Edward hoped most fervently that Gretorex would make a last-moment confession. Not that the Home Secretary really doubted the fact of the young man's guilt. But he felt the kind of anxiety which must possess any sensitive, conscientious human being who has the onerous gift of life in his hand, if he knows that the mind of a friend he trusts as deeply as he did trust Sir Joseph's powerful mind, is convinced of a condemned man's innocence.

The execution had been fixed for a Thursday. Deliberately Sir Joseph arranged to cross to Calais on the Wednesday in order to meet his wife, who was coming back the next day from the south of France.

Though Lady Molloy was an invalid, a tiny, fragile little body, and no longer young, her husband adored her, and when he was parted from "the woman who owned him," as he sometimes oddly expressed it, he seemed at times only half himself. His Eileen, so he told himself now, would know how to heal the ache at his heart.

For one thing, Lady Molloy was deeply religious in a happy child-like way. Heaven seemed to her a beautiful place, just hard by, and so she would naturally view Roger Gretorex's terrible mode of exit from life as the certain gateway to a happier existence than he could have hoped for on this earth.

"The day after tomorrow-the day after tomorrow."

Those four words seemed to beat themselves on Enid Dent's brain. Sometimes would come a variant —"What can be done, surely something can be done, before the day after tomorrow?"

Early on the Tuesday morning she wandered out of doors and walked for miles in the cold, still empty streets. At last she went into Westminster Abbey for a while, and then into the vast Catholic Cathedral. But she found she could not pray. She felt as if abandoned by God, as well as by man.

Reluctantly, she at last turned her feet towards Ebury Street. She shrank from seeing Mrs. Gretorex. To Enid there was something horribly unnatural in the calmness and appearance of strength shown by Roger's mother. It was, as the girl knew, by Roger's plainly expressed desire that they were going home tomorrow down to Sussex. By his wish, also, they would be in the parish church, which was actually an enclave in the grounds attached to what was still his house, when nine o'clock struck out his hour of doom on Thursday.

As Enid came in to their sitting-room Mrs. Gretorex held out an open letter.

"This has just reached me-sent on from Mr. Oram's office this morning. It's from the old woman who used to look after Roger." And as the other took it from her, "Rather a touching letter, but I don't feel I can bring myself to go to Ferry Place, my dear. I went there once, and spent such a happy, happy day with Roger. This Mrs. Huntley waited on us. Perhaps you will go instead of me? See what she says."

Enid took the letter, and this is what she read:

6 FERRY PLACE.

Tuesday.

Dear Madam,

I don't know what to do about the doctor's things, and I should be glad if you could spare time to come here. Also there is something on my mind that I'd like to tell you, Mrs. Gretorex. But I gave my word, I even swore my oath to the doctor not to. So perhaps I oughtn't to.

I've tried to keep everything tidy, but the police pulled everything about so.

Yours respectfully,

Bertha Huntley.

"I wonder what she wants to tell you?"

"I can form a shrewd guess," said Mrs. Gretorex in a low voice.

The girl looked at her with eager eyes. "It may be something tremendously important," she exclaimed.

The older woman shook her head.

"It might have had a certain importance before the trial, but it would have no importance now. I have no doubt that what Mrs. Huntley wants to tell me is ——"

Then she hesitated, for Mrs. Gretorex was an old-fashioned gentlewoman, who considered that certain things which unfortunately do happen in life should not be dwelt on, much less mentioned, by "nice" women.

"What do you mean, Mrs. Gretorex? Do tell me!"

The girl was looking at her with perplexed, unhappy eyes. Perhaps, after all, it would be better to tell her the truth? It might cause her to forget Roger more quickly than she could otherwise do.

"I have very little doubt, Enid, that Mrs. Lexton, at one time, often went to Ferry Place. Naturally Roger bound the old woman to silence. He may have even made her swear that she would never reveal a fact so damaging to Ivy Lexton's reputation. I don't know if a knowledge of what I feel sure was the truth would have made any difference, one way or the other, at the trial. In any case, it won't make any difference now."

"May I go off to Ferry Place now?" asked Enid eagerly.

"Do, if you like. But be careful what you say, child." She gazed into the girl's flushed face. "I think we ought to do what we know Roger would wish us to do-and not to do."

And then, with a slight break in her even voice, she quoted the fine line —"For silence is most noble to the end."

As Enid Dent walked with what, to one passing her, would have appeared to be the happy, eager steps of youth towards Ferry Place, she more than once felt strongly inclined to turn back.

The thought of going to the house where Roger Gretorex had lived and worked during the months when he and she had become so entirely estranged was bitter to her. Also, she now had to endure the incessant talking and the kindly meant, but to her almost intolerable, sympathy of the landlady of Mrs. Gretorex's lodgings. The thought that she would now endure more sympathy, and more garrulous talk, on the part of Mrs. Huntley was well nigh unendurable. Why not go back and write a nice letter to the old woman, explaining that Mrs. Gretorex was ill, but wished Mrs. Huntley to know how deep was her gratitude for everything she had done for her dear son?

And then, just as she was going to turn around, Enid felt ashamed of her strained nerves. If this old woman had been fond of Roger, then she must be very unhappy now.

She had to ask the way twice to Ferry Place, and each time she asked the question she saw a peculiar look come over the stranger's face, showing, plainly enough, that he had recalled the fact that this was where Roger Gretorex had lived, the man who had committed murder for the sake of the woman he loved. The name of the obscure thoroughfare had been constantly mentioned, bandied to and fro, during Gretorex's trial.

Enid soon found the double row of shabby little houses. It was strange to remember that Roger had lived for over a year in this sordid-looking place.

She walked slowly down the middle of the roadway till she reached No. 6. It looked just a little cleaner and "better class" than the houses on each side of it.

She knocked, and the door was opened almost at once, revealing a grey-haired, sad-faced old woman, who, before the visitor could speak, said sharply, "You've made a mistake. No one lives here now."

"I've come from Mrs. Gretorex," said Enid in a low voice.

And then the door, which had been nearly closed in her face, was opened widely.

"Come in, miss. Come in, do!" and the old woman opened a door to the left, and showed the visitor into what had been Roger Gretorex's consulting-room. It was bare and poor-looking, but the girl, with a stab of pain, saw at once a small piece of furniture which had always stood in what was still called "the day nursery" at Anchorford Hall.

"Mrs. Gretorex is ill, or she would have come herself. But she has given me a message for you, Mrs. Huntley. She wishes me to tell you how grateful—how grateful——"

And then all at once Enid Dent broke down, and burst into a storm of tears.

She had not so "let herself go," at any rate not in the day-time, since the end of Roger Gretorex's trial. But somehow now, with this stranger, she didn't care. It was such a comfort to have a good cry, and something seemed to tell her that this sad, anxious-looking old woman would understand, and sympathise with, her grief.

Mrs. Huntley pushed the sobbing girl gently down into the worn leather arm-chair in which Gretorex would sometimes put a delicate-looking woman patient-the sort of patient who did not care to go into the surgery.

"I suppose," said Mrs. Huntley in a troubled voice, "that you was the doctor's young lady, miss?"

It somehow comforted Enid to hear those simple words, uttered in so quiet, if pitying a tone.

"I think I was," she sobbed. "Indeed, I am sure I was-though that was a long time ago, Mrs. Huntley."

"I know," came the low-toned answer. And the old woman did know, perhaps better than anyone else in the world, why Roger Gretorex had left off thinking of the girl who now sat, the picture of despair, before her.

Enid suddenly got up. She dabbed her eyes with her handkerchief.

"And now," she said, "let me deliver the rest of my message, Mrs. Huntley. Mrs. Gretorex knows how good you were to her son, and she wants me to tell you that a little later on she would like you to come down to Anchorford, for she does want to see you."

"Later on?" echoed the old woman in a strange voice. "But that would be too late, miss. I has to see Mrs. Gretorex today for it to be of any good. Can't you take me to her? Not that I likes to leave the house alone. I never do leave it-not since I got the message from Mr. Oram that I was to regard myself as caretaker, that is."

"I am afraid you can't see Mrs. Gretorex today," said Enid firmly. "But I'll give her any message, and-and you can trust me, Mrs. Huntley, you really can!"

"I wonder if I can? I wonder if I dare?"

"Have you anything to say that we don't already know?" she asked.

"Yes, I have, miss. But in telling it I may be doing wrong."

"D'you mean something about Dr. Gretorex? Something that might, even now, make a difference?"

"I don't know. I can't tell. I fear me it may be too late."

"Let me judge of that," said Enid Dent.

She had become quiet, collected, though she was filled with a feeling of suspense and, she dared not call it "hope."

"Shall I tell you?" said Mrs. Huntley as if asking herself the question. And then, all at once, she answered it, "Yes, surely I will!"

Alfred Finch was reading a copy of an old complicated will. But though he was trying to concentrate on the business in hand, he found his mind straying persistently to the prison cell where Roger Gretorex sat waiting for the morning of the day after tomorrow. For one thing, he had heard by a side wind that the warder who had Gretorex in his special charge believed him innocent, and this made a great impression on him. That warder had had charge of over thirty men condemned to death, and this was the first time he had ever believed one of them to have been innocent of the crime for which he was to suffer death.

The telephone bell at his elbow rang.

"Miss Dent is on the line, Mr. Finch. Can you speak to her? She says it's very urgent."

"Put her through at once."

And then he heard an eager, quivering voice, "Is that Mr. Finch? Can you come at once, Mr. Finch, to 6 Ferry Place? I believe I've got some new evidence."

"New evidence?"

Mr. Finch, though he was alone, shook his head. Had he not himself done everything that was in the power of mortal man to procure new evidence in the last three weeks, and had he not entirely failed?

"I don't wish to say more over the telephone, but can you come now, at once, to take a statement from Dr. Gretorex's day maid, Mrs. Huntley?"

Mrs. Huntley? Why, that was the old caretaker woman! He remembered distinctly reading over the record of her short, colourless, unimportant interview with Inspector Orpington.

Mrs. Huntley could have nothing new to say of the slightest value. Stop, though-she probably knew certain facts which might have been regarded as greatly to Mrs. Lexton's discredit, had they come out at the trial. Facts which would certainly have added pungency to Sir Joseph Molloy's speech for the defence. But Mrs. Huntley could have nothing to reveal that could make any real difference, now, to the fate of Roger Gretorex.

However, if only because he had come to like and respect Mrs. Gretorex's young friend, Mr. Finch made up his mind he would do what Enid Dent desired.

"I'll be with you within twenty minutes," he called out.

"Be as quick as you can. I'm so frightened, Mr. Finch."

"Frightened?" he repeated, surprised.

"Yes." The voice dropped. "Supposing Mrs. Huntley were to die, suddenly, before you've heard what she's got to say? I dare not tell you what it is over the telephone. But it is very important — —"

Now Mr. Finch thought so little of what he was going to do, and, presumably, hear, that he simply left word for Mr. Oram that he had had to go out. And when he reached Westminster, he did not dismiss his taxicab; he left it at the end of Ferry Place.

Enid Dent stood waiting for him at the open door of the little house, and he noted at once the strained, excited look on her face.

Had she been a young man, and not a young woman, Alfred Finch would have exclaimed, "Come, come! What's all this pother about?" But as it was, he looked at her very kindly, and made up his mind that he would "let her down" as gently as might be.

"I hope she'll tell you all she told me," murmured Enid as he shut the door. "Mrs. Lexton told a lie when she said she had never been here but once, and then with a woman friend. Mrs. Huntley swore to Roger Gretorex that she would say nothing about that, and she feels that she is breaking her oath. But I doubt if she realises herself the fearful importance of something else she told me, something Roger may suspect, but which only she actually saw."

And then she opened the door of the consulting-room.

Mrs. Huntley was sitting all in a heap in a chair, staring before her. She looked up when the two came in, but she did not get up.

"Here is Mr. Finch. I want you to tell him exactly what you told me."

"You tell him, miss," muttered the old woman. "I've told you everything and-and I feels very upset."

"Mrs. Huntley is ready to swear," said Enid quietly, "that she once found Mrs. Lexton alone in the surgery here, with a jar labelled arsenic standing on the table before her."

Alfred Finch, startled, looked hard at the old woman. Was she telling the truth, or had she invented this ingenious story?

"When did that happen?" he asked quietly. "Is there any way in which you can fix the date of that occurrence, Mrs. Huntley?"

She looked up at him. "Yes," she said dully. "'Twas the last time Mrs. Lexton ever had supper here. The doctor got a messenger boy, and sent him up to a grand shop in Piccadilly for some cold fish-sole, I thinks it was-done up in a newfangled fashion. Also there was a game pie, likewise an ice."

"But how does that fix the date in your mind?" asked Alfred Finch rather impatiently.

"I can't fix it. But you could, sir, from the messenger boys' office. I heard one of them boys once tell the doctor that they kep' all their receipts. 'Twas early last summer when that happened."

He felt suddenly convinced that she at least believed she was telling the truth.

"The last time Mrs. Lexton had supper here?" It was that statement which in a sense impressed him. And had he been another kind of man he would undoubtedly have explained, "But you yourself signed a statement declaring that Mrs. Lexton had never been here, at 6 Ferry Place, excepting on one occasion to tea?"

But, instead of saying that, he observed encouragingly, "Now listen to me, Mrs. Huntley. You say, I notice, 'the last time.' Would Mrs. Lexton have been here to supper as many, say, as three or four times?"

"Much oftener than that!" exclaimed the old woman, rousing herself. "At one time, Mrs. Lexton was here constant. She'd come in just for ten minutes. 'Nother time, maybe, for a couple of hours. She'd 'phone first, to see if the doctor'ud be in. Mostly I couldn't help knowing about it, though the doctor always made an excuse to get me out of the place before she come."

"And on that last occasion, what exactly was it that happened? Are you sure this jar of arsenic was on the table, in front of Mrs. Lexton?"

In his eagerness he came and flung himself across a chair, close to the old woman.

"I'm sure 'twas there, though I don't know how it come there, excepting that the doctor had maybe some medicine to make up. I come in to clear up, and as I puts my key in the surgery door-that's our back-way in, sir-she didn't hear me. When she did, she was awfully put about. I begged her pardon, and I went away. And when I come round to the front of the house, I saw the doctor letting a man out. That was why Mrs. Lexton was alone, then, in the surgery. She was waiting for the doctor, maybe to get her a cab. He often did that."

"I suppose you can give me nothing that would afford any corroboration as to what you have just told me? I mean that would make anyone know that you are now telling the truth? *I* believe you, Mrs. Huntley, but you know that, in a matter of this sort, belief doesn't go very far. People want proof."

"I knows that. But I can't say no more than I have said."

"Is there nothing? Think, Mrs. Huntley!" exclaimed Enid Dent. "Did you never tell anyone outside that you'd found Mrs. Lexton in the surgery under such curious circumstances?"

"I give the doctor my word I'd never tell on either of them. He said I could do a great thing for him in doing that, and I've kep' my word till today."

And then Alfred Finch had something like an inspiration.

"Of course, I know the police made a thorough search of this house," he observed. "But I ask myself, Mrs. Huntley, if they overlooked anything —*anything in the way of a letter or letters?*" And he looked very hard at the old woman.

Mrs. Huntley blinked at him, and for the first time she looked uneasy and ashamed.

"I've got summat," she said in a low reluctant voice. "Summat I've no business to have. It's two love-letters Mrs. Lexton wrote to the doctor. As was his way, poor young gentleman, he tore them up in little pieces, and ——"

"You pieced them together," observed Mr. Finch pleasantly.

Enid Dent gave a gasp, as he went on:

"If you can produce those letters, I think I can promise you, Mrs. Huntley, that Dr. Gretorex will not hang the day after tomorrow. They, together with a sworn statement made by you before a Commissioner of Oaths, will provide what is called 'new evidence.' I want you to go with me now into the surgery, to tell me exactly where Mrs. Lexton was standing when you surprised her. You are sure that she was alone?" he added quickly.

"She was quite alone," said Mrs. Huntley positively. "I come in softly like, and there she was! I can show you exactly where she was standing."

She got up and led the way down the passage, and through the two doors which shut off the surgery from the house.

"Is everything here just as it was?" asked Mr. Finch quickly.

"No, sir. They took away everything as was in that cupboard, but they left the books."

He glanced up at the row of shabby volumes in the hanging bookcase, but made no comment.

"Is that the same table where stood the jar labelled arsenic?"

Mrs. Huntley put her work-worn hand on a certain spot on the deal table.

"The jar was here; the light was full on it, and I saw it plain as plain."

And then she acted, or, rather, enacted, the scene with some spirit, making Enid Dent stand exactly where Ivy Lexton had stood.

"I noticed particular how she was dressed," she went on eagerly. "She always dressed very dainty-like, lovely clothes they was! And she had the most peculiar looking bag I ever did see. 'Twas exactly like mother-of-pearl. Lovely it was! I noticed it when she turned round. Says she, 'Why, Mrs. Huntley, how you did startle me,' or something like that, sir."

Alfred Finch was writing down every word that came out of her mouth. He was one of those men who never lose a chance, and he had invented a kind of shorthand for himself. Everything the woman had said since he had come into the room had been put on record by him.

"And now," he said quietly, "I'll trouble you to show me those two letters."

Finch noticed that Mrs. Huntley gave just an imperceptible glance towards the girl who stood a little aside, gazing into vacancy, as if her thoughts were far away, as indeed they were-with Roger Gretorex in his prison cell.

"Yes, sir, I'll go and get the letters, but I do hope Dr. Gretorex won't ever know I did such a thing as that, sir? I was very attached to the doctor, and that made me feel curious, I suppose. I oughtn't to have acted so, sir; I knew I was doing wrong."

"All I can say now is, thank God you did do wrong, Mrs. Huntley! But don't you worry-we won't let him ever know you did what you did. After all, anyone who found those pieces might have put them together, eh? Why people don't burn compromising documents always beats me! I've got a cab at the end of the street, and I want you to come along this very minute to a Commissioner of Oaths. I've got all you've told me in black and white. You'll only have just to repeat word for word what I've got down here before the gentleman, and then swear it's true."

"But do you think I ought to leave the house, sir?"

"We can leave Miss Dent here, while I go on to your place to get those letters."

When, within a quarter of an hour, the three were standing outside the queer little office of a Commissioner of Oaths, with whom Alfred Finch happened to be acquainted, Mr. Finch said something which surprised Enid Dent. "I think you'd better not come in here with us," he muttered. "You see, it's better, in such a case, to have the witness alone. Prevents her being nervous."

She did not guess the truth, which was that, in the few minutes he had been away with the old woman, she had spoken more freely than she had cared to do before the girl whom she regarded as Gretorex's "young lady." And some of the things she had then told him Alfred Finch determined should be embodied in her statutory declaration. Mr. Finch was keenly alive to the value of prejudice. He was aware that the Home Secretary was a man of rigid, some would have said too rigid, moral principle.

So it was with considerable satisfaction that he had exclaimed, after reading through the two letters, "My word! Mrs. Lexton's what *I* call a hot cup of tea. Eh? Mrs. Huntley?"

125

Solemnly she had nodded her head. She had always known that such was the fact, though she wouldn't perhaps have put it in just those words, for she was a refined, delicate-natured old woman.

Chapter Twenty

The morning after these events had taken place, the Home Secretary, Sir Edward Law, was moving about his fine room in Whitehall. He felt restless and thoroughly ill at ease, and that, although he was a statesman noted for his calm and cool temperament.

Within a few moments from now he expected his door to open and three persons to be shown in. First there would be a solicitor named John Oram, whose name he vaguely knew as that of a man of the highest standing in his profession, and who, the year before, had been President of the Law Society. Mr. Oram was the legal adviser of Roger Gretorex, a man convicted of murder, whose execution had been fixed to take place the following morning at nine o'clock. Then Sir Joseph Molloy, the most famous advocate of the day, known by the cynically minded as "the murderer's friend," who had defended Roger Gretorex at the Old Bailey would accompany Mr. Oram, though his presence could not be regarded as being quite in order. However, Sir Joseph was a very old friend of the Home Secretary, and he had pleaded urgently to be allowed to come this morning. The Judge, Mr. Justice Mayhew, who had tried Roger Gretorex, was the third visitor expected, his presence at the forthcoming conference being, very properly, regarded as essential.

An odd thing had happened only the previous day in connection with this Gretorex case. Sir Edward Law had received an envelope, marked "Private," and containing a letter signed "Roger Gretorex." With it, a plain piece of paper bore the following words: "The enclosed was written to Mrs. Lexton only last November, after the beginning of Jervis Lexton's illness. It reads like the letter of an innocent man."

That touching, in its way noble, love-letter had much impressed him, and had added a note of real mystery to a story with all the details of which he was by now painfully familiar.

At last Sir Edward stopped in front of his writing-table. There, in a place by themselves, stood five white cards. Each was marked with a name and a date; and they formed a perpetual reminder that four men and one woman were now lying under sentence of death. For the date on each of those death-cards was the day on which the person named was to suffer the last penalty of the law.

The Home Secretary's eyes became fixed on the card bearing the name of Roger Gretorex, the young man of gentle birth who had been sentenced to death at the Old Bailey for the murder of one Jervis Lexton. And, as he gazed at the rather unusual name, the Minister, in whose hands the fate of these men and one woman still reposed, asked himself, with a tightening of the heart, whether Sir Joseph Molloy might not be right after all in his belief that there had been a grave miscarriage of justice.

Sir Edward Law was a man with a high sense of duty. At first he had naturally accepted the verdict at the trial as conclusive of Gretorex's guilt, and he had daily expected to hear the news that there had been a full confession, especially after he learnt that the condemned man had refused to enter an appeal. But he had been unwillingly impressed by Sir Joseph Molloy's strong conviction of his client's innocence, and now he understood that certain extraordinary new evidence was to be laid before him this morning, at what was indeed the eleventh hour.

That was why, as late as the day before, the Home Secretary had conscientiously read once more all the documents, and they were many, connected with what had been called "The Lexton Mystery." He had felt it to be his plain duty thus to prepare himself for the critical examination which it would be his business to apply to this new evidence.

And yet? And yet, he could not imagine what new evidence could possibly be adduced of a nature strong enough to upset the apparently conclusive case built up against Roger Gretorex at the trial.

The door opened, and Sir Edward's principal private secretary came in.

"Sir Joseph Molloy to see you, sir, by appointment. And there is another man with him."

Thus announced, Sir Joseph Molloy, who was followed by Alfred Finch, entered the room and, after greeting his old friend, the Home Secretary, came at once to business.

"Mr. Oram is unfortunately ill, so I have ventured to bring in his stead his head clerk, Mr. Finch, who has had all the threads of the Gretorex case in his hands. Indeed, it is to Mr. Finch that I believe we owe the proof of a fearful miscarriage of justice. I hope he will be able to convince you, Sir Edward, of the innocence of his most unfortunate client, Roger Gretorex. 'Murder, though it hath no tongue, will speak!'" added Sir Joseph in a dramatic tone.

The Home Secretary slightly raised his eyebrows. Sir Joseph was going just a little bit too fast, as he sometimes did, especially when he had any kind of audience. But the famous advocate realised that he was not going quite the right way to work, for quickly he changed his tone:

"I think, Sir Edward, that after you have seen the statutory declaration made by a certain person who was closely connected with Gretorex's London life, as well as other new evidence which Mr. Finch is about to lay before you, you will agree that there is a strong case for, at any rate, the postponement of Roger Gretorex's execution."

And then the door of the room opened again, and the Judge who had tried the Lexton case came in.

Mr. Justice Mayhew appeared outwardly his usual calm and dignified self. But within he was full of interest, and even a certain excitement. Unlike the Home Secretary, he thought nothing of Sir Joseph Molloy's belief in his client's innocence; what had profoundly impressed him had been the condemned man's refusal to appeal.

A few moments later the three men-for Alfred Finch was standing a little aside, he had done his part and he knew the documents which he had brought with him almost by heart-were gazing with intense curiosity at Mrs. Huntley's statutory declaration. Each, in turn, read the pasted-up fragments of Ivy Lexton's two passionate love-letters. They belonged to an early period of her friendship with Roger Gretorex, and each letter proposed a meeting at Ferry Place. On each occasion she had chosen an evening, or rather a night, when her husband was to be with an old friend who had a fishing place some way from London.

And then the Home Secretary took out of a drawer, and handed to the Judge, Gretorex's own piteous letter to Ivy Lexton, the letter which had remained so long hidden in Mrs. Berwick's desk.

It took quite a little while for Sir Edward Law and Mr. Justice Mayhew to make themselves fully acquainted with what had been laid before them. And then they looked at one another in silence for a moment. As for Sir Joseph, he wisely said nothing, though he was longing intensely to express something of the triumph and exultation which filled his heart.

"I read a full report of the case over again yesterday," said the Home Secretary. "There seemed to me, then, no doubt as to the guilt of Roger Gretorex. But this Mrs. Huntley's report of what she swears she saw the very day before, it is now ascertained, Jervis Lexton had his first attack of illness, does, I admit, entirely alter the complexion of everything. But I should not have attached very great importance to a statement which rests on the word of one person, who, if she tells the truth now, certainly lied before, had we not also these three letters. They prove that Mrs. Lexton has committed gross perjury."

As the two men he was addressing remained silent, he went on: "I suppose the police made a thorough search of the flat in which Jervis Lexton met his death?"

And then all at once Alfred Finch took a hand.

"No, Sir Edward, the flat was not searched," he answered deferentially.

"Are you sure of that?"

"Quite sure. It is not usual to institute a search unless there is cause for suspicion against a person actually living in the house or flat where the murder has been committed. Now, the first C.I.D. man, who was in charge of the preliminary inquiries, undoubtedly formed the definite opinion that Roger Gretorex had poisoned Jervis Lexton. From his point of view there was no need to go further, the more so as his view was confirmed by a conversation he had with Gretorex just after he had taken a statement from Mrs. Lexton. The inspector, a day or two later on, interviewed Mrs. Huntley. You have that first statement of hers, gentlemen, in that bundle of papers I have laid down over there, marked 'I.' Mrs. Huntley then perjured herself, apparently because she had made a solemn promise to Dr. Gretorex to reveal nothing as to his association with Mrs. Lexton. She was, of course, quite unaware, at the time, of the fearful injury she was doing her employer."

The Home Secretary opened the bundle marked "I." He read through first the notes which Inspector Orpington had made during his first interview with Ivy Lexton-that interview during which she had gone out of her way to volunteer the fact that Roger Gretorex entertained for her a hopeless, unrequited passion.

Sir Edward next read most carefully again Mrs. Lexton's two letters to Gretorex, as well as the letter which had reached him anonymously only yesterday.

"This Mrs. Lexton appears to be, in any case, a most hypocritical and abandoned woman," he observed tartly.

Sir Joseph Molloy laughed a merry, hearty, boyish laugh, and Mr. Justice Mayhew looked round at him with an expression of shocked disgust on his stern face.

But "divil a bit," as he said to himself, did Sir Joseph care for that.

"Do you agree," said Sir Edward Law, looking at the Judge, "that these various documents provide sufficient reason for further inquiries?"

Mr. Justice Mayhew waited for what seemed a very long time, both to Sir Joseph and to Alfred Finch. Then reluctantly he answered:

"Yes, I think we have certainly cause here for the execution to be postponed, and for further inquiries to be made."

"Now that we are on what I may term the right track," exclaimed Sir Joseph, "I trust that my unhappy friend Roger Gretorex will not be allowed to languish in the cell of a condemned felon a moment longer than is absolutely necessary?"

The great advocate felt that he had now done all he could, and he was well aware that he had only been admitted to this conference by favour. And so, after a word of thanks to his old friend, and a sly look of triumph at the Judge, he went away, taking Alfred Finch with him, and leaving the Home Secretary and Mr. Justice Mayhew alone together.

Inspector Orpington looked not only serious but also very grim, as, early that afternoon, and accompanied by the same colleague as had been with him here before, he rang the bell of Mrs. Lexton's flat.

He felt extremely incensed for, turn the facts round in his mind as he might, there was no doubt that the childishly simple-looking, lovely little woman had completely taken him in. She had certainly, as he put it to himself, bamboozled him to the top of her bent.

Yet, even now, he found it almost impossible to believe that Ivy Lexton had poisoned her husband. Even so, he had been very much startled and impressed, not so much by Mrs. Huntley's new statement, for he knew her to be a liar. No, what had astounded him had been Ivy's letters to Roger Gretorex. Though these two letters had been written at a time when the writer was passionately in love with her correspondent, they revealed quite a different type of woman from what everyone connected with the case had taken her to be.

Inspector Orpington had also been unwillingly impressed by the letter written by Gretorex to Ivy in evident answer to one in which she had begged him to leave off coming to see her. The date, that of November the 6th, inscribed on Gretorex's letter, proved that she had written the note to which it had been the answer after she had started her cruel work of poisoning her husband, if indeed she had poisoned her husband. The inspector realised that the letter was what might have been called a bull point in the writer's favour. It breathed sincerity in every line.

It seemed a long time, to the two men standing there, before the door of the flat was opened by the cook. She looked surprised when she saw the inspector standing there, and then she smiled amiably.

"Want to see Mrs. Lexton?" she inquired. And, as he nodded, "Then want will be your master! She's away in the country, and not coming back yet awhile."

Orpington had already walked through into the hall.

"All alone in the flat?" he asked casually.

"I am this minute. There don't seem any reason for keeping a young girl here all day just to do nothing," said the woman tolerantly. "She works pretty hard when Mrs. Lexton is at home, that I will say."

"Where is Mrs. Lexton staying?"

"I've got it down on a bit of paper. It's near Brighton. A place belonging to the Lady Flora something or other. I'll go and get it."

"Wait a sec. We've come on what isn't a very pleasant job, cook. We've got to search this place of yours."

"Search this place?" Cook looked taken aback. "Whatever for?"

As no answer was vouchsafed to that question, "I'll just go and tidy my room then," she exclaimed. "I've been taking things easy since Mrs. Lexton went away. Where will you begin? How about the dining-room just here?"

"All right. We'll begin with the dining-room, and work down towards the kitchen."

He added in a perfunctory tone, "No need to tell you to hide nothing, eh, cook?"

"There's nothing to hide!" she exclaimed with some heat. "Everything's always left open. Mrs. Lexton isn't a lady to lock up her jewellery, like some do. She trusts us, and we are worthy of the trust, same as everyone is who is trusted."

"If that's so 'twill make our job easy. Then there's no lock-up at all?" and he looked at her rather hard.

"I keeps my box locked up, but you're welcome to the key!"

"Don't you be afraid. We'll let your box alone. I meant, is there no lock-up this end of the flat?"

She waited a moment. "There's half the big hanging cupboard in Mrs. Lexton's bedroom always kept locked, just because there's nothing in it. She keeps all her fine clothes-my, and she has got a lot, fit to stock a shop with!—in a little room that no one uses, next door to the bathroom."

"Have you got the key of that part of the hanging cupboard?"

"I've never even seen it. But I expect it's about somewhere. Maybe in the dressing-table drawer."

It takes a long time to search a room thoroughly, and by the time the two men had done with the dining-room and the drawing-room, they felt tired.

"Perhaps we'd better do Mrs. Lexton's room next? Not that I expect to find anything there. The room in which that poor chap died was searched, and thoroughly too, though not till after the post-mortem."

Cook brought the bit of paper on which Ivy had written down her country address. Then she went off again into her kitchen.

The two men walked, in a rather gingerly way, into Ivy Lexton's charming bedroom.

There the searchers had an easy task, for everything was unlocked, as the cook had said it would be.

But suddenly Orpington exclaimed, "Why, this must be the room where, according to that good old soul, there's a lock-up? I'd forgotten that! It's the half of this big cupboard. Seen any keys about?"

The other shook his head.

Orpington, stepping back, looked dubiously at the big handsome inlaid piece of furniture. It was a fine bit of early Victorian cabinet work, and had belonged to the mother of the Miss Rushworth whose room this was. Though it was not in modern taste, Inspector Orpington thought it a beautiful object.

"I wonder if we've any call to force this lock?" he muttered to himself. "I wouldn't like to hurt that cupboard in any way. It's a good piece ——"

"I bet you I can open it all right without doing it a bit of harm," said the other man confidently.

He went up to the cupboard. Then he did something to the lock with a bit of wire he happened to have in his pocket, and the big door swung open.

Orpington came forward quickly. He peered into the mahogany-lined cavity. It was empty, save for a shabby-looking red-leather despatch-box, on which, so faded as to be practically indecipherable, were embossed three gilt letters.

"That's a rummy looking thing! One wouldn't expect Mrs. Lexton would have such an object as this about," and he lifted the despatch-box out of the cupboard.

It was surprisingly light.

"I wonder if she kept Gretorex's love-letters in there," said the other with a laugh. "If so, we may find something useful, eh?"

Orpington shook the box. Though it was so light he could feel that there was something in it which rolled about.

"You won't find it as easy to open this box as you did that cupboard," he observed, "but it has to be done."

"The only way we could open this," said the sergeant, decidedly, "would be with a kitchen knife, unless they've got a chisel."

"You go and get what you can from the old woman."

A minute or two later the man came back. "She's in her room tidying up," he said with a grin, "so I just took this without saying 'by your leave.'" And he held up a short stout kitchen knife.

"You just lock that door," said Orpington quickly.

And then, the two men, by exerting a great deal of strength, managed to prize open the hinges of the old despatch-box which had belonged to Ivy's father. The lock stayed fast.

The inspector felt a pang of disappointment, for there only lay on the rubbed green velvet lining a lady's fancy handbag.

And then Orpington suddenly remembered Mrs. Huntley's sworn statement. In that statement was actually a description of the bag Ivy had had with her when the old woman had found her alone in the surgery with the jar of arsenic on the table before her. A bolster bag that "looked like mother-of-pearl." This was the same one without doubt.

He took the odd little bag out of the despatch-box and pressed the jewelled knob—to find nothing in it but a cable from South Africa. The signature, "Rushworth," meant nothing to him, though of course he knew of the famous Rushworth Line.

Then he opened the little white leather-lined, inner pocket of the bag. It, too, was empty. A faint scent, that of a popular face powder, rose from it.

And then, suddenly, he noticed, with a queer quickening of his pulse, that a few grains of what looked like kitchen salt clung to the white leather sides.

Moistening his finger, he put it against the leather, and a few grains stuck on to his wet finger. Face powder? No, not face powder. He touched his finger with his tongue, and then the colour rushed up all over his face.

"I'd like Sir Bernard to have a squint at that!" he exclaimed, holding up the open bag.

"D'you mean you've found something?" the other cried excitedly.

"Hush!"

Carefully Orpington put the rather absurd-looking mother-of-pearl bolster into a big black bag which he had brought with him. Then he put the empty despatch-box back into the cupboard.

"Let's get out of this," he murmured, "before the old woman sees us. Can you manage to shut the cupboard as cleverly as you opened it?"

"I think I can," said the other. And sure enough he did shut it, though it took him longer to lock up the half of the great early-Victorian cupboard than it had done to unlock it.

Orpington took a card out of his notebook. He wrote on it: "We've seen everything we wanted. Shan't be troubling you any more," and left it in a prominent place on the hall table.

Then he shut the front door rather loudly behind him, and, together, the two men went down the stairs by the side of the lift.

When they were safely out of the Duke of Kent Mansion, the inspector stayed his steps.

"I've got her!" he said exultingly. "Little Ivy will live to be sorry she bamboozled 'yours truly,' my boy!"

Chapter Twenty-one

With a sudden cry of fear Ivy Lexton sat up in the Jacobean four-post bed, where she had spent a broken night.

She was still plunged in sleep, but anyone standing, say, by the large half-moon window of the delightful old-world country bedroom would have thought her awake, for her violet-blue eyes were wide open and dilated, as if with terror.

How lovely she looked; how child-like was the pure, delicate contour of her face, and the droop of her little red mouth. Her dimpled shoulders rose from what she called a "nightie" of flesh-coloured crêpe de Chine. The sleeveless bodice was edged with a deep band of real lace, and, to the eyes of the old-fashioned maid who waited on her in this, her friend's, Lady Flora Desmond's, country cottage, it looked more like a ball-dress than a nightgown.

There were tens of thousands of human beings who, had they been privileged to see Ivy as she was now, this morning, would have felt their hearts contract with intense pity for the woman they regarded as having been the innocent victim of an extraordinary set of ironic circumstances. There were also tens of thousands of other human beings who, though they had had strong doubts as to the part she had played in the singular story, would have told themselves that their suspicions had been cruelly unjust, could they have looked into that flower-like face, and heard the words now escaping from her half-opened mouth.

Those words were uttered in an appealing, broken tone, "Don't hurt him! Please don't hurt him!" And then: "Oh, Roger, I am so sorry for you!"

Ivy's soul was not here in this delightful country bedroom. It had travelled a long long way, to a prison situated on the outskirts of London.

She seemed to be gazing through the door of a small, bare room, which she knew to be now occupied by one on whom judgment of death was to be executed that morning.

There stood by the pallet bed the tall, sinewy figure of a man who had loved her with a passionate and absorbing love, and whom she, in her own fashion, had also loved. By his wish, at his trial, not a word concerning what she had called their "friendship," had been uttered in extenuation of anything he, Roger Gretorex, had done, or left undone.

There he stood, the man whose arms had so often cradled her, on whom she had made the limitless demands that a woman only makes on the man she loves. Never once, in great or in little things, had he failed her.

This morning he looked strange indeed, for though dressed, he was collarless, and clad in an old tweed suit —a suit which Ivy remembered well, and which she had once told him caressingly she liked to see him wear.

He held himself upright, with his head thrown back in what had been a characteristic attitude.

In Ivy's vision two men were pinioning Roger's arms, and it was to them that, living through this terrible nightmare, she had just addressed her piteous plea. And then with slow steps the chaplain, together with the governor of the prison, walked in . . . .

It was all happening exactly as Ivy had once seen something happen, in what had then appeared to her just a thrilling scene in a play, in London about a year ago.

And now Roger left the cell and began walking, with steady steps, his head still thrown back, down a narrow way . . . .

And then the woman in the bed gave a stifled shriek, for suddenly she saw the gallows through an open door at the end of the passage.

She covered her face with her hands, yet something seemed to force her to peep through her fingers and-for a fleeting moment-Roger Gretorex turned and looked at her . . . .

So had the condemned man turned and looked at the woman in the play.

But Roger's face was so charged with mute, terrible reproach that, with an anguished cry of protest, Ivy awoke-awoke to the blessed reality that she was sixty miles from the place where that awful drama was to be enacted this morning.

Her shaking hand felt for her diamond-circled watch on the Chippendale table standing by her bed. Having found it, she held it up close before her eyes.

It was only eight o'clock. She sighed heavily, for that meant that there was another hour of misery and suspense to be lived through. Nay, maybe even as much as an hour and a half-for the morbid-minded woman pal of hers who intended to stand near the prison gate till the death notice was put up, and had promised faithfully to telephone to her from a house near by, had thought it unlikely she could get a trunk call through before half-past nine.

The tears began rolling down Ivy Lexton's cheeks; yet it was not for Roger Gretorex, and his awful fate, that she was weeping. It was for pity of herself, for all she had gone through, and for what remained for her to go through, till she knew for certain that Roger Gretorex had died, as he had lived, silent.

She was well aware, deep down in her heart, that not only his counsel, Sir Joseph Molloy, who believed him innocent, but also that Roger's mother, would hope up to the last moment of his sentient life that he would clear himself by shifting the burden of guilt on the one who was guilty.

Ivy had written the condemned man a letter three days ago, and she had made so many rough copies of that short letter that she knew it, now, by heart.

She repeated that touching letter over to herself, rocking her slight body this way and that in the large bed.

Sunday night.

Dear Roger,
I am ill, so I cannot come to you. Otherwise I would do so. You know that I believe you innocent, and I want now to tell you how grateful I am for all your kindness to me, and for the love, however wrong it may have been, that you lavished on me.

Ivy.

She hoped that letter had given poor Roger pleasure and, above all, that he had read between the lines and seen how really, truly sorry she was-how dreadfully grieved that everything had fallen out as it had fallen out. Indeed, she had twice underlined the word "grateful."

And then she suddenly felt that she could not go on remembering any more. It was too horrible-too horrible! So she took a bottle off the little table, where her watch was lying, and measured out a small dose into a medicine glass. Lady Flora would wake her, she knew, when that secretly longed-for message came through.

Soon she was once more plunged into uneasy slumber. But alas! again there came that hideous, hideous nightmare.

Once more she seemed transported to the condemned cell. But this time, in addition to the warders, the governor of the prison, and the chaplain, there was the horrid, cruel, fat-faced man, Sir Joseph Molloy, who had cross-examined her. True, he had dealt with her gently, kindly, but only because he had been adjured to do so, and, as well she remembered, with now and again a tigerish glare in his blue Irish eyes.

She listened with a feeling of indignation and pitiful dread to his voice uttering the words: "I adjure you, Gretorex, to tell the truth, now, for the sake of your poor mother who has always believed you innocent!"

There was a pause. Ivy clasped her hands together in supplication. But the collarless prisoner had turned his sunken eyes away from her pleading face. Was he going to obey Sir Joseph Molloy? Yes! For she heard Roger's deep voice answer: "It is as you have always thought it was, Sir Joseph. I die innocent. Ivy Lexton poisoned her husband."

Outside that quiet bedroom Lady Flora, already on her way down to breakfast, heard a fearful cry—"No! No! *No!* —that isn't true!"

134

She opened the bedroom door and saw that Ivy was asleep. "Poor child," she murmured. "No wonder she talks in her sleep. Thank God! that unhappy man is to be hanged this morning."

And, being the manner of woman she was, she offered up a silent prayer for the murderer, that he might make his peace with God.

There came a sharp knock on the bedroom door, and Ivy woke with a stifled cry. She jumped straight out of bed and stood, her hands clasped together, waiting.

There came another knock, and then, "Come in!" she cried shrilly, and Lady Flora's old parlourmaid entered the room.

Ivy had never liked the woman, and the woman had never liked her. She did not understand, and she never quite knew how to treat, those of her own sex whom she regarded as inferior to herself; yet some of the kindest letters written to her in the last few weeks had been from domestic servants, warmly sympathising with the heroine of their favourite Sunday paper.

"Mrs. Doghill is on the telephone, ma'am. Her ladyship is holding the line till you come."

Ivy snatched up her periwinkle-blue satin dressing-gown and wrapped it about her. Then she thrust her little white feet into slippers that matched the dressing-gown, and ran downstairs, telling herself, not for the first time, how stupid it was to have the telephone in so public a place as the hall.

Lady Flora was standing, the telephone receiver to her ear. But when she saw Ivy she silently handed her the receiver and, turning into the dining-room, shut the door.

"Is that you, Millicent? Yes-yes! I can hear quite well——"

She waited in an agony of mingled hope and fear till, with startling distinctness, came the measured words that were being uttered sixty miles away.

"There's been a reprieve. The story goes that important new evidence was laid before the Home Secretary yesterday."

Ivy remained silent. She felt stunned. New evidence?

At last she managed to get out, in a low, strangled voice, "I—I don't quite understand."

But instantly she heard a cross voice interject, "You've had six minutes-can't allow you to have any more now."

"Indeed I haven't! I've only just come to the telephone," she said pleadingly.

"I can't help that. The call was put through six minutes ago——" And ruthlessly she was cut off.

Ivy turned towards the room where she knew her hostess was waiting, full of sympathy. She opened the door, and then she cried, "He's been-he's been——" and before she could say the word "reprieved" she had fallen fainting at the other woman's feet.

Lady Flora would not have believed an angel, had an angel come and told her, that her dear little friend Ivy Lexton had fainted, not from relief, but from sheer, agonising fear.

Ivy spent the rest of the morning in bed, a prey to frightful anxiety and terror.

New evidence? What could that mean? Had Roger really failed her at last?

At twelve o'clock the parlourmaid came in with a telegram.

> Hope to be with you tomorrow evening.
>
> Miles Rushworth.

The telegram had been sent from Paris the day before, and delayed in transmission.

"There is no answer," said Mrs. Lexton in her soft voice. And then she lay back, feeling much less unhappy.

Whatever the mysterious reprieve might portend, Rushworth would very soon, in fact tomorrow, be here to help and to protect her.

As she read the telegram over for the third time, Ivy told herself how noble, how generous, how devoted the sender had proved himself. Also, what a wonderful life lay before her as his cherished, sheltered wife! Rushworth was all-powerful. New evidence? There could be no "new evidence" for the simple reason that nothing, nothing, *nothing* had ever happened-that could possibly be found out.

Chapter Twenty-two

As he walked up the gangway of the cross-Channel boat at Calais, Miles Rushworth's heart was full of two women. The one was his dead sister, the other Ivy Lexton, the woman to whom he was hastening, and whom he expected to see today. Every fibre of Rushworth's being longed consciously, hungrily, thirstily, for Ivy.

It was a source of real grief to him that these two could never now meet and love each other. He had been painfully aware that his sister hoped he would marry her own dearest friend, Bella Dale, and he had not dared to speak to her of Ivy.

During his long, dreary journey home he had often asked himself if all she had gone through had changed her from the deliciously pretty, kind-hearted, rather irresponsible little creature he remembered her as being, into a more serious woman. Not that he wanted Ivy different. To him she was already absolutely perfect. But her letters had grown shorter, as his had grown longer, and vaguely they had disappointed him.

Roger Gretorex? How often had Rushworth tried to visualise the young man who had committed so dastardly a crime in order to set free the woman he had loved hopelessly, and without return, from the degradation of being tied to such a waster as had been Jervis Lexton.

Though even the South African papers had been full of the wretched fellow's photographs, proving that he had a singularly handsome face, Rushworth had no clear vision of him. Also, Ivy had never once mentioned him in any of her letters.

Suddenly that fact, Ivy's absolute silence concerning Gretorex, struck him as being strange. He also realised, what he had not realised till now, that poor lovely Ivy could not but be, all her life long, even after she changed her name, a marked woman. She would be always pointed at, and that wherever she went in English-speaking lands, as the heroine of a great *cause célèbre*.

Yet stop! In the circumstances, would it not only be right, but reasonable, that she should marry him, Miles Rushworth, almost at once? He would beg her, entreat her, to consent to an immediate marriage. And then he would take her away in his yacht to the South, to some quiet place where they two could be hidden in a trance of love, while people forgot the sordid story of the murder of which she had been the innocent cause.

It was a fine winter day, though bitterly cold, so the home-coming traveller found himself a comfortable spot in a sheltered place, on the upper deck of the steamer, where was just room for three.

Two deck-chairs were already occupied, one by a big man with whose powerful, humorous face Rushworth felt he was vaguely familiar, the other by a delicate, fragile-looking, little grey-haired lady. The third chair was unoccupied, and so he sat down in it.

Perhaps because he was in a sentimental mood today, he felt queerly moved when he saw that, under their rug, the big man was holding the hand of the grey-haired little lady. They were talking together eagerly, happily; obviously, so Rushworth told himself, an old-fashioned husband and wife, never so happy as when they were together.

His heart swung back to Ivy Lexton, and to the bliss of their coming meeting.

Poor, precious darling! What a terrible ordeal she had been through! He would regret all his life, all their joint life, that he had been far from her during the weeks that had followed the strange death of Jervis Lexton.

And then-for a moment he thought his ears had misled him-he heard that very name of "Lexton" uttered aloud by the man sitting one from him.

"That Lexton affair? Come now. If you really read your loving husband's letters —I sometimes suspect that you don't, you naughty little thing-well, there'd be nothing left to tell you! It's hunting I should be today, instead of coming to meet an ungrateful woman."

"I want to know what's happening now, Joe. Also, most of all, what led to the extraordinary reprieve on the very day this man was to have been hanged?"

A reprieve? Miles Rushworth felt a sudden rush of anger and surprise. He was, of course, aware that Roger Gretorex, the man whose name and personality he loathed, and for whom he felt he would ever feel an intense, retrospective horror, was to have been hanged this very morning. That fact had been stated in both the daily papers which are published in English in Paris.

If it was true that there had been a reprieve that morning, how had this stranger already become aware of the fact?

"You know I told you, Eileen, long ago, that the poor chap had refused to appeal?"

"Yes, I remember that," she murmured.

"Well, there seemed nothing left to be done! I was in despair, and it was only the day before yesterday that by-well, I suppose old-fashioned folk like you would call it an intervention of Providence, some astounding new evidence was produced. And what's more, I've been proved right!"

And there was a tone of triumph in the, now low, organ-like voice.

"D'you mean that what you half suspected was true all along, Joe?"

She had turned her head round, and was gazing up into her husband's face.

Rushworth saw the big man bend his head as jovially he exclaimed, "Bedad! I think we've got her cold!"

A tremor ran through the lady. "What a horrible expression," she murmured.

"Still, so far there's something lacking, me dear, and it's causing me a bit of anxiety."

"What's that, Joe?"

"Motive!" the man exclaimed, in a voice that had become suddenly grave. And then he went on: "I don't mind telling you that everything fair and-well, a bit near the wind, also, was done to try and find out if our lovely, clinging Ivy had another man in tow. She is a"—the speaker sought for something in place of the Biblical word trembling on his lips, but he gave it up, and said instead:

"We heard that there was one chap who went about with her a good deal last autumn, and who was far more often at Duke of Kent Mansion than Gretorex ever was. But though we ran him to earth and gave him-at least I hope so—a pretty bad quarter of an hour, it was clear that he would never have married her, not if she had been a hundred times free! Also, though he's a gay bachelor, and manages to give his lady friends a scrumptious time, he's not a rich man, and our practical little Ivy wants money, money, money all the time."

"Then what's going to be done now? You don't want your man, if he's really innocent, to languish in prison half his life," observed the little lady shrewdly.

"I do not," he answered, in his rich, Irish voice. "What's more, I want to shift that noose. Once we get her in the dock I'll see there's no recommendation to mercy; trust me for that! The woman's a double-dyed murderess. She poisoned her husband, and she as good as hanged her lover."

"You haven't got her in the dock yet, and maybe you never will," said his wife calmly.

"Hold on! Hold on! Did you ever see me miss a kill I'd set my heart on? There's another woman whose neck I'd like to wring-that of an old charwoman, who, if she'd told the truth when Gretorex was first arrested, might have made all the difference, for there would still have been time, then, to find out something."

"Has that poor, pretty woman had a chance of saying anything for herself?" asked his wife slowly.

"That artful little Jezebel is staying with a woman friend in the country at present, and the police are determined that everything is to be O.K. this time. It's for hell she's making——" and he laughed a jolly laugh. "Ivy's held all the cards in her hand up to now, but she's going to lose the rubber."

"I do wonder, Joe, what her motive can have been-her husband had just got a good job, hadn't he?"

For a few moments the speaker remained silent, then he said in a singular voice:

"If Gretorex had hanged this morning, I'd have betted a hundred to one that within a year we should have seen, in all the papers, a paragraph announcing that the beautiful Mrs. Lexton, whose husband had died in such tragic circumstances, was about to be married very quietly to Mr. Dash, a gentleman of great wealth and considerable position!"

Rushworth moved slightly in his seat. He felt as if, within the last few minutes, the whole world, his world, had stopped going round, and that when it began again it would be in quite a different world that he would find himself.

"Then you think it will come out, now, that Mrs. Lexton was in love with some man ——?"

"I don't think anything of the kind! My view is that among the innumerable young fools who have made love to her in the past year or two, she marked down some rich man as a possible husband, *were she only free*. One thing we learned only the other day. This was that two or three years ago she did her best to persuade that rotter Jervis Lexton to consent to an arranged divorce. He refused, unluckily for himself, for, though he was a poor mutt, he adored his wife. She's the sort of woman over whom men go fantee ——"

"It's unlucky that you can't put a name to the happy man, Joe! Eh, my dear?"

"Unlucky? I should think it is unlucky! Still, someone's been supplying pretty Ivy with plenty of money during the last few weeks."

"It's strange she wasn't suspected."

"Of course she was! But not by the right people. My word, Eileen, she is a clever little woman! You should have seen her in the witness-box! Why, butter wouldn't melt in her mouth. But she overplayed her part. I think a good many people found it difficult to believe that she's been what she made herself out to be —a kind of plaster saint."

"Is there any evidence to show that she was not that?" asked Lady Molloy quietly.

"There you go! Hate to believe anything of a certain sort about a woman! You're a regular suffragette. A cold-blooded poisoner, yes-but naughty? Oh dear no, not that, if you please."

Half to himself, he added, "She wrote Gretorex two letters the poor chap's servant got out of his paper-basket and pieced together. The minute I'd read 'em I knew there'd be a reprieve!"

"Why?"

"Because Eddie Law is a highly moral man. He loathes the sins he's not inclined to." Sir Joseph added candidly, "Most of us do, me dear."

As Rushworth walked down the gangway at Dover two or three of his fellow-passengers nudged one another and smiled. They thought he was "a sheet in the wind," for he did not seem to know quite what he was doing, or where he was going.

The moment Mr. Oram received the wire informing him that the execution of Roger Gretorex had been postponed, he hurried back to London, full of surprise and curiosity.

What an amazing-he almost felt it to be, even now, an unbelievable-story, was that told him with deferential clearness and dryness by Alfred Finch.

"God bless my soul!" he repeated at intervals.

And then at last, with some magnanimity, he observed, "Then you were right, Finch, and I wrong, all along. Though I thought her a vain little fribble, murder is the last thing I'd have suspected that young woman capable of."

"I didn't suspect her either, sir. I was looking for a man-the successor to Dr. Gretorex in the lady's affections. The police believe they're on the track of what may be styled Mrs. Lexton's motive. It's a man, right enough! Orpington wouldn't tell me his name. He simply said he was very rich, and seemingly infatuated with her."

He gave the old solicitor a rather odd look. But that gentleman did not take up the challenge, though all Rushworth's cables, both to Ivy and to the lawyer himself, had been traced. And Mr. Oram had just become aware of the fact.

"Well-well-well ——"

"I suggest, sir, that you appeal to Sir Edward Law to consider the release of Dr. Gretorex on licence. The letter which he wrote to Mrs. Lexton-you have a copy of it here-which someone, I suspect one of the maids at the flat, sent anonymously to the Home Secretary, though one can't exactly call it evidence, makes it clear to any impartial mind that our man was absolutely innocent of the whole business. As soon as she got busy, Mrs. Lexton wanted him out of the way. That's as plain as a pikestaff. After all, he is a doctor, and he might have spoilt her game. Also he must have known, if he stopped to think a bit, that she had had access to the poison."

"More fool he to go to the flat on that last day," said Mr. Oram crustily.

It was that fact which, as soon as he had learnt it, had seemed to fix the guilt definitely on Gretorex.

"He was dotty about her! When a chap's in that peculiar condition, sir, it's as if he can't keep away," murmured Mr. Finch.

And then, it might have seemed irrelevantly, he observed: "Mr. Rushworth will be back in London in a day or two. Earlier, if he travels overland from Marseilles."

But even Alfred Finch felt a thrill of surprise when that same afternoon he was told that Mr. Rushworth was closeted with Mr. Oram. Indeed, he made a quick mental calculation. Either this must mean that their important client had come to Mr. Oram's office straight from Victoria Station, or that he had flown from Paris.

Mr. Finch would have given a good deal to have been present at the interview which was taking place within a few yards of where he was working on a tiresome right-of-way case.

Mr. Oram's head clerk had never much liked Miles Rushworth, and he could not help smiling to himself, as he considered the very awkward position in which that gentleman would find himself, if he was called as a witness for the Crown, as he most certainly would be if Mrs. Lexton were ever put on trial for the murder of her husband.

Alfred Finch knew that something of a most incriminating nature had been found in Ivy's bedroom, when the flat in Duke of Kent Mansion had been searched yesterday. He thought it probable that this consisted of a series of letters between Mrs. Lexton and Miles Rushworth. Even a man of huge wealth does not give something for nothing to an attractive woman.

Lawyers are apt to overlook the exception which proves the rule in life.

Had Mr. Finch been able to look through a blank wall, he would have seen Mr. Oram sitting at his writing-table, and looking across it straight at Miles Rushworth. And could he have heard what was being said, he would have realised that his employer was speaking in a tone that was, for him, oddly hesitant and uneasy.

"I'm sorry to say, Rushworth, that I've no doubt at all but that there's been a terrible miscarriage of justice. I take it that you knew comparatively little of Mrs. Jervis Lexton, even though her husband was in your employment?"

Miles Rushworth made a conscious effort to appear calm and unconcerned. But he failed in that endeavour, and was aware that he failed.

"I knew them both fairly well," he answered at last.

Mr. Oram began playing with a paper knife. He was wondering how much the man who sat there, with overcast face, and anxious, frowning eyes, was concerned with this horrid business.

"What's going to be the next move, Oram? I take it that you've been informed?"

"Well, yes, I have been informed, though quite unofficially. The-ahem! authorities are very naturally perturbed. An innocent man was very nearly hanged. It was, in fact, a matter of hours — —"

Should he tell this old friend and client the truth? All his life long John Oram had cultivated caution, and technically he was now bound to silence. But he made up his mind that he owed the truth to Rushworth. Even now the solicitor had no suspicion of how really close had been the relations between the woman he now believed to have been a cold-blooded murderess, and this man whom she had so completely deceived. He was aware of how carelessly generous Rushworth could be and often was.

Still, a glance at his client's face, now filled with a painful expression of suspense and acute anxiety, showed that this matter was of great moment to him.

"Mrs. Lexton," he said in a low voice, "is going to be arrested, I understand, this evening, or tomorrow morning. The Criminal Investigation Department of Scotland Yard are completing what they consider a very strong chain of evidence against her. I have here copies of three letters which have come into their possession. You had better glance over them, Rushworth."

He got up and, leaning across his table, handed a number of typewritten sheets to his client.

How strange looked those burning words of love and longing, transcribed on a bad old typewriting machine! But the man now reading them could visualise Ivy's pretty flowing handwriting, and, as he read on, he turned hot and cold.

Then he started on Gretorex's letter; the letter acquiescing in Ivy's decision that there should be a break between them.

"That was written," observed the solicitor, "after Lexton's mysterious illness was well started. I think you will agree that it is the letter of a man who was certainly unaware of what was going on?"

He waited a moment, then he added: "They've unluckily traced all your cables to the lady, Rushworth, as well as yours to me. I fear that you are certain to be called as leading witness for the Crown, if Mrs. Lexton is sent for trial, as seems now inevitable."

"That would be monstrous! What is my connection with the case?" exclaimed Rushworth. "Surely I had the right to give all the help in my power to the wife of one of my own people?"

"They will call you in order to prove that Mrs. Lexton had a strong motive for wishing to get her husband out of the way," returned Oram in a doleful tone. "I hope you refrained from writing to her? If you did, I trust she had the sense to destroy your letters."

"It is this man Gretorex, if, as you seem to think, he is entirely innocent, who should be called, not I," said Rushworth in a hard voice.

"Roger Gretorex will certainly refuse to give evidence against her. They'll try to make him. But they'll fail. He worshipped Ivy Lexton, and I fear he still loves her."

Then the old man sighed. "It's an awful story, Rushworth," he observed, "however you look at it."

The other threw the typewritten sheets of paper back on the table. He rose, and rather blindly he felt for, and found, his hat and stick.

"I must be going now," he said shortly. "If I'm wanted, you know where to find me, Oram."

He felt humiliated to the depths of his being. His passion for Ivy Lexton had turned to bitter hatred. Yet he knew that their fates were linked together, and that through what had been his mad infatuation for this woman, a name which was known and honoured all over the world, was not only going to become a laughingstock, but also to be smirched and befouled for ever.

As he went down the fine staircase of the old house, he exclaimed wordlessly, "By God, that shall not be!"

He waited a moment in the hall, and in that moment he thought of a way out.

It was a way made possible by the fact that an unpleasant experience at the beginning of August, 1914, had taught him the value of gold. Since the Saturday which had preceded the outbreak of war, he had always kept a thousand pounds in gold, and a thousand pounds in Bank of England ten-pound notes, in the private safe of his London office.

He walked quickly to the corner of a quiet street where he had left his car, and threw the chauffeur the address.

Then he looked at his watch. If what old Oram had said was true with regard to the probable arrest of Ivy Lexton, there was just time to accomplish that which he had planned to do in what had seemed but one flashing second.

"Stop at the nearest telephone box," he called out. And the chauffeur drew up at a tube station.

Rushworth was in the telephone box for a long time, for he had to a certain extent to speak in parables. But the young man whom he had called up, and had had the good fortune to find at home, at last understood exactly what was wanted of him. He was an airman to whom Rushworth had once been magnificently generous.

"Right-ho!" came the young voice down the line. "I'll be quite ready. I understand you want me to take my wife, too, and that you'll motor her down here from town. Her passport's always O.K. You can trust me. Afraid? Not much!"

Rushworth's face looked strained and white as he came out of the telephone box.

He was well aware that he was inciting that lad to do, from pure gratitude, a very wrong thing. Well? If it "didn't come off," he, Rushworth, would take all the blame, of course. But he felt pretty sure that the plan he had made would succeed, for it had the two essential qualities which spell success. His plan was bold and his plan was simple.

True, he wondered uncomfortably if the police had traced that last wire of his from Paris. He was glad indeed that Ivy had had the wit to telegraph her country address. And then, as he evoked her lovely face, her beckoning eyes, his own darkened, and filled with wrath and pain.

He did not go himself into his London office. Instead he sent in his chauffeur, with the key of his private safe, and armed with minute instructions as to what he was to take out of it.

Then, when the man had brought him the heavy little canvas bag, and the envelope containing a hundred ten-pound notes, he threw him the address of some lodgings in a quiet street off Piccadilly, where he knew Lady Dale and her daughter were staying just now. His sister had made him promise that he would see Bella the moment he reached London, and he was fulfilling that promise.

When he was told that her ladyship was out, but that Miss Dale was in, and alone, he suddenly felt as if his luck was holding, after all!

Ivy had insisted on coming back to London before luncheon.

Not only was her mind now full of vague, unsubstantial fears, but she was aware that Miles Rushworth would call at her flat some time this evening. That, indeed, was a fact to which she clung and constantly returned with a feeling of reassurance and hope. Even so she had not allowed Lady Flora to telephone the fact that she was returning unexpectedly to the flat. She felt, somehow, that she wanted no one to know about her movements just now. She was beginning to feel that most terrifying of sensations-that of being hunted.

Even when settled comfortably, and alone, in a first-class carriage of the train taking her to town, she found she could not rest, and she actually got up and began moving about.

It was such an awful sensation-that of feeling that human hounds might be hot on her scent . . . .

She had bought her favourite picture paper at the station, and then she had had a shock, for a large photograph of Roger had confronted her on the front page.

Underneath the picture ran a long paragraph, stating that Dr. Gretorex, who was to have been hanged this morning for the murder of Jervis Lexton, had had his execution postponed on the very eve of its being carried out. Such a thing had not taken place in England for close on eighty years. But important new evidence had been placed before the Home Secretary at the eleventh hour . . . .

"New Evidence"—Ivy turned those two ominous words over and over again, in her troubled, anxious mind. They now forced her to do what she had believed she would never, never have to do-live over again, in imagination, a certain fortnight of her life, the first fortnight of last November . . . .

She found herself imagining, suspecting, wild, crazy things. For instance, the existence of minute peepholes in the ceilings of certain rooms in the flat? Even that seemed more likely than that Roger Gretorex should have "given her away" with regard to the fact that she had been once left alone by him with a jar of arsenic on the table of his surgery.

Besides, even if he had done such a cruel, despicable thing, what he had it in his power to reveal *proved* nothing, and could prove nothing. She knew herself to have been not only very clever, but also very very careful.

And yet, as the train sped nearer and nearer to London, she became more and more afraid.

The old cook was quite pleased to see "the missus," and volubly she described the visit of Inspector Orpington and of his sergeant.

"No, they didn't find nothing. How could they-when there was nothing there?"

This Ivy believed to be nothing but the truth, and yet the fact that the two men from Scotland Yard had come to search the flat, filled her with a terrible foreboding.

And then, suddenly, she remembered Mrs. Huntley! With a sensation of sick fear she recalled how Gretorex's servant had surprised her on what she now perceived to have been the most dangerous day of her life.

Vile, wicked, cruel old woman! However, she, Ivy, had already replaced the cap on the jar labelled "Arsenic" when Mrs. Huntley had crept into the surgery so slyly and softly behind her. But the jar had been there, on the table before her, and no doubt the old fox had noticed it.

Yes! It was probably some sort of gossip traced to Gretorex's day-servant which had been the cause both of the reprieve, and of the presence yesterday of the Scotland Yard inspector here, in the flat. But, thank God, there was nothing-nothing —*nothing* that could be found, and for the best of reasons, that there was nothing to find.

Even so, all this was very frightening, as well as very annoying, if only because it meant new trouble and worry, just at a time when she, Ivy, would be wanting to pick up the old, and create the new, links, between herself and Rushworth.

She went into her bedroom feeling a little reassured. It is always better to know the worst, and Ivy Lexton thought she did know the worst now. And it was not so bad as she had feared.

Already she was mentally preparing the tale she would tell. And it ran somewhat like this: She had gone just for a moment to see Gretorex on the evening Mrs. Huntley had seen her in the surgery, with a message from Jervis, who was waiting for her hard by Ferry Place in a taxi. They two were on their way to a dance, and Jervis had suggested that Gretorex should come with them. But the fact had made so little impression on her mind that she had forgotten all about it, when asked if she had ever been to Ferry Place alone. If Mrs. Huntley mentioned the supper, she would simply deny that she had been the lady entertained by Gretorex. Mrs. Huntley had not actually seen her with her host. She had only seen her for that moment or two in the surgery.

But, even so, Ivy's nerves were so far upset that she made an involuntary and violent movement of recoil, when she heard a sudden loud knock on the front door of the flat.

There followed a moment of delay, and then she heard the cook waddling down the passage. She told herself that it was probably Inspector Orpington, and she mentally prepared her story, the explanation, that is, of that unfortunate encounter with Mrs. Huntley.

And then her heart leapt with joy in her bosom, for, "Is Mrs. Lexton at home?" was uttered in Miles Rushworth's voice.

"I don't know that Mrs. Lexton can see you, sir."

"I think she'll see me. Will you kindly say Mr. Rushworth has called to see her?"

Ivy heard him go into the drawing-room, and, after a few moments spent before her dressing-table in making up her face, she followed him.

Miles Rushworth was standing in the centre of the room, and when the door opened, and Ivy came through it, she looked so innocent and so appealing, as she advanced towards him in her plain black dress, that suddenly he felt as if all that had happened today had been only an evil dream. Almost he held out his arms.

And then he took a step backwards, for alas! he knew all that had happened today was no dream, but stark reality.

In silence she held out her hand, and perforce he took it in his, for a moment.

"I felt so sad, even in the midst of my own troubles, when I heard about your sister," she murmured.

"Don't speak of her!" he exclaimed violently. And involuntarily she shrank back.

She had put down that terrible, stern, sorrow-laden expression on his face to grief for his sister. But all at once she saw that he was gazing at her with an alien look-the look of a stern judge-on his sunburnt face.

What had he heard? What did he know? As she met that awful, accusing shaft of contempt, and yes, of loathing, a sensation of icy despair began slowly to envelop her.

"Do you remember Bella Dale?" he asked suddenly.

She answered in a faltering voice, "The girl on the yacht? Of course I do."

"She was my sister's dearest friend," his voice sank. More strongly he said, "I went to see her this morning, and-and now we are engaged."

And then he could not but admire her, for Ivy threw back her head, and in a hard, clear tone she exclaimed:

"I wish you joy, Mr. Rushworth! Also I do want to thank you from the bottom of my heart, for all you have done for me."

She knew now why he looked "like that." He was ashamed, and well he might be.

Quickly she told herself that he wasn't married yet. The fact that he was so moved showed the power she had over him. It had been foolish of her to suppose, as she had done for a moment, that he had heard something to her disadvantage-why, there hadn't been time!

But what was this he was saying?

"I'm the bearer of bad news, Mrs. Lexton."

His voice had become almost inaudible. She moved, timorously, a little nearer to him.

"Bad news?" she echoed uncertainly, and once more terror filled her burdened, fluttering heart.

"You are to be arrested tomorrow morning on the charge of having caused the death of your husband by poison. The police claim to possess ample evidence to ensure a conviction; so you are in frightful danger."

Arrested? In one fleeting moment she saw herself a prisoner in the dock where Roger Gretorex had stood. She visualised the Judge, the jury, the lawyers in the well of the Court, even the pitiless crowd of sightseers. The lifting of the black cap on to the Judge's wig-his awful words of admonition-the condemned cell . . . the gallows . . . .

She who now had always fainted so easily, why did she not faint now? Because she was tasting the bitterness of death.

Yet she made no sign, though she was staring at Rushworth with dilated eyes. But for those large, terror-filled eyes, he would have thought that she had not understood the purport of his awful revelation of what now awaited her. And something like a spasm of pity shook him to the depths of his being.

"I think, nay, I'm sure, I can save you," he exclaimed confidently.

Then he went on, speaking in low, quick tones: "I've arranged with a friend of mine who has got an aëroplane-you remember Jack Quirk, on the yacht? —to take you by air now, at once, today, to Spain. You will travel as his wife, on her passport. I've brought you a thousand pounds in gold, and another thousand in notes. From Spain you ought to be able to get a passage to South America without too much trouble. Quirk will arrange it all for you, and he will give you an address, where, if in need of help, you can write to me, once you are safe, far, far away."

His voice broke. He was remembering a moment-an immortal moment-in their joint lives, when Ivy had certainly loved him, in her fashion.

He saw her lips, which were quivering under the dab of lipstick rouge, try to form the words, "Thank you."

"I'm afraid there's no time to be lost. We'd better not be seen leaving the flat together. I'll say good-bye to you in the hall, and you'd better follow in about five minutes. My car is in Palace Row. *Don't bring anything with you.* The front door may be watched, but I think not, as you are believed to be in the country."

Epilogue

For the first few moments, spent alone by her in her bedroom, Ivy could only feel relief-sheer, sobbing relief.

Then there came over her a sensation of utter, numb despair.

She had lost everything that makes life worth the living to such as she . . .

But there was no time left her, now, to remember the past, or dread the future. She must hurry-hurry.

So it was that, in less than five minutes after Rushworth had left her, she was standing outside the flat, clad in a small pull-on black hat and a big fur coat.

The lift came up, and then, just as she was going to step into it, she remembered suddenly the bolster bag Rushworth had bought for her at Dieppe. On the morning of Jervis's death she had shaken out of the inner *pochette* the two or three pinches of-of "stuff" which remained in it, into the fire, and then, hardly knowing what she was doing, she had put it back in the red despatch-box. It would be all right, there, till she went out of her widow's mourning.

She couldn't leave *that* behind. Why it was worth a lot of money! Besides, she would give up wearing black as soon as she reached the place of safety Rushworth had promised her.

"Wait a minute," she said to the porter. "I've forgotten something. I won't be a second!"

She put her key in the lock, and rushed back to her bedroom.

Meanwhile there began an insistent ringing for the lift from the bottom of the shaft, in the hall of the Mansion.

The porter knew pretty Mrs. Lexton's ways. He felt sure that when she had said: "I won't be a second!" she meant probably five minutes, maybe even longer than that, especially if she had forgotten something.

The bell was ringing continuously now, and with a shock the man remembered that the agent for Duke of Kent Mansion was coming to see a leak in the roof this very afternoon.

Quickly he pulled the cable, and the lift slid down.

Meanwhile Ivy had run back into her bedroom, turning up the electric light as she walked through the door. Quickly she took the three keys she always carried about with her in her embroidered black vanité case, and, unlocking the half of the great cupboard, she seized the despatch-box.

The lid fell back the wrong side, queerly. Someone failing to force the lock had prized open the hinges, and the bag with its beautiful emerald and pearl clasp was gone-gone!

She threw a wild look round her. What could she take with her? Then she remembered what Rushworth had said. No, she mustn't take anything. Nothing, apart from that little bolster bag, was of any real value. . . . She turned out the light, and, running blindly through the dark hall, opened the front door of the flat. She hadn't been more than two or three minutes, after all.

She was trembling now; she felt strung-up and terrified, hardly conscious of what she was doing.

She opened wide the lift gates. They were already ajar, and then-her little feet stepped through into the void.

The man below heard a terrible scream, followed by an awful thud, thud, on the iron top of the lift.

And, at once, with a fearful sensation of dismay, he knew what he had done. He had omitted to shut the gates for the first time since he had been on this job.

For one thing, apart altogether from that little matter of the agent's visit, he, too, was excited-he, too, had been wondering what was going to happen. Everyone in Duke of Kent Mansion had been thrilled by the news of the reprieve. And, in his excitement at seeing the heroine of the Lexton Mystery, and in his certainty that he would be up again in less than a minute, he had left the lift gates ajar.

In one rushing moment, while on his way to the house-telephone to ring up the engineer, he visualised with dreadful clearness the Coroner's court, the censure passed on him by the jury, his dismissal from this good situation, and the consequent angry despair of his wife.

Poor, pretty, pleasant-spoken "Ivy," as he, in the company of thousands of other men of all ages, conditions, and kinds, had fallen into the way of secretly calling her-she had brought bad luck on everybody who came in touch with her. Well! Now she wouldn't be able to harm anybody, man or woman, any more.